"We can't share a bed!"

Joe came over to take her hand. "You have to do it, because we have to make this marriage of ours look as real as possible."

"Well, I'm not going to." Emma jerked her hand away from his. "You are not the boss of me."

A challenging glint appeared in Joe's amber eyes. "I am, however, your husband," he pointed out.

Her heart began to speed, but Emma refused to give ground. "So?"

"So I'm too tired to argue about this anymore, Emma." Without any warning, Joe scooped her up in his arms and held her against his chest.

"What are you doing?" Emma demanded, incensed.

"Exactly what you think," Joe said, turning sideways to go through the bedroom doorway. He looked down at her determinedly. "I'm taking you to bed."

D0249741

Dear Reader,

All moms want their kids to grow up happy, healthy and secure in the knowledge they are loved. Given their druthers, they also want their children to be happily married one day, with loving families of their own.

Helen Hart, the owner of The Wedding Inn in picturesque Holly Springs, North Carolina, is no exception. Helen was lucky enough to marry her true love and have six children with him. When her husband died, she went on to rear her brood alone. They've all grown up now, but not one is currently happily married, and Helen worries her five sons and one feisty daughter will never find the love they so richly deserve, unless they begin taking some risks. It won't be easy. Hockey star Joe has never gotten over his secret love, and seems to care only for his career. Bakery owner Janey is still reeling from the death of her husband and struggling to bring up her sports-obsessed son. Orthopedic surgeon Cal won't admit it, but he and his physician wife seem to be separated. Easygoing veterinarian Fletcher spends more time tending to animals and making everyone laugh than pursuing the woman Helen suspects is the love of his life. The inveterate observer/sportscaster Dylan seems to prefer to watch life from a distance in lieu of getting into the thick of the action himself. Sheriff Mac is so busy keeping law and order that he nearly misses a chance to help the damsel in distress who could be right for him.

As you might have guessed, the path to love is never easy for the members of the Hart family, but it is fun and exciting and yes, oh so romantic. I hope you enjoy all six of these books as much as I've enjoyed writing them! For more information, visit me at www.cathygillenthacker.com.

With warmest regards,

Cathy Gillen Thacker

Cathy Gillen Thacker

THE VIRGIN'S SECRET MARRIAGE

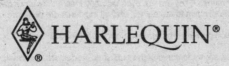

HARLEQUIN®

TORONTO • NEW YORK • LONDON
AMSTERDAM • PARIS • SYDNEY • HAMBURG
STOCKHOLM • ATHENS • TOKYO • MILAN • MADRID
PRAGUE • WARSAW • BUDAPEST • AUCKLAND

If you purchased this book without a cover you should be aware
that this book is stolen property. It was reported as "unsold and
destroyed" to the publisher, and neither the author nor the
publisher has received any payment for this "stripped book."

Alexander John Hodges, this one is for you.

ISBN 0-373-75001-3

THE VIRGIN'S SECRET MARRIAGE

Copyright © 2003 by Cathy Gillen Thacker.

All rights reserved. Except for use in any review, the reproduction or
utilization of this work in whole or in part in any form by any electronic,
mechanical or other means, now known or hereafter invented, including
xerography, photocopying and recording, or in any information storage
or retrieval system, is forbidden without the written permission of the
publisher, Harlequin Enterprises Limited, 225 Duncan Mill Road,
Don Mills, Ontario, Canada M3B 3K9.

All characters in this book have no existence outside the imagination of
the author and have no relation whatsoever to anyone bearing the same
name or names. They are not even distantly inspired by any individual
known or unknown to the author, and all incidents are pure invention.

This edition published by arrangement with Harlequin Books S.A.

® and TM are trademarks of the publisher. Trademarks indicated with
® are registered in the United States Patent and Trademark Office, the
Canadian Trade Marks Office and in other countries.

Visit us at www.eHarlequin.com

Printed in U.S.A.

ABOUT THE AUTHOR

Cathy Gillen Thacker married her high school sweetheart and hasn't had a dull moment since. Why? you ask. Well, there were three kids, various pets, any number of automobiles, several moves across the country, his and her careers and sundry other experiences (some of which were exciting and some of which weren't). But mostly, there was love and friendship and laughter, and lots of experiences she wouldn't trade for the world.

Books by Cathy Gillen Thacker

HARLEQUIN AMERICAN ROMANCE

HARLEQUIN BOOKS

*The McCabes of Texas
†The Lockharts of Texas
**The Deveraux Legacy
∆∆The Brides of Holly Springs

Chapter One

Joe Hart had made one crucial mistake in his long climb to success, and now finally—seven years after being caught in the wrong place at the wrong time with the "boss's daughter"—he was finally being given the chance to undo the damage caused by his foolishness.

He figured if he could come to terms with the heiress who had deliberately misled him and crushed his heart, see her for the deceitful manipulator she really was instead of the starry-eyed virgin he recalled every single night in his dreams, he might finally be able to move on. Because if there was one thing Joe wanted, it was a wife and kids of his very own. And to achieve that, he had to put Emma Donovan out of his heart and his mind once and for all.

In the meantime, though, he had the rest of the Hart clan to satisfy his craving for a family. His mom, his four brothers, his sister and her son. Now that he was back in the United States, back in his hometown of Holly Springs, North Carolina, he would be able to see a lot more of them. Joe was looking forward to interacting with them on a daily basis—as an adult, instead of a kid. That was if this meeting ever ended, he mused, in mounting frustration.

The Carolina Storm hockey team owner—multimillion-aire Saul Donovan—seemed to have no end to the rules and regulations he wanted to go over, before he and Joe signed their names on the dotted lines of Joe's contract.

"All team members are expected to give back to the community that supports them and participate in local charities. You can select your own. Or my wife, Margaret, and the rest of the team's public relations staff will help you."

"No problem," Joe said, looking over at his new boss. The fifty-something man was just under six feet, and a little soft around the middle. But there was nothing soft in his light green eyes. "That's something I've always done whether it was required or not."

Saul looked at Joe over the rim of his half glasses. "And the team sponsors a hockey camp for young kids. You'll be expected to help out with that this summer, as well."

Joe nodded, not sure why he felt as if he were being called out on the carpet like an errant teenager. Although Saul had been nothing but businesslike and professional thus far in his treatment of him, he was waiting for the proverbial ax to fall.

Swallowing around the tension in his throat, he looked Saul in the eye and imparted sincerely, "I have a nephew who might want to participate in that." Assuming, Joe amended silently and ruefully to himself, if he could convince his older sister a burning interest in athletics was a good thing for her twelve-year-old son. Not an easy task, given the way Janey's marriage to Christopher's dad had turned out.

Saul nodded approvingly, then glanced down at the sheet of paper in front of him. "And that brings us to the last item on our agenda." Saul put down his pen, set his jaw.

Ah, shoot, Joe thought. Here it comes. The dressing-down I've been waiting for.

"I'm willing to overlook what happened years ago on one very important condition," Saul continued sternly. He took off his glasses and dropped them on the desk, giving Joe the full benefit of his decidedly lethal glare. *You stay away from my daughter.*

Like he wanted to get in that kind of mess again? And

be sent back to the minors or benched? At the height of his pro career? "Believe me, I intend to keep my distance, and then some," Joe promised. He not only wanted to exorcise Emma from his soul, in the most expedient practical way possible, he had no desire to speak to the beautiful brunette heiress ever again.

"I mean it," Saul reiterated, frowning. "I don't want Emma hurt."

Joe didn't want to be hurt, either. And Emma Donovan had torn his heart apart. To the point Joe had more or less sworn off love ever since the night he had been caught trying to sneak a sobbing, angry Emma and her suitcase back into her college dorm. Only to come face-to-face with her equally angry father. To this day, Saul Donovan still did not know the full extent of what had happened—or almost happened—that night. When Joe had learned the truth, he had come immediately to his senses, much to the rebellious Emma's chagrin.

As the increasingly uncomfortable staring match between Joe and Saul continued, Coach Thaddeus Lantz leaned forward and interrupted. "I think Joe gets it, Saul."

Joe nodded obediently, indicating that was indeed the case. Boy, did he get it. If he screwed up this time, there would be no second chances. Saul would do everything in his power to see Joe was finished in the world of professional hockey. And as owner of one of the best teams in the NHL, and soon to be solely in charge of Joe's destiny, Saul was powerful enough to accomplish it.

Saul Donovan backed off only slightly. "Given the line of work Emma has chosen, and where she has located her office, it may not be so easy to avoid her," he warned Joe.

No kidding, given the fact Emma had chosen to work alongside Joe's mother, who still did not know that Emma and Joe had ever been personally acquainted or even dated!

"You leave that to me, sir. I have no intention of running into your daughter at the Wedding Inn. Or anywhere else.''

His mother owned and.ran the premier wedding location in all of North Carolina. And Emma was now—according to his mother, anyway—the best, most sought-after wedding planner in the state, as well. The two women worked side by side more often than not. But that did not mean Joe had to get involved in the family business. Or ever put himself in a position where he actually had to speak to the impulsive heiress.

''Emma is over there this evening, you know.''

One of many reasons why Joe hadn't told his mother he was in town. Yet. ''I'm planning to crash at a hotel in Raleigh, until I can get the rest of my stuff moved here,'' Joe said. He already owned a home. He had purchased one a year ago in his hometown as an investment, but he'd never gotten around to furnishing it. Mostly because he hadn't expected to be living here again quite so soon. And wouldn't be now if Saul hadn't come through with the offer to play right wing for the Carolina Storm.

''Have you checked in at that hotel yet?'' Saul asked, a little more kindly.

''Uh, no.'' Joe had been picked up by his Raleigh-based sports and entertainment attorney, Ross Dempsey, and come straight to this meeting from the airport.

''Then stay here,'' Saul encouraged, accurately reading Ross Dempsey's wordless entreaty to be more cordial to his newest player.

Joe cast a confused look at his attorney, who nodded encouragingly, then turned back to Saul. Making sure he had understood the invitation correctly, Joe asked, ''You want me to stay here, at your estate?''

Talk about going hot and cold and hot again. He was beginning to see where Emma got her mercurial changes of mood.

Saul nodded, all cordial businessman and paternal kindness once again. "We've got plenty of guest rooms upstairs."

Joe hesitated. He knew from the talk among other athletes that this was par for the course for any new players on the Carolina Storm hockey team. Saul Donovan wanted the team to feel like family. And he did everything in his power to keep morale high and engender player loyalty, to him personally, as well as the team. His methods worked. The Storm had the highest re-signing statistics, and best player-satisfaction survey scores, in the league. The mess with Emma aside, Joe knew he was lucky to be signing on here.

"You'd be doing us a favor," Saul continued. "My wife and I are going to Southern Pines for a golf tournament. And—given the rash of mysterious break-ins in Holly Springs lately—I'd prefer the house not be empty." Saul paused. "There is only so much a state-of-the-art security system can do."

Joe knew from his brother Mac, the Holly Springs sheriff, that the savvy bandit—or bandits—recently plaguing the central Carolina area were able to get past electronic security systems with ease.

"I'd be glad to look after the place for you," Joe volunteered. He figured, given past mistakes, it was the least he could do.

"We'll be back tomorrow evening, so it would just be for the next twenty-four hours," Saul continued.

"No problem," Joe said easily. "Emma…?"

"Is rarely here. When she does come over, she calls first. She knows we're going to be out of town, so she won't be stopping by the estate." Otherwise, Saul made it pretty clear by the look he gave Joe, there would have been no invitation.

Joe breathed a sigh of relief.

Saul nodded at the general counsel for the team. He handed over the contract that Joe and Ross Dempsey had already scrutinized, and a pen. Joe glanced through the pages, too, and noted it was just as they had agreed. Five years, with a no-trade guarantee. Aware again of the enormity of the risk he was taking, but equally aware of the jump in salary and chance to play on a better team, under a much better coach, he signed on the appropriate line. Saul Donovan followed suit.

It was done. He was now a member of the Carolina Storm hockey team. The two men stood, shaking hands in a way they never would have done seven years ago, when Saul had nearly derailed Joe's pro career. "The press conference announcing your return to Raleigh is set for Monday morning at 9:00 a.m. at the arena in Raleigh."

"I'll be there," Joe promised.

Emma's mother, Margaret, appeared in the doorway. Joe had never had any dealings with her, but he knew her by reputation. Margaret was a public relations whiz. She had helped her husband turn his sandwich shop into a franchise of successful restaurants nationwide, and now headed up the Carolina Storm's PR department. With her dark hair and pretty green eyes, she was as beautiful as her only daughter. Margaret was dressed for the drive to Southern Pines in tailored yellow golf slacks and matching sweater set. "Saul, are you about ready to leave?"

Saul nodded. "Just let me get my suitcase and golf clubs."

They all said good-night and Saul walked Coach Lantz and the two attorneys out.

Margaret smiled at Joe. If she blamed Joe for what had happened with him and Emma when they were just nineteen, she wasn't showing it as she handed Joe a piece of paper that held the security code for the house. "Let me show you around." She escorted him upstairs to the guest room she wanted him to use, then back down, through the back hallways, into the kitchen. Along the rear of the house was a separate wing that included a personal gym, weight room, indoor swimming pool with retractable roof, whirlpool tub and dressing rooms. "Feel free to use any of this that you like," Margaret told him graciously.

"Thanks," Joe said.

Margaret paused.

"What is it?" Joe asked, reading the worry in her soft eyes.

Margaret sighed. "I hate for you to be all alone in this big place, given what has been happening lately."

The break-ins again. He wished everyone would stop talking about it. But Joe supposed that was a hazard of living in a small town, some thirty minutes out of Raleigh. The residents weren't used to crime. So to them it was a very big deal.

"Not to worry, Mrs. D. I'm a big guy," Joe told her reassuringly. He could take care of himself.

"WELL, THAT WENT VERY WELL if I do say so myself," Helen Hart murmured, shortly after nine-thirty, as the last of the Shephard-Crowley wedding guests drove away.

"I think so, too," Emma Donovan agreed wholeheartedly with Joe Hart's mother. "Everything was just perfect, down to the last detail." And thanks to the fact that the two families involved were socially and politically prominent in the state of North Carolina, and had possessed the foresight to time the ceremony for maximum press coverage, the highlights of the celebration were going to be on the eleven o'clock news.

"We're both going to get a lot more weddings because of this one," Helen murmured happily.

Emma nodded as the catering crew continued to clean up the last of the glasses, and the twenty-seven-piece orchestra disbanded for the evening. Hard to believe that she and the widowed mother of the ex-love-of-her-life had become fast friends, as well as business associates. But then, the fifty six year-old mother of six with the short red hair and amber eyes did not know that Emma had ever dated or even met Joe. It wasn't that Emma meant to keep anything from Helen Hart. Just that she had never known how to bring it up, when Joe obviously hadn't. And maybe it was for the best, anyway, since Emma was still bitter about the quick and easy way Joe had dumped her, for the sake of his career.

"It's just too bad all our clients aren't as easy to work with," Emma murmured, as she headed toward the office she leased in the business wing of the Wedding Inn.

Helen sent her a sympathetic glance as Emma took out the secret-service-style earpiece and microphone she wore during weddings and put them away. "You're thinking about the Snow-Posen nuptials next week, aren't you?"

Emma nodded. Gigi Snow, the mother of the bride, was a real pill. And then some. Emma knew that she and Helen would both have their hands full the following week, pulling everything together for what was shaping up to be central Carolina's most expensive wedding of the year. "But tonight I am not going to think about that," Emma stated determinedly. Tonight, she was exhausted. So much so, in fact, she was thinking about doing what she rarely did, and nixing the drive back to her apartment in nearby Raleigh.

"You headed back to Raleigh?" Helen asked as she walked with Emma out onto the wide front porch of the palatial three-story white brick inn. They stood on the semicircular pillared portico, with the black wrought-iron railing and a half dozen steps down on each side.

"Actually, no. My parents are out of town for the weekend, so I think I'm just going to go over to their estate and spend the night there," Emma said, watching the employee cars and service vans continue to leave the parking area at a steady rate.

Helen's face creased with concern. "Be careful. It could be dangerous going into such a big house late at night, alone. And that place of your parents is so isolated." Helen paused, acting as much like Emma's mother as her own.

"Do you want me to call Mac and have someone from the sheriff's department escort you?"

Emma shook her head. "Don't be silly. There's no reason to bother your son. I know the recent spate of burglaries are all anyone has been talking about, but honestly, it isn't as if the thieves have done much but help themselves to a few very expensive sets of golf clubs, and the occasional pantry or wet bar. No one's been hurt in any of the break-ins."

"Because no one's been home when any of the break-ins occurred," Helen countered sagely. "The victims have all been out of town, or away for the evening. There's no telling what could happen if the thieves came face-to-face with someone they were burgling."

A shiver went down Emma's spine as she considered the possibility of that happening to her. Forcing herself to remain calm, she countered, "My parents have a state-of-the-art security system."

Helen frowned, even more worriedly. "Mac told me the thieves have been getting around those."

And as Holly Springs sheriff, Mac Hart would know, Emma realized uneasily. With effort, Emma pushed away her fear. "Really," she promised Helen. "I'll be fine." All she needed was a long soak in a hot bath, some cozy pajamas and a good night's sleep.

Determined to achieve all three within the hour, she strode wearily out to her BMW. As she made her way through the sleepy little town and drove out to the estate her parents had purchased just two years ago, Emma couldn't help but think how much her life had changed from the time she was a little girl. Her parents were rich now beyond their wildest dreams, but when she had been in elementary school her father and mother—both of whom had come from modest middle-class backgrounds themselves—had still been struggling to turn Saul's Sandwich Shops into a national chain. Margaret and Saul had traveled so constantly, in fact, that they had been forced to put Emma in an all-girls boarding school in Virginia.

Always a serious student, Emma had excelled in the rigorous academic atmosphere. Free to devote themselves to selling franchises and opening new Saul's Sandwich Shops, Margaret and Saul had achieved the nationwide success and fame they wanted. By the time she'd graduated from high school and had gone on to Brown University in Rhode Island, her father had realized yet another long-held dream of his and purchased an NHL hockey team, the Carolina Storm.

Emma had been excited about the purchase and wanted to attend the games, meet the players, but her father—ever protective—had strictly forbidden it. Hockey players were bad news for women, he had said. If only she had listened to him all those years ago… But she hadn't. And instead had directly disobeyed him, and had regularly gone to see a minor-league AHL team in Providence, Rhode Island. She had been enthralled by the physical agility, speed, skill and determination of the young, handsome players. One in particular, a sexy southern boy and North Carolina native, had really caught her eye.

Emma sighed. She knew better than to let herself think about that. If she did, she would be up all night, dreaming of a guy with tousled light brown hair and golden brown eyes….

Scowling at her inability to get past what might as well have happened in another lifetime, she punched in the security code, watched the gates open, then drove up the lane. To her relief, the ten-thousand-square-foot house and grounds were as quiet and tranquil as ever.

She let herself in the slate-blue southern colonial, with the white shutters and slate-gray trim, and made her way up the front stairs to her bedroom at the far end of the hall.

Emma pinned her hair up on the back of her head. She washed the day's grime off her face and took off her clothes while the tub filled, then sank chin-deep into the fragrant bubbles.

As she soaked, her thoughts turned once again to Joe Hart, and the sexy, frustrating-as-all-get-out havoc he had wreaked on her life. They had never made love. But she still couldn't forget the heat of his kisses, or the tender evocativeness of his touch. Still couldn't stop wanting him or wishing they'd...

Scowling, Emma got out of the tub. And that was when she heard it. The sound of something—someone—moving around on the first floor, directly below her. In the workout room, or sauna...maybe.

Emma froze, panicked at the realization she was not alone. Then reached for the phone on the bathroom wall and, still dripping water and bubbles everywhere, swiftly punched in 911. She barely had time to whisper what was happening before Sheriff Mac Hart himself was on the line. "Emma. I want you to sit tight," he warned briskly. "Don't even think of going to confront whoever is in the house."

In the utter silence of the big house, Emma heard the distinct sound of a door shutting. Another opening. A deep-throated male cough. A crash as something dropped. A muffled exclamation, swearing. She knew what Mac had said, but she was not going to sit there like a sitting duck and wait for whoever was in the house to find her, alone and unarmed. Shaking with a mixture of adrenaline and fear, she pulled her floor-length navy-blue robe on around her and belted it tight. She needed a weapon with which to protect herself. And she knew just where to find one.

JOE WAS HALFWAY UP THE REAR staircase when he heard the thud of someone crashing into something in the dark, and then the faint, scuffling sounds of someone moving stealthily along the upstairs hallway. Since there was no staff there, no one from the Donovan family, it had to be an intruder.

His body still glistening from the long swim in the indoor pool and the soak in the hot tub, he ducked back, out of sight. Heart pounding, he leaned against the inner staircase wall, wishing he had a lot more on than a towel around his waist. Damn it. The last thing he needed was a thief successfully burgling Margaret and Saul Donovan's place when he was house-sitting.

That would be a great way to begin his tenure on Saul's team!

On the other hand, saving the day might win him a few brownie points. And those he could use.

Easing his way soundlessly back down to the first floor, he slipped into the kitchen pantry, figuring he had surprise on his side. He needed protection, and as his hands closed on a wooden handle, he knew he had found it. Now all he had to do was wait for the intruder to come a little closer and turn his back, and Joe would take the broomstick and knock the interloper flat before he knew what hit him.

Joe stood next to the crack in the pantry door, peering out.

The large kitchen windows had no covering, but the moonless night offered little illumination. The room was so dark he could just barely make out the figure of a person, a half a foot or so smaller than he. Wrapped in some sort of dark garment or clothing that went all the way to the floor and obliterated even a hint of skin. The interloper had his back to Joe and was rummaging around in the kitchen drawers, a little too noisily and in too much of a panic for Joe's comfort. Figuring he had to act fast before his opponent found the sharp blade of a knife to use on him, Joe rushed out of the pantry. The shadowy figure whirled and came at him, arm raised. He ducked. And something heavy—a marble rolling pin—whacked the counter beside him.

Joe swore, swung his broom. His opponent sidestepped briskly and the handle grazed the cabinet before he could get it behind his opponent's knees. The rolling pin came up in the air again. Joe used the broom like a sword to knock it away. It hit the floor with a loud clatter.

Mission accomplished, Joe thought as he grunted in victory. Then winced as a knee jabbed viciously toward his groin. He blocked the devastating blow with his thigh, and grabbed his rather puny opponent by the arms, but could do nothing about the towel slipping free from around his waist. A small bare foot jabbed his instep. He grunted, his towel falling completely away as he shoved his opponent up against the counter. The terry robe fell open. Trapped, body to body, in struggling combat, Joe felt the warm, damp softness of female breasts, tummy, thighs. Inhaled the clean scent of soap and a distinctly flowery, female perfume. Shocked to realize this might not be a burglar after all, he dropped his hold on his opponent abruptly and stepped back.

Before he could speak, she'd grabbed a heavy ceramic cookie jar from the counter and was again trying to whack the hell out of him. Not about to sustain a career-wounding injury in such an ignominious way, Joe caught the woman's hands, fighting off the skull-shattering blow as cookies flew everywhere. "Jeez, wait! I—"

"Go to hell, you thug!" she muttered right back. "What right do you have to break in here?"

"Crimony, lady! I'm not..." Joe swore again, even more virulently as she kicked him hard in the shin and they struggled fiercely for possession of the jar. He almost had possession of it, too, when his surprisingly lush, female opponent let out a long, terrified scream.

Refusing to let himself get brained by a hysterical female, Joe struggled all the harder, yanking it free, putting it safely aside. To his frustration, she immediately made a grab for something else on the counter—a bottle of wine? He intervened, and she pulled away. He caught her sleeve before she could reach for anything else.

Not about to let him declare victory, she twisted and turned like a wild thing, her open robe going the way of his towel in their frantic tussling. As her clothing fell free of her and she kicked it away, Joe tried again to reason with her as she frantically grabbed for something else while still screeching loudly.

Ears ringing, he stopped her and their naked bodies collided, chest to chest. He grabbed onto her arms, to calm her. To no avail. No matter what he did or said, he couldn't get her to listen to him or stop that deafening screaming.

Perhaps never would have if not for the sudden blinding burst of light, shining in through the kitchen windows, illuminating them from head to toe, in the shockingly bright and revealing glow of the police spotlight. Shocked speechless, they froze, like two kids playing statue in the yard.

Joe turned back to his opponent. Caught a glimpse of dark tousled hair, familiar pine-green eyes and soft, stubborn lips, falling open in dismay. He had one second to register just whom he had been tussling with. Oh, no, he thought. ''No!''

And then the all-too-recognizable voice of the local sheriff boomed at them over the loudspeaker. ''All right, you two! Hold it right there!''

Chapter Two

"You just can't stay out of trouble, can you, little brother?" Holly Springs' sheriff, Mac Hart, demanded in an exaggerated southern drawl as he dropped the bullhorn, punched in a security code and burst in through the kitchen door. Three uniformed deputies were behind him.

Not when it came to Emma Donovan, Joe thought in chagrin as he moved instinctively to shield his female companion. Keeping his taller, stronger body positioned between the glare of the police spotlight and Emma's lithe but curvaceous frame, he helped her retrieve—and then shrug on—her robe. Not that his gallantry helped all that much. There was enough light reflected off glimpses of her silky smooth skin to let everyone there see she was naked as a jaybird, as was he.

Keeping his bare backside toward the glare of the spotlight, Joe swiveled from the waist, turning his head and shoulders slowly, so he could get a better look at the group assembled, on the other side of the glass windows. Was it his imagination, or was that a TV news station truck in the drive, and—holy bananas!—were cameras pointed his and Emma's way?

Stifling a litany of swear words that came to mind, Joe used his lazy Carolina drawl to disarming affect. "Mind if I grab my towel, big brother?" Aware the light should have been shut off by now, to afford them some much-needed modesty, Joe glared at Mac. He could see that his law-and-order brother was as quick to jump to erroneous conclusions about his baby brother's behavior now as he had been about the scrapes Joe had inadvertently gotten into as a kid. "Or were you planning to shoot me?" Joe finished sarcastically. Joe knew Emma Donovan would like to do so.

A deeply disapproving look on his face, Mac holstered his gun and waved the two deputies to do the same. "Get something on—both of you," Mac responded, then turned around to face the news crew that had tagged along and pushed their way into the spacious kitchen, too. "And turn those cameras off!" he ordered sharply.

"No way!"

Joe recognized Trevor Zwick, the reporter from W-MOL.

"We're responding to the 911 call over the police radio, same as you. And this is the estate of Saul Donovan, Carolina Storm's owner, so it's news."

"It's also his daughter," Joe interjected grimly, warning the news crew what they already should have known, that Saul and Margaret would not take kindly to this.

The young, red-haired cameraman stepped forward to zoom in, as Joe wrapped the towel around his waist and continued to stand, blocking the crew's view of a still trembling and shaken Emma. "Hey, Joe! Rusty Crowley here. Are the rumors true? Have you signed with the Storm for next season?"

Joe grimaced. Of all the places to meet with a hockey afficionado. "I can't comment on that," he said firmly. Not when the official press conference had yet to be held. Not when he hadn't had time or opportunity to get his family together and tell them.

"Then can you comment on why you're here in a state of undress with Mr. Donovan's daughter?" Trevor Zwick asked, like the indefatigable reporter he was. "Or why the sheriff's department was summoned here this evening on a breaking-and-entering report, phoned in by Miss Emma Donovan?''

Joe looked to Mac for help. If anyone had the authority to disperse them, his brother did.

"That's enough questions, guys," Mac said, reading Joe's mind and waving the news crew away. "Off the property. Now."

The entire three-person news crew looked deeply disappointed.

"You heard me," Mac continued, with the full authority of local law enforcement. "There's no story here."

Mac's deputies moved to enforce his orders. The crew was shooed away, still protesting. Emma turned and disappeared into the adjacent hall, out of sight of the windows. Joe did the same.

Mac followed and loomed in the doorway from the kitchen. He hit the wall switch, so the room was bathed in soft yellow light. Then he glanced pointedly at Emma, who was now leaning weakly against the wall, an expression of unmitigated anger on her pretty face. "Everything okay here?" Mac asked gently, still studying Emma with professional dispassion. "Or you want me to stay and check it out?"

Joe turned to Emma and got a really good look at her for the first time that evening. Seven years had passed since the two of them had laid eyes on each other. Whereas before she had been a young girl, still in her late teens, now she was all woman. And he wasn't just taking in the lush curves of her five-foot-six frame. There was a wisdom and maturity in her long-lashed emerald-green eyes, a knowing curve to her soft ripe lips, a new stubbornness to the set of her chin. She was wearing no makeup. But then, with her elegant features, soft peachy-gold skin and dark, sexily upswept hair, she really didn't need any to look drop-dead gorgeous. Tucked in the plush navy bathrobe, her bare feet planted determinedly apart, she looked like the rich, pampered heiress she was.

Joe realized that even though emotionally he could care less about her and wanted nothing to do with her, he was as physically drawn to her as ever. And more telling still, she couldn't seem to stop hungrily staring at Joe any more than he could stop drinking in the sight of her.

Which could only mean one thing. Saul Donovan had been right to worry and warn Joe away from his only daughter.

Because if the two of them were around each other for any time at all...

Mac cleared his throat. "Well?" he prodded again, impatiently.

Aware his brother still hadn't received a full explanation, and deserved one for having been called out to the estate on a false emergency call, Joe turned back to Mac and said, for both their benefit, "I'm a houseguest here."

Emma harrumphed in a way that had Joe pivoting back to her. She glared at him resentfully. Like this—as well as everything else—was all his fault! "So. Am. I." She pushed the words between tightly gritted teeth.

"Yeah, well, I had no idea she was staying here, too." Not about to take sole blame for anything that had happened between them—not again—Joe jabbed a thumb at his bare chest. "The Donovans told me I would be alone here this evening, when they left for Southern Pines a few hours ago." So if anyone was at fault here, he figured grimly, it sure as heck wasn't him!

Emma huffed at him contemptuously. "You think I knew?" Emma spouted right back incredulously, tightening the belt on her terry-cloth robe.

Joe shrugged, trying not to notice how quickly—and heatedly—his body was responding to her. "How the heck should I know? It wouldn't be the first time you accidentally on purpose got me in a heap of..." Trouble, Joe had been about to say.

Curious, Mac lifted his brow. Looked from one to the other. "Something here I should know?" he queried dryly.

Joe shook his head no. He didn't want anyone in his family learning about the mistake that had sent him back to the minor league, seven years ago, just hours after being called up to the NHL for the very first time. They didn't know it was something he had impulsively done—with Emma, no less—that had nearly derailed his pro career before it ever really got off the ground. Joe had gone on to make up for his mistake, and devoted himself and his energy to his career. The shame he still felt, was his own. As far as he was concerned, no one else ever had to know about the depth of his stupidity and naïveté back then. And the same went for Emma's machinations.

"Look, we're fine, Mac," Joe assured stiffly. "You can go. Emma and I will sort this out by ourselves."

Mac looked at Emma, still weighing his options and what was the wisest thing to do. "You okay with that?" he asked plainly.

Emma nodded stiffly. "I apologize for dialing 911. Had I known who it was, prowling around downstairs…"

"You would have told 'em to shoot first and ask questions later?" Joe quipped.

Emma glared at him and folded her arms in front of her like a shield. "Har-de-har-har, hotshot." She turned back to Mac. "Suffice it to say, I would not have called you all out here or created such a ruckus."

"Have I missed something?" Mac asked sarcastically, narrowing his eyes at them both.

Only the biggest catastrophe of Joe's entire life. "Nope," Joe stated with a glibness he couldn't begin to really harbor. "So if you'll excuse us, big brother, Emma and I would like some time alone."

EMMA HAD TO HAND IT TO Joe for one thing—he sure knew how to get rid of an audience. Fast. And for that she would be eternally grateful. She folded the lapels of her robe, one over another, covering as much of herself as possible. "If you'll excuse me," she murmured, hand pressed against the cloth covering her collarbone, "I'm going to get dressed and get out of here."

"Not so fast." Joe clamped a hand on her shoulder. "I want to know what you're doing here." He searched her face. "Was this an elaborate ploy? Was the punishment your father bestowed on me seven years ago not enough? Is he still trying to get even with me for 'robbing you of your virtue and then dumping you'?"

Not that any of that had actually happened, but it was what her parents thought had happened that night. She had never bothered to set her folks straight, figuring she wouldn't be believed, anyway. Joe had actually been trying to do *right* by her—in his convoluted mind, anyway—by reneging on all his promises to her and bringing her back to college. Joe hadn't come to her rescue, either. At least until now, anyway. "I have no idea what you're talking about," Emma said bluntly. "Or why you would ever be invited to be a houseguest here, of all places!"

Joe folded his arms in front of him and regarded her skeptically. "You're telling me you honestly don't know what transpired here tonight."

Emma tried to keep her eyes off the sinewy lines of his shoulders and chest, the satin hue of his bronzed skin. She did not need to recall how it felt to be held against the warm, strong body of his. Never mind think about how well, how passionately, he kissed! Doing her best to slow her racing pulse, she shrugged. "Should I?"

Joe stared at her. Still debating, Emma guessed, if he could trust her.

He compressed his lips grimly, then stated in a low, matter-of-fact voice, "I signed a contract with your father's hockey team."

It was Emma's turn to be skeptical, even as she struggled to ignore her reaction to his nearness.

Seven years might have passed since she had last seen him on anything but a television screen, but he still had the same magnetic effect on her. One glance at his handsome, All-American-guy-next-door face was enough to command her attention. Try as she might, she couldn't tear her eyes from the crescent-moon scar at the corner of his right eye or the dimple in his chin. She didn't want to be affected by his sexy smile or penetrating golden-brown eyes. She didn't want to notice how his six-foot-two, two-hundred-pound frame dwarfed her, or be aware of his powerful athlete's body that was honed for maximum agility, strength and speed. Nor did she want to be anything but immune to his exceedingly confident presence. Or recall the playfulness that lurked just beneath the surface of his ever-present determination to have everything he wanted, when he wanted it. But he mesmerized her just the same....

"I thought my dad said you would never play for him again, ever, that night—"

Joe interrupted. "When he caught me trying to sneak you back into your dorm?"

They glared at each other, remembering. Finally, Joe scowled at her accusingly. "If you had told me your connection to the NHL team-owning DONOVANS to begin with."

Emma rolled her eyes. "You would never have gone out with me if you had known I was Saul Donovan's nineteen-year-old daughter."

Joe nodded and affirmed dryly, "No kidding, Sherlock."

Stung all over again by his readiness to dump her, Emma lifted her shoulder in a delicate little shrug. "So you proved me right about you, in the end." That he wasn't a man to be depended upon. At least not in a romantic sense. "So what?"

Joe leaned back against the wall, the towel looped around his waist sliding a little lower on his hips. "You're telling me you don't know what was in the contract I signed this evening?"

Emma moved her eyes away from his exposed navel,

and the T-shaped line of golden-brown hair on his midriff. "How could I? I didn't even know you were *here* this evening."

"And I shouldn't be here now, either," Joe muttered, shoving away from the opposite wall and beginning to pace.

"Now what's the matter?" Emma demanded, wishing he didn't look so damn sexy in a towel, the hint of an evening beard lining his face.

Joe ran a hand through his hair. "I don't suppose there is any way we're going to be able to keep tonight's mishap quiet in a community as small and tight-knit as Holly Springs."

"Given the fact we were damn near caught en flagrante by the police and the press?" Emma echoed drolly. "I rather doubt it."

Joe looked her square in the eye. "We weren't doing anything!"

Aware Joe smelled like a mixture of chlorine and the musky masculine scent that was unique to him, Emma released a long, pent-up sigh. "Except wrestling with each other. Not that it matters. We weren't 'doing anything' the night my father caught us returning to my dorm at Brown, either. He simply assumed the worst when he saw me coming back in with a suitcase, crying my eyes out, and heard you telling me it was over, that you were never going to see me again—ever—despite my wishes to the contrary. Because you, big guy, looked guilty as all get out."

Joe's lips curved smugly. "As did you, Miss Emma."

"Naturally, he assumed we had done the deed. Just like tonight. I'm sure those deputies took one look at the both of us and thought, well, you know…

"That we were really getting it on?"

Emma flushed, as she was pretty sure Joe meant her to. "I'm just speaking the truth," she said stubbornly. "By tomorrow this will be all over town."

Joe closed his eyes, then slowly opened them. "Then I am in trouble."

Emma waited for the rest.

"I promised your father I would steer clear of you," Joe said in a flat, dispassionate voice.

To her stunned amazement, Emma found his willingness to ditch her now hurt just as much as it had years before. Unable to help herself, she lashed out sarcastically, "Good job."

Joe glared at her resentfully. "My standing with the team depends on me not hurting you any more," he said.

Emma shook her head disparagingly. "Well, that's a comfort."

Joe gave her a look. "Help me out here, Emma."

Emma lifted her chin. "Why should I?" she demanded right back.

"Because your reputation is at stake, too," Joe said heavily.

"I don't care about that." Emma cared about her heart. And her heart had been smashed all to pieces by this handsome athlete who lived and breathed only for his time on the ice. She didn't care what it did to his career—she had no intention of letting him do the same thing to her again! And giving him no chance to say anything further, she turned and exited the hall.

EMMA CAME BACK DOWNSTAIRS fifteen minutes later. Her dark brown hair was brushed and down, the clothes she had been wearing earlier—a sexy pale pink cocktail dress and heels—were on. Joe was dressed, too, in a navy sport coat, coordinating pale blue shirt and tie and stone-colored dress slacks. He was sitting on the sofa, his duffel bag on the floor to the left of him. If possible, he looked even grimmer than he had when she left. She knew just how he felt. This evening had *disaster* written all over it, even without anyone else witnessing it, which they surely, and irrevocably, had.

Joe compressed his lips together dejectedly and tossed a grim look her way before announcing desultorily, "We're on the eleven o'clock news."

Emma blinked. Please, let her have heard wrong. "What?"

"My brother Cal just called me on my cell," Joe explained a trifle impatiently. He leaned forward, hands clasped loosely between his spread knees. "He was in the doctor's lounge, over at Holly Springs Regional Medical Center, when he saw a promo about the nighttime antics of Joe Hart and the Storm owner's daughter, Emma Donovan. The full story should be coming up after this commercial."

Her spirits plummeting as swiftly as the strength in her legs, Emma sank down on the arm of the sofa. No sooner had she gotten comfortable than the news program came back on. At the anchor's urging, Trevor Zwick, the reporter who had been at the house just thirty minutes ago, began a breathless recounting of the situation from a remote location. He was interrupted when the TV station began to roll the tape.

Emma gasped as her hopes for mercy from the local media faded. Too late, she realized she should have called her mother, the public relations expert, on her cell phone as soon as this happened. And asked Margaret Donovan to intervene. But she hadn't. And as a result... Emma's eyes widened as the spotlight came on and the images on screen suddenly became so much bigger and clearer. She clapped a hand over her heart. "Oh, my heavens..."

Joe said something else, in a much saltier vein. And then they both stared in horrified silence as the Technicolor tape of them first putting their hands above their heads, then scrambling for cover, rolled across the screen.

"As you can see, it was quickly deemed to have all been a big misunderstanding," the eager reporter continued. "Although, what free agent Joe Hart was doing at Storm owner's estate is definitely something we sports fans

want to look in to. Does it mean the rumors are true—that
Joe Hart is going to sign with the Carolina Storm? Or was
his presence there more of a…uh…romantic nature, with
local wedding planner extraordinaire, Emma Donovan.''

Blushing, Emma clapped both her hands over her face.
Damn it, she had hoped not to be identified in the frame.
Hoped not to have her business hurt by her getting caught,
in a state of undress, with a hunky athlete.

''Well, there you have it,'' the anchor concluded. ''Exclusive film of the tumultuous goings-on at the Saul Donovan home this evening. Available only on W-MOL. Your
local Action News team!''

''Oh, my lord,'' Emma muttered, even more emotionally.

Joe punched a button on the remote and the TV screen
went blank. ''My feelings exactly.''

The only thing she had to be grateful for was the fact
that Joe's tall, muscular body had blocked any view of her
body. She hadn't known it prior to this—since she hadn't
had occasion to see him naked, and she promised herself
sternly, never would again—but in addition to his ruggedly
handsome face, he had an Adonis-beautiful body, with
broad shoulders and a powerfully sculpted chest, amaz-
ingly taut buttocks and long, sturdy legs.

''I suppose it's too much to hope tonight's catastrophe
will end here with this one showing of the tape,'' Emma
gulped. She could only imagine what her parents were going to do when they heard about—or worse—saw this
tape!

Joe sat back against the cushions and raked both his
hands through the tousled layers of his ash-brown hair.
''The only good thing is it's Friday.''

Emma bit her lip. ''I don't—''

Joe sighed. ''If it does hit the national news, it will hit
it on the weekend news cycles, which not too many people
watch.''

Emma groaned all the louder, as she thought about that

tape being picked up and shown on the network and cable shows. "Y-you really don't think…" she stammered, feeling hideously embarrassed. "I mean. Nothing actually happened here."

Joe smirked, shook his head, as if he couldn't believe her naïveté. Even now. "Face it, Emma," he warned her tiredly. "The tape's a hoot, and sordidly appealing. It's going to be everywhere." Prediction made, he picked up his bag and headed for the foyer.

Emma's lower lip trembled as she stood and followed him, albeit somewhat unsteadily, to the front door. She watched as he opened it, wishing he wouldn't just take off at the first sign of trouble with her. "So what are we going to do?" she asked plaintively.

"That," a stern male voice said from the shadows, as two very familiar figures came rapidly up the sidewalk, "is exactly what we'd like to know."

Chapter Three

Well, this family drama was oddly familiar, Joe thought, as he stared into the grim, set face of Saul Donovan. Beside him, his wife Margaret looked just as distressed.

"How did you find out?" Emma blurted out, looking—to Joe's chagrin—every bit as upset and guilty as he felt.

"The sheriff's department called us on my cell as soon as the 911 call from the house came in," Saul said. "Your mother and I turned the car around immediately."

"And then, your brother Mac," Margaret Donovan continued, talking to Joe, "telephoned us to let us know everything was okay. It was all a misunderstanding. Albeit a rather unfortunate one."

No kidding, Joe thought.

"The third call came just a minute ago, from Coach Lantz, telling us the whole sorry incident was on the eleven o'clock news!" Saul fumed.

Joe was sorry about that, too. Sorrier than he could ever say.

Saul glared at Joe. "This is what you call staying away from my daughter?"

Emma looked at her folks, interjecting before Joe could respond. "I didn't know he was here. I really did think he was a burglar."

"And I didn't know she was here," Joe added hotly in

his own defense. "I thought someone had broken in while I was working out in the pool."

"And I'm supposed to believe that?" Saul bellowed sarcastically.

"Yes, Dad!" Emma declared. "You are!"

Saul turned back to Joe and stuck a lecturing finger beneath Joe's nose. "Is this why you agreed to be on our team? Because of Emma? Because I swear if you think I am going to let you hurt and lead her astray again, you have another think coming. I don't care how many millions we just agreed to pay you! You'll be sitting out the games in the locker room! Or sent back to the minor leagues again."

Yet another reminder of the balance of power. Joe regarded Saul aloofly. "You don't have to tell me the many ways you can ruin my life, sir. I'm well acquainted with all of them. Believe me, when I signed with the Storm it was not my intention to ever so much as cross paths with your daughter again. Which is why I never should have stayed here this evening."

Saul lifted a thin, disapproving brow and continued regarding Joe over the rim of his bifocals. "No argument there," he muttered disparagingly.

Another car pulled into the driveway. It stopped just short of the sidewalk they were all standing on. Storm coach Thaddeus Lantz got out of the SUV and walked over to where they were standing. Joe didn't even have to ask. He knew Coach Thad Lantz showing up here now was no accident. Coach was here at Saul Donovan's request. To tell him he was already going to be fired, at worst, or at best, put on waivers for another trade?

The thirty-six-year-old Thad crossed his hands over his chest and regarded Joe silently. The youngest coach in the NHL was a Tom Selleck look-alike, and the idol of many a swooning female. "Hell of a mess," Thad stated finally, in the low, patient tone he was known for. "You better figure out how to fix it, kid. Fast."

FIX IT? THAT WAS A LAUGH! Joe thought as he drove over to the house of the family member who was likely to be the most help to him.

"I was wondering if and when you would show up," Janey Hart Campbell said, ushering him inside. Although it was twelve-thirty at night, the chestnut haired Janey was still wide awake and hard at work as her jeans, T-shirt and white chef's apron attested. Owner of her own bakery, Delectable Cakes, she also provided wedding, groom and engagement cakes for the Wedding Inn, owned and run by their mother, Helen.

Janey led the way back to the kitchen, where she was busy putting the finishing touches on a four-tiered wedding cake.

"That for tomorrow?" Joe asked, swiping a bit of butter-cream frosting from the edge of the bowl.

Janey swiped his hand away, but not before he got a taste of the delicious vanilla topping.

"Yes. It's for the Thermonopoulos-Thornton wedding that Mom and Emma are both working on."

Joe knew this was his lead-in to tell Janey all he knew about Saul Donovan's daughter. But he wasn't in the mood to go into his dating history.

Undaunted, Janey kept right on icing the cake. "So have you talked to Mom yet?" she asked, as she flattened butter cream over the top and sides of the final layer of the sugary confection.

Joe shrugged and shoved his hands in the pockets of his dress slacks. "I thought she might be asleep."

Janey lifted a telltale brow and aimed it his way before picking up the pastry bag. "One can hope she hasn't seen the news yet," she murmured.

Joe watched as she put piping around the edges. "But you obviously have," he noted with a beleaguered sigh.

"Oh, yes." Janey's knowing amber eyes narrowed with disapproval. "Mac called me from the sheriff's office. He wanted to make sure that Christopher wasn't watching the eleven o'clock W-MOL news."

Joe tensed. The last thing he wanted to do was set a bad example for his only nephew. "Did Chris see it?" Joe asked uncomfortably.

Janey compressed her lips together in a way that reminded Joe his seven-years-older sister had suffered her own travails. And regrets. Mostly, Joe thought, due to the fact she had married young, and married wrong. And then been left a widow when her only child was ten.

But she had her life back on track now. Or at least she was getting there, Joe thought.

"No. Not yet, but it's unlikely I'll be able to keep it from him. And at twelve—well, he's bound to have a lot of questions when he does see it."

As well as some misplaced male envy, Joe thought. Damn it all. This was not the kind of example he had wanted to make for the starry-eyed adolescent.

Joe sighed and repeated an old family homily, "Good news travels fast."

"And bad news even faster." Janey finished it for him with a roll of her eyes and wry smile.

Joe helped himself to a beer from her refrigerator. "Does everyone else in the family know?"

Janey shrugged as she picked up another piping bag and began carefully decorating the cake with yellow icing flowers. "Cal saw it—he was in the doctor's lounge over at the hospital. Last I saw Fletcher, he was headed out on an emergency call—the Petersons' mare is in breech, and they needed a vet out there for the delivery. Dylan, well, because he's a TV sports commentator, if he hasn't seen it yet, he will soon."

Joe sighed. That covered himself and all five of his siblings. He jerked loose the knot of his tie. "I was hoping it would remain a local story."

Janey shook her head in silent disagreement, her own naïveté long since faded by a flawed marriage to a guy much more reckless, and self-involved, than Joe.

"I...don't think so. That backside of yours, with the black bar placed strategically across it? Who could resist?"

Feeling like a victim on a humorous-videos TV show, Joe grimaced. "Very funny."

"I wasn't laughing earlier, believe me, and neither, I'm betting, will Mom. Especially if that clip hits the national news, or worse, ends up featured on the 'Bad Boys of the Week' portion of Tiffany Lamour's TV show."

Joe tensed. He hadn't given any thought to that, but now that Janey brought it up, he knew his big sis was right. The footage of him being caught buck naked, with a towel draped around his ankles, was exactly the kind of embarrassing clip the cable sports network commentator liked to use to end her often sensational interview show.

"Unless you think you could sweet-talk Tiffany into not using it," Janey asked hopefully.

Not likely, given the air play it had already had and the laughs it had engendered, not to mention the possibility of other networks picking it up and running it again and again. "I'm not even going to try," Joe decided, signaling the subject was closed. He took another swig of the icy-cold beer, let it cool his parched throat. "Besides, I'll live this down." It was just another way of being put in the penalty box. The public censure wasn't fun while it was happening, but it always ended eventually. And then it was promptly back to business as usual.

"Let's certainly hope so." Janey bit her lip.

Joe took another sip of beer. "What?" he demanded irritably when the silence between them continued.

Janey wrinkled her nose at him. "What do you think? I'm worried about the impact something like this is going to have on my son!"

"In terms of example-setting," Joe guessed.

"It's not as if I don't have enough troubles with Christopher already," Janey lamented anxiously.

Joe studied his sister, knowing that she was now wrestling with the same demons his own mother had encountered when he was growing up, determined to nix college and even some of his high school for a career in professional sports. "Chris still wants to become a pro hockey player when he grows up, hmm?" Joe remarked.

The corners of Janey's lips turned down. "Worse. He wants to follow in your footsteps all the way."

Here they went again. "And that's a bad thing?" Joe prodded dryly.

Janey looked down her nose at him. "It is when you end up on the evening news, buck naked."

Silence.

"Anything else you want to say?" Joe preferred to get it over with.

Janey began piping on perfect green leaves. "If you must know, I'm concerned about Emma, too. She's a good friend of mine."

That, Joe hadn't known. He regarded his sister contentiously. "Since when?"

"Since I moved back to Holly Springs last year. We've worked together on a lot of weddings." Janey paused, before turning curious eyes his way. "She must have been very embarrassed."

"That's putting it lightly." And Joe figured he knew why. There couldn't have been a more shocking way for them to see each other naked for the first—and only—time.

"Have you apologized to her?"

Joe shrugged his shoulders restlessly. "Didn't really have a chance. We were too busy dealing with the calamity."

"Then I suggest you make an apology as soon as possible."

Maybe later, when things cooled off, he'd send her some flowers or something. "Somehow I don't think she wants to hear from me at the moment," Joe drawled thoughtfully after a moment.

"Probably not, but that doesn't mean an apology is any less called for in this situation." Janey shook her head.

"It's not as if she can slink away and hide for a few days, either."

Joe looked at her.

"It's June, Joe," Janey explained in exasperation. "The height of wedding season. The Thermonopoulos-Thornton wedding is going on this weekend. The ceremony and reception are tomorrow afternoon and evening, and the bridal breakfast is on Sunday morning. It's a fairly large group—two hundred and fifty guests—and Emma has to be there to oversee all the details. Plus, it's a local wedding, so I imagine everyone will have seen the news or heard about her humorously unfortunate run-in with you tonight."

Including their mother, Helen. Joe knew his mom would have a few words of her own to deliver on the subject. He wasn't ready to hear them. "Listen, my camping gear is still in Canada, at my apartment in Montreal. The super agreed to pack up my belongings tomorrow and ship 'em to me, but I won't get 'em until Monday or Tuesday. So you got a sleeping bag and backpack I can borrow in the meantime?"

"Oh, Joe. You can't just run away and leave Emma to deal with this all alone."

Joe knew if he was there it would just make things worse. Holly Springs was too small a community for him and Emma not to run into each other. And the press would be looking for him in Montreal, too. "Coach Lantz told me to lay low until the Monday morning press conference." At which point, Joe was supposed to handle the situation with such finesse that it would fix everything. Although how in heck he was going to do that, he didn't know.

"So you're going backpacking?" Janey asked.

Joe nodded.

"Why not use the family cabin?"

Joe shook his head. The family's mountain retreat just outside Blowing Rock would be ideal. Unfortunately, it was the first place any truly nosy reporter would look. "I need the exercise," he said. And he needed time to think. Because he had no idea what he was going to say come Monday morning that would in any way, shape or form begin to get him out of this mess.

"WE JUST CAN'T HAVE SOMEONE of your dubious... reputation...overseeing our daughter's wedding," Gigi Snow told Emma bright and early Monday morning, in her office at the Wedding Inn.

As much as Emma was loathe to admit it, she had been expecting the dismissal from the image-conscious Raleigh socialite. The equivalent of the white-gloved slap across the face, however, changed nothing in a business sense. A contract was a contract. "You understand it's too late now—with the wedding just six days away—to cancel my services and simply walk away," Emma warned the petite, reed-thin woman.

"Oh, we still want to have it at the Wedding Inn," Gigi said, smoothing her short jet-black hair, then the jacket of her Donna Karan suit. "We just don't want *you* anywhere on the premises."

"I'm sure I can find someone to step in at the last moment, but I must warn you, you'll be liable for two planning fees," Emma stated kindly.

Michelle Snow, Gigi's daughter, a pretty and sweet young woman who rarely spoke up for herself or defended herself against her mother's overbearing nature, began to look embarrassed. As did Gigi's generally indifferent husband, Mason Snow.

Benjamin Posen—the thirty-year-old groom—looked mortified at the additional expense. "But that's going to be another—" he sputtered.

"Twenty-five-thousand dollars, minimum," Emma said, quickly doing the math. Her standard fee was ten percent over the cost of the wedding, and the wedding now had a quarter-of-a-million-dollar price tag, and was still inching upward every single day.

Benjamin Posen began to sweat. He tugged at the collar on his starched blue shirt as if it were choking him, along with the silk designer tie. "I really think we ought to reconsider." The handsome groom glanced at Emma, silently pleading for help. "After all, Miss Hart has done such a superb job for us and worked so hard for months now."

"Are you balking at the extra expense?" Gigi Snow stared down her future son-in-law with lethal ebony eyes. "Because if you are saying what I think you are, Benjamin, that our only daughter's happiness and reputation aren't worth an additional $12,500 on your behalf—"

"It's fine, Mother Snow," Benjamin said in a low, strangled tone. His fair skin turned beet red, below his white-blond hair. "Really, I'll be happy to help out with this."

"Good, I'm glad this is settled. I'll look forward to hearing about your replacement—" Gigi glanced at her watch "—by noon today. Now, if you'll excuse us, we have a final fitting to go to at Vera Wang in New York City."

The Snows filed out, Benjamin taking up the rear, somewhat desultorily.

No sooner had they left, than Helen Hart appeared in the portal. "Your father is on the phone, Emma."

Emma looked at the clock. Eight-forty-five. And already the day sucked rocks. "Thanks, Helen." Emma picked up.

Saul's voice rumbled over the line. "There's a press conference this morning at the arena at 10:00 a.m."

Emma rubbed the tight skin above her eyes. She wished she could do what Joe Hart had allegedly done this weekend—go somewhere and hide. Or what her parents had done: issue a brief, carefully worded press statement about the fiasco and then head for a golf tournament in Southern Pines.

But she'd had to stay and face the music. "What does

the press conference have to do with me?'' she asked her father tensely.

''Absolutely nothing,'' Saul growled sternly, ''which is why I want you to stay clear of it.''

Staying clear of the brouhaha hadn't done much for Emma thus far. In fact, it seemed only to have generated more interest in her side of the story. ''Who's going to be featured?'' Emma asked casually. As if she even had to ask, after the weekend scandal.

''Exactly who you'd think, Emma! Joe Hart.''

At the mention of his name, Emma's pulse kicked up a notch. Pushing the sexy image of Joe—naked—from her mind, she drew in a steadying breath. ''How's he doing?''

''That is precisely the kind of question I don't want you asking, Emma.''

Emma knew that. It didn't, however, deter her in the least. ''Was his weekend as bad as mine?'' Frankly, she didn't see how it could have been.

She had been dogged by the press from Saturday morning on. Local reporters from all four networks had showed up to try to get an interview from her concerning the Friday night incident at her parents' estate. Sheriff Mac Hart'd had to set up a perimeter around the inn, which saved her from having to answer questions by curious media. And of course as her luck where Joe Hart was concerned, would have it, it was a slow news weekend. So their unexpected late-night run-in with each other had gotten a lot of air play.

Emma knew her parents were hideously embarrassed— and so was she. It seemed whenever, wherever Joe Hart came into her life, trouble soon followed. But this time her heart went out to him, because he had been publicly embarrassed at a level only a professional-athlete-slash-celebrity could be. And was suffering the same professional ramifications she was. Like it or not, that gave them something in common. Something to try to jointly deal with.

As if reading her mind, and the direction her emotions were headed, her father repeated firmly, "This is Joe Hart's problem. Let him handle it."

Emma knew her father would be happy to see Joe hang, and part of her would like that, too—for the way Joe had unceremoniously taken her right back to her dorm when he'd found out she was not only forbidden to have anything to do with hockey players but related to his brand-new boss, to boot. But the other part of her decided she was not going to hide.

So Emma said a cheerful goodbye to her father and told Helen where and how she could be reached. Then she grabbed her pager and her cell phone, got in her car and drove to the Professional Sports Arena in Raleigh where the hockey games were held. The guards knew her— everyone there knew her—and they let her in one of the back entrances. Emma stopped briefly in the ladies' room, to make sure she was camera ready, and saw how pink her cheeks were. And knew, as long as the subject was Joe Hart, she would continue to be flushed.

After applying a little lipstick, she headed for the room where press conferences were always held, slipping in through the side door. Joe was standing with his agent and one of the team's publicists. He was wearing a pair of jeans that molded every powerful inch of his lower half, and a short-sleeved silk-jersey T-shirt in a light charcoal gray, that delineated his broad shoulders, six-pack abs and nicely shaped pecs. He looked sexy and ready for anything that came his way, and as she stood there watching him Emma was aware of two things. One, she was glad her mother was apparently not here this morning. She didn't want to have to face her, too. Or deal with Margaret's attempts to steer her away from "trouble." And two, Emma realized, whenever she was near Joe, whenever she laid eyes on him, she immediately began to feel more alive. Alert. And ready for anything, too.

Joe stopped in midsentence when he saw her. Their eyes

met for a breathtakingly long moment. Held. And then he was moving through the crowd of reporters and TV and newspaper cameramen to her side, a polite smile fixed on his face.

As he neared her, Emma could see he apparently hadn't shaved since she had last seen him—a quarter inch, maybe more, of golden-brown beard lined his ruggedly handsome face. She wasn't sure what that meant. Had he decided to grow a beard? Was it a statement regarding his attitude about the circus here today? Did he just want to look tougher, more ready to rumble, when dealing with the press?

Whatever the reason, she was sure it had nothing to do with grooming. The rest of him was impeccably put together. He smelled good, too, as if he had just gotten out of the shower. "What are you doing here?" he demanded.

Emma wished there had been just a tad of warmth in his molten amber eyes. She smiled at him as if they were old friends, instead of adversaries. "I came to see the announcement," she murmured politely, aware their conversation was beginning to generate a lot of interest among the casually chatting sports reporters in the room.

Joe slid a hand beneath her elbow and guided her as much out of earshot of everyone else as he could. "You know they'll pounce on you like piranhas."

Trying not to feel bereft when he dropped his hand, Emma tilted her head up to his and smiled even more sweetly as she murmured back, "I also know I have to answer questions, Joe, about what happened the other night, because if I don't make myself available to reporters, they are going to keep right on dogging me, too. The way I see it—this is the safest venue in which to do it." The fact she was Saul's daughter, and Saul controlled his team's access to the press, would make them wary of angering Saul. Hence, Emma figured she could expect—and answer—some softball questions, go on the record and be done with it.

Joe frowned, clearly seeing the wisdom of what she was saying, even as he wanted to argue with her. For purely argument's sake? "It's a team press conference, Emma," he reminded her.

And her father, the team owner, had already forbidden Emma to be anywhere near here. But then, Emma thought, Joe didn't know that. And what he didn't know...

Aware all eyes in the room were on them, and that many ears were straining to hear what they were whispering about, Emma continued to smile and look into his eyes. They were so close she could smell the sandalwood-and-leather fragrance of his cologne. "You want to hold two separate ones, then?"

Dread shone in Joe's eyes. "No."

Emma drew a deep breath, and leaned in closer, to talk in an even quieter, more conciliatory tone. "Then, here is the plan...."

By the time Emma had finished, it was time to start the press conference. Her father and Carolina Storm coach Thad Lantz, and his coaching staff, walked in. As he looked at the two of them, Saul Donovan's expression did not change, but the look in his eyes did. He wanted to kill Joe. And he wasn't too pleased with Emma, either. But that was just too bad, Emma thought resentfully, because she had a reputation to salvage here, too.

A flirtatious look on her face, Emma stepped up to the microphone first. "I wish you all were baffled about why I might want to make a statement today, but unfortunately—" Emma smiled and shook her head in an exaggerated display of rueful disbelief "—I know you all know what little mishap I'd like to talk about here today."

Acting as if she were Scarlett O'Hara holding court amid a bevy of suitors, Emma batted her eyelashes flirtatiously as laughter rumbled through the room.

The mostly male reporters leaned forward expectantly. Cameras whirred and clicked as Emma went on to explain more seriously, "Everyone around here is aware there have been some robberies in this area lately. So everyone is a little on edge to begin with. I wasn't supposed to be staying at my parents' estate on Friday night, but it was late, and I knew they were headed to Southern Pines, and I just wanted to crash. I thought I was alone in the house. I had no idea they had a houseguest—one Joe Hart.''

Emma paused and lifted a hand toward Joe as more chuckles resonated in the room. ''And, as I gather you have all figured out by now, poor Joe had no idea I had come in there, either. A lot of you have been out to the house for parties, so you know what a big place it is. About ten thousand square feet. Anyway, when I realized I wasn't alone in the house, I got very frightened and I panicked, and Joe reacted with equal zeal to protect the place.''

Emma wrinkled her nose in a playful mea culpa once more, making it all into a private joke she was letting the media in on. ''Anyway, had I not dialed 911 before heading bravely down to get a rolling pin to protect myself, and run smack dab into the man I thought was a burglar, fresh out of the hot tub, and had the local police not been so quick to respond, or the indefatigable W-MOL Action News crew been at the ready, there would have been no film of the infamous event to put on the late news. But it did happen, and everyone has seen the most embarrassing moment in my entire life—'' Emma turned and winked sympathetically at her ''partner in crime'' ''—and probably Joe's, too. And I thought you all deserved an explanation from me personally. As for what I learned from this, next time I want to crash at my parents' place—'' Emma jabbed a thumb at her chest ''—I'm calling first!''

The room erupted in laughter. And then applause.

Blushing, Emma waved off the amusement and thanks of the reporters—for giving them a hot lead to use in their coverage of the story—and stepped back to a corner of the room.

JOE HAD TO HAND IT TO EMMA. She was not only gutsy as heck, she was all grown-up. And it was the grown-up part that had spiked his pulse the most. Before, when he had known her, she had been a confused, albeit incredibly pretty girl with a penchant for hiding who she was. Now she was all woman, and confident as could be. Ready to put it all out there and let the chips fall where they may. It made her a lot harder to deal with, and a lot harder to forget.

But enough of that, Joe thought as the team's general manager finished the formal announcement and Joe stepped up to the microphone. It was time to get down to the business of why they were really all here. His future on the Carolina Storm hockey team. Assuming he still had a future. The set, closed look on Saul Donovan's face at this moment guaranteed nothing except the fact that there would be hell to pay if Joe ever hurt his daughter again.

Sobering, Joe looked out at the crowd. In the second row, was Tiffany Lamour, the Cable Sports News sports show host famous for making—and breaking—careers with her no-holds-barred interview style, and penchant for revenge. Joe had noted that Tiffany'd had a cynical smile on her face while Emma was talking, and an even more evil smile on her face as she listened to the team's general manager go over the details of the three-year, seven-and-a-half-million-dollar contract he had signed on Friday night. The two-and-a-half mil a year was by far more than he had ever earned.

"Any qualms about the no-trade clause?" the reporter from the Raleigh newspaper asked.

"None," Joe lied through his teeth.

"Anything you want to add about what happened Friday night?" the W-MOL TV station reporter, Trevor Zwick, asked with a lascivious wink.

Joe shook his head. "Emma's already set the record straight. She's told you what happened. I have nothing to add in that regard, except—" Joe flashed a regretful smile that was immediately caught on film by about fifty still and video cameras "—that I sure wish I'd found a better way to get on the evening news. Say with a hat trick during my first game for the Carolina Storm?"

The crowd of sports-minded reporters laughed. They knew a three-goal game was every player's dream. And rarely happened.

Joe spent the next twenty minutes answering questions about what he hoped to bring to the team, how his style of play would fit in, and how good it felt to be back home, after the last ten years away from North Carolina.

Finally, Tiffany Lamour took the floor. "Where are you planning to live, Joe?" she asked with a casual smile Joe didn't begin to trust. "In Raleigh, close to the arena, or here in Holly Springs with your new family?"

New family. What the hell was she talking about? "I'm not sure what you mean by 'new,'" Joe hedged carefully, suddenly feeling as if he had stumbled across an angry copperhead in the woods and was about to be subjected to a lethal bite. "As far as I know I don't have any more brothers and sisters," he joked, and saw Tiffany Lamour's expression grow inexplicably even more triumphant. "Or nieces or nephews, either, in the last twelve years," Joe continued in his jovial tone as everyone else around him continued to look as perplexed and caught off guard as he felt.

"What about wives then?" Tiffany asked smugly.

You could have heard a pin drop in the silent room.

Although he felt as if the floor were now dropping out from under him, Joe did his best to keep his poker face. He shrugged his broad shoulders amiably. "I'm not married, Miss Lamour. You know that."

"Au contraire, Joe." Tiffany rifled through some papers in her hand. She studied the page in front of her. "Because, according to reports I've just received, you eloped with a young girl seven years ago."

Joe stared at her. *How the hell had Tiffany found out about that? How had anyone? He had paid handsomely to make that mistake go away.* But knowing there was no way he could deny it now the press knew, he finally cleared his throat, shrugged again, as if it were so long ago he could barely remember, and said, "A youthful mistake." And then some.

Out of the corner of Joe's eye, he could see that although her posture was still as self-assured as ever, the color was draining slowly but surely from Emma's face, as well.

While everyone watched with bated breath, Tiffany edged closer to the podium where Joe stood. "Is that how you still feel about your wife, Joe, because as far as the records show, you are still married to that young girl. Except she is no longer as young as she was, either."

Joe swore virulently and silently to himself as Tiffany continued her speculation triumphantly. "Although perhaps your wife *is* just as irresistible to you today as she was seven years ago. *As was readily proved Friday night.*"

At the direct reference to the incident with Emma, Joe's heart began to pound. He felt sick inside at the thought of what was about to be revealed.

"What are you trying to say here, Ms. Lamour?" Saul Donovan thundered, getting angrily to his feet. He looked as if he had heard enough!

Tiffany Lamour turned to Joe's boss with a smile. "I'm just asking, Mr. Donovan, how you feel about your former, current and future son-in-law."

Chapter Four

Pandemonium broke out in the press room. Her heart pounding, Emma caught the look of shock and outrage on her father's face. Knowing she had to do something to save herself and Joe even further embarrassment, she stood and glared coldly at Tiffany Lamour. ''I don't know where you got your information—''

Tiffany glanced calmly down at the papers in her hand. ''Ye Olde Wedding Chapel in Nooseneck, Rhode Island. That's a little town about thirty minutes or so outside Providence. At the time you were apparently in your freshman year at Brown University and Joe was playing for the Providence AHL team.'' Tiffany flashed Joe and Emma a dazzling smile. ''Which must be how you two met, right? At a minor league game?''

Emma pushed aside the memories of the many nights she had eighty-sixed studying her freshman year to go to the arena to watch Joe drive the puck up the ice and into the net. She had been so wildly in love with him then, so naive…she'd thought the passion they felt for each other was strong enough to endure anything! Little had she known…just how quickly he would dump her in favor of his career.

''Anyway, back to the chapel…'' Tiffany Lamour continued her recitation with a self-satisfied smile. ''Apparently that establishment is famous locally for doing a lot of uh—let's just say—hasty or middle-of-the-night wedding ceremonies. As yours apparently was. Not that it's hard for two nineteen-year-old-kids to get married in Rhode Island, in any case. The legal age is eighteen, and there are no blood tests or waiting period required.''

The rest of the reporters regarded Tiffany in awe. Mostly male, none of them had thought to look into Joe or Emma's private life after the Friday night brouhaha at the Donovan estate.

But Tiffany Lamour had.

And her questioning was reaping a lot of attention. Emma had no doubt this little Q and A would be replayed on news shows across the country. Probably reported in newspapers and magazines as well, since it was the kind of juicy, unexpected gossip the public reveled in about celebrities. And as one of the rising stars of the NHL, Joe Hart was indeed a celebrity.

Joe smiled wryly, even as he laced a hand around Emma's waist and dragged her near. He leaned down to murmur in her ear. ''I guess we've been found out, sweetheart,'' he said, loud enough for everyone to hear.

The men in the room chuckled in equal parts speculation and sympathy. Saul Donovan looked as if he was going to leap across the room and punch out Joe. Coach Thad Lantz just shook his head, as if he couldn't believe the messes his players could get themselves in.

''And now that the secret is out,'' Joe continued, taking her other hand securely in the warmth and strength of his and squeezing it hard, ''I think I'd like some time alone with my—with Emma.''

The assistant coaches and trainers stepped aside, forming a gauntlet so Joe and Emma could exit the room without the reporters and their cameras following. As soon as they hit the outside corridor where security men with badges were standing around, Joe took Emma's hand. ''You know the back way out of here?'' he asked.

Emma nodded. As eager to flee her father's wrath and

earn them some time to regroup as Joe, she tightened her fingers in his and led the way.

WHEN THEY REACHED THE STAFF parking lot outside the arena, Joe pulled the keys from his pocket and hit the unlock button on the remote. ''Let's get out of here before we talk,'' he said, yanking open the door of his low-slung sports car.

Knowing the reporters couldn't and wouldn't be far behind, Emma agreed. ''Where are we going?'' she asked.

''My attorney's office. I have a feeling we're going to need Ross Dempsey's help to get us out of this mess.''

Emma knew Ross Dempsey. The handsome bachelor was one of the most prominent sports-and-entertainment attorneys in the area. He represented a lot of the Carolina Storm hockey players and managed their business affairs. He had been at her parents' Holly Springs estate for numerous social gatherings. Plus, he understood the rigorous demands of professional hockey, on the ice and off. And would know exactly how devastating a revelation like this could be to someone like Joe.

''So what did you ever do to Tiffany Lamour to get her to come after you—us—like that?'' Emma asked as Joe drove away from the arena.

Her question had been rhetorical. But she could tell by the way Joe hunched his shoulders that she had hit a nerve. ''It's a long story,'' he muttered, refusing to so much as slant her a glance.

Emma knew guilt and the desire to keep something private when she saw it. She tugged the hem of her yellow summer suit down toward her knees. ''We've got time.''

Lips tightening, Joe just kept driving.

His silence irked her. ''And given the fact I am now—by association with you—one of her targets,'' Emma continued as she tried to get a little more comfortable in her seat by pushing some of the electronic buttons on the side, ''I think I have the right to know.''

Joe sighed as they came up to a traffic light. He tightened his hands on the steering wheel and cast a glance over at her. "What do you know about Tiffany?" he demanded in a low, gruff tone that made her even more aware of him.

Emma shrugged as Joe's gaze swept over her, head to toe, in a boldly assessing manner that had her skin heating wherever his eyes had touched. "Nothing really, except that she hosts that popular sports show on the Cable Sports News network." Which featured a segment at the end called "Bad Boys of the Week." Emma had a feeling who the next Bad Boy was going to be.

"A network that her daddy owns," Joe interjected meaningfully.

Emma paused, not sure what Joe's point was. "So?"

"So—" Joe pushed down on the accelerator as the light changed and roared out into the intersection "—nothing Tiffany does is 'out of line' because she knows her father isn't going to fire her."

Emma curled her hands around the armrests, tension stiffening every inch of her five-foot-six frame. "You're scaring me."

Joe shook his head and shrugged off Emma's complaint. "Tiffany Lamour's a scary lady."

My opinion exactly, Emma thought, recalling the deliberate way Tiffany had set out to humiliate them both, and gain maximum advantage out of her sensational discovery.

The question was why she had done it that way. Why Tiffany had seemed to be gleaning some sort of personal satisfaction in publically embarrassing both Joe and Emma that way. It had seemed to go beyond the normal newshound on a story thing. To cross over into the personal-feminine-vendetta sort of thing.

Which begged Emma's next question. "Did you ever date her?" And if so, why did Emma care? Why was she already feeling just a tad jealous at the thought?

"No. I did not date Ms. Lamour. And therein," Joe continued in a low, clipped tone, "lies the problem."

Emma paused as Joe turned into the parking garage adjacent to the Hanover Towers building in downtown Raleigh, where flashing signs directed them up to the sixth floor. "I don't get it."

Joe drove slowly, looking for a space. "Tiffany likes to sleep with the men she interviews."

Emma gulped. She wasn't sure she wanted to hear this, but also knew she couldn't afford to get blindsided again by facts of which she was not aware. She turned to Joe as he located a space and guided his sports car into it. "Have you ever been on her show?"

"No." Joe cut the engine and removed the key. "And I don't intend to go on it, either."

"Because you're afraid she will sexually harass you?" Emma got out of the car, into the warm humid morning air. Joe did the same.

Joe hit the automatic lock button on the keyless entry pad on his key chain, and the car responded with a flash of headlights and an affirmative beep. Joe held out his arm, gesturing Emma to walk with him. "Because I know that if I do go on the show, and she does interview me, and I don't go out to dinner with her afterward and take her to bed, that she will then A, never have me on her show again, and B, do everything in her considerable power to trash me to TV viewers and within the league."

Emma was shivering as Joe wrapped his arm protectively around her shoulders, and led her to the elevators that would take them down to the ground floor. "You're serious."

"Dead serious." Joe released a weary breath and punched the down button next to the painted steel doors.

The doors slid open. Emma stepped inside. "She does this all the time?"

Joe followed her and punched ground floor. "Every day." He leaned against the back wall with Emma.

"And no one at her own network stops her." Emma was amazed at that. Even if her father did own CSN, one would think the powers that be would be worried about lawsuits and bad publicity. Not to mention the new sexual harassment laws.

Joe closed his eyes and rubbed at the tense skin over his brows. "First off, no self-respecting jock is going to go to the media claiming he can't fend off the passes of some woman. He'd be laughed out of this country. And probably off his team. Secondly, there's really no way to prove this is what Tiffany is doing. She's very subtle in her approach. It's just understood. It's eye contact. A brush of her hand against the back of yours. She knows the fine legal line and she stays on her side of it."

The doors opened and Joe and Emma stepped out. Mid-morning, the cavernous garage was mostly deserted. "Do people at CSN know what's going on?" she asked as she fell in step beside Joe.

Joe rested his hand on the back of her waist as he guided her through the shadowy labyrinth of parked cars toward the exit. "I'm sure they've figured out by now who is on the top of her hit list and who is not."

Emma lengthened her strides in an attempt to match his. "And they haven't done anything to stop her, either?" Emma asked, amazed.

Joe shrugged. "There was a female producer a few years ago who tried. She was immediately fired from the network, her own professional reputation trashed. Tiffany accused the woman of sleeping with a player who had been on the show."

Emma edged closer to Joe as they hit the sidewalk. Speaking even lower, she looked up at him and asked, "Was it true?"

"Yeah—" Joe's eyes were grim as he leaned down to whisper in Emma's ear "—but they were dating. It wasn't like the producer was hitting on every jock that came on the show."

Emma sighed as they approached the sidewalk. There were other people there, waiting for the light to change, and they had to put off their conversation until they had crossed the street, moved through the marble-floored lobby of the Hanover Building and were in an elevator again, on the way up to Ross's office.

"But it didn't matter in the end, that the whistle-blowing producer wasn't really guilty of sexual harassment, that her affair with the player was a mutual thing, apart from his appearance on Tiffany's show," Emma surmised.

"Nope." Joe's lips were set in a harsh, unflattering line. "The producer was still canned because her daddy didn't own the network."

Emma studied Joe. She could tell by the way he wasn't looking her right in the eye that he still hadn't told her everything. "Just out of curiosity—has Tiffany Lamour ever hit on you directly?"

Joe grimaced in a way that let Emma know she had just made it to the bonus round. "Only because I've never let her get physically close enough," Joe said.

From any other man, Emma might have thought that was just ego talking. The distressed look in Joe's eyes said differently.

Tiffany Lamour was doing her best to get Joe to take her where he didn't want to go. He wasn't going to let it happen. It was that simple.

To EMMA'S RELIEF, ROSS SAW them right away. Speaking for both of them, Joe brought him quickly up to speed about what had just occurred at the press conference. Like everyone else in Raleigh who watched the news or read the papers, Ross already knew what had happened Friday night at the Donovan estate. "So what I—what we—need to know is, was Tiffany Lamour telling the truth?" Joe asked Ross. "Are we still married?"

"Then you're not denying you eloped when you were nineteen?" Ross regarded them both solemnly.

Joe and Emma looked at each other. Both nodded reluctantly.

"And then what?" Ross said. "Did the two of you get divorced? Was the marriage annulled? How long were you married?"

Emma and Joe exchanged glances. "Thirty minutes," Emma replied, making a wild guess.

"About that," Joe agreed.

The normal poker-faced Ross did a double-take. "I'm all ears."

Emma recalled that awful moment of truth as if it were yesterday. The stunned, then angry look on Joe's face when he discovered who her father was....

"Emma?" Ross's patient voice drew her out of her pensive thoughts.

Emma blinked and swallowed around the knot of emotion in her throat. "What?"

"Is that the way you recall it?" Ross asked.

"Recall what?" Emma flushed, embarrassed she had been so caught up in the past she had completely lost track of the conversation.

"That as far as you and Joe knew, after you talked to the justice of the peace who married you, that the papers had been torn up, the marriage wiped completely off the books."

"Yes." Emma nodded vigorously. "Yes, that's exactly what happened."

Joe continued his pacing by the windows, overlooking the Fayetteville Street Mall, the state capitol and sundry other downtown high-rises. "Except it's still on the books somewhere. Otherwise, Tiffany Lamour never could have found out about it," Joe murmured. He raked both his hands through his sandy-brown hair, looking as distressed and disgruntled as Emma felt about that.

"Well, that's easy enough to confirm one way or another. If you two will excuse me a moment, I'll go make a few calls, check public records.'' Ross exited his private office and shut the door behind him.

Once again, silence fell between Emma and Joe. "What a mess," Emma murmured eventually.

"You're telling me." Joe thrust his hands in his pockets. Funny, he thought. He hadn't thought about any of this stuff in years. Or at least he had tried not to. But now it was as clear in his mind as if it had happened yesterday.

He was still deep in thought remembering the past when Ross came in the room.

"The marriage is still on the books. There is no record of it being annulled or expunged in any way."

Joe swore virulently beneath his breath. He thought, but couldn't be sure, Emma did the same. "So now what?" Emma said, abruptly looking every bit as soul weary as Joe felt.

Ross sat down behind his desk. "That depends on whether or not the marriage was ever consummated."

Emma flushed a becoming pink. "We told you. As soon as we walked out of there, we had a fight and Joe walked back in and told the JP to tear up the papers."

"So the answer is no," Joe affirmed.

"I meant in any time since then," Ross explained. "In the last seven years."

Joe could see how that would complicate things, if the marriage was still on the books. Fortunately for him and Emma both the answer was still the same. "No. We haven't seen each other until last Friday."

Ross continued looking at them, waiting. Not quite believing…

"So you're saying—" Ross phrased the query as delicately as he could.

Joe scowled. "No. Nothing happened," he reiterated flatly.

"But you don't believe us, do you," Emma guessed slowly, still blushing, a little bit.

Ross put down his pen. "I do. Others might not."

"And that could complicate things?" Joe asked.

Ross nodded grimly. "More from a public relations point of view than legally, as long as your accounts of the events of Friday evening's mishap are in accordance with each other's."

Seeing where Ross was going with this, even if Emma didn't—yet—Joe swore silently to himself. He hadn't even thought of that. Although he should have.

"What do you mean?" Emma asked.

Ross and Joe exchanged telltale looks.

Finally, Ross continued, "The Storm runs a very clean, scandal-free operation, Emma. What happened Friday night—Joe turning up naked with any woman not his wife—was not good. But that at least could be explained. Your secret seven-year-long marriage, on the other hand…"

Emma turned back to Joe.

His heart going out to her for the mess they were both in, Joe explained carefully, "I think what Ross is trying to say is that people are going to speculate that you and I have been carrying on with each other all along and hiding it from everyone. For kicks, I guess."

"But we know that's not true," Emma protested, incensed.

"In the arena of professional sports, perception is what counts," Ross said quietly. He and Joe continued to look at each other in silent understanding.

"I won't kid you about this, Joe," Ross continued finally. "Saul's protectiveness toward Emma is legendary."

"No joke. After he caught Emma and I breaking up, he sent me back down to the minors the very next day. I never even made it to Raleigh. The Storm traded me soon after to the lowest-standing team in the AHL."

"I remember," Ross said. "I had just started working in Raleigh. Everyone wondered what you had done to ire Saul."

"Well now they know," Joe said glumly. He looked at

Emma pointedly. "It took me another two years to get back into the NHL, Emma."

"And it wasn't your playing," Ross said.

"No, my stats were good." Joe recalled how hard he'd had to work, just to get back to where he was, career-wise, when he had first met Emma. "But there was this perception put out there that I was trouble. I had to disprove that." And it had taken a while. A long, butt-busting while. Joe had no wish to return to that kind of uphill battle.

Emma swallowed hard. She looked even more distressed. "I'm sorry. I had no idea. I mean—my dad never discussed it with me. He didn't even ask me what happened that night. He just told me to never see you again. I said not to worry, I had no intention of doing so, and that was that."

"But you were aware I had been sent back to the AHL," Joe said.

Emma looked abruptly guilty. "I told myself it had nothing to do with me. Or my dad. I mean, it happens all the time. Players get called up to the NHL for a trial, then sent back down. I really wasn't paying attention. Since then, I've spent very little time watching or following hockey."

Joe could believe that.

He had tried not to know anything about what Emma was up to, either. Tried to pretend as if his brief romance and marriage to her had never existed.

For all the good the head-in-the-sand approach did either of them now.

Ross and Joe sighed in unison. Emma looked equally distressed.

"What do you think I should do?" Joe asked Ross tiredly.

Ross lifted his hand, let it fall. "Figure out how to fix it, I guess, within the perception of the public."

Emma snorted in disgust. "Like that's possible," she muttered, rubbing the back of her swanlike neck.

Never one to give up easily, on anything—except maybe his relationship with Emma—Joe turned back to the woman who was still his legal "bride."

"Maybe it is," he murmured as inspiration hit.

Chapter Five

"I'd like to talk to Emma alone for a few minutes," Joe said to Ross, his frustration shifting into the same type of cool determination he showed on the ice, when reacting to some down-and-dirty play by his opponents. "Is there somewhere we could have a few moments alone?"

Emma wasn't sure she wanted that. Not that it appeared it was up to her...

"Sure." Joe's attorney smiled at them both reassuringly, as if he, too, thought it were a great idea. "There's a conference room down the hall." Ross escorted them to a small windowless room with an oblong table and chairs, got them both a couple of diet sodas from the refrigerator in the corner and shut the door behind them.

Aware her pulse was suddenly racing, Emma circled around to the opposite side of the table. She pulled out an upholstered chair with a swivel bottom and sank into it, grateful for the piece of furniture between them. Pretending to be as coolly confident as he, she looked him straight in the eye and murmured, "I take it you've got an idea."

Joe nodded as he popped open the lid on his soda. "The way I see it we can keep on playing defense or we can go on the offense."

Emma had a bad feeling about where this was headed. She had never been a strategy-over-heart kind of person. Joe, however, was. "Spoken like a true right winger."

"Hey." He looked her up and down before returning to her eyes. "Those points I score are no accident. You want to get ahead in this life, you've got to get out there and mix it up."

Make that a really bad feeling. "You want us to scrimmage with someone?" Emma countered dryly, not liking the ornery glint in his eyes one bit.

Joe's chair squeaked as he tipped it back as far as it would go. He rubbed his hand across the sexy stubble on his jaw. "I want us to catch the opposition off guard and do exactly what they aren't expecting us to do."

Emma kept her gaze away from his delectably soft lower lip. "Which would be?"

Joe shrugged his broad shoulders lazily. "Stay married."

Emma choked on her drink, just barely managing to avoid spraying the table. She pressed her hand to her lips as she fixed him with a withering glare. "I don't find that suggestion at all amusing, Joe."

The amusement left his amber eyes. "It's no laughing matter for me, either, sweetheart," he said as he leaned across the table.

Emma gulped, not sure whether to laugh or cry, just knowing she felt like doing both. "Y-you're serious," she stammered finally.

Joe nodded and sat back in his chair, all business once again. "The way I see it, Em, we can keep denying there is anything between us until we're blue in the face. But because people now know that we ran away and secretly eloped when we were nineteen—"

Emma saw where this was headed. "—no matter what we say to the contrary, they're going to speculate that there is still some chemistry between us."

"Right." Joe looked happy they were on the same page, at long last. "And that puts us in a high-pressure situation. So," he continued as pragmatically as if they were discussing the weather, "the logical thing to do is just stop fighting the inevitable gossip. Go with it and stay married. That way, there will be talk for a few days. And then, after a few news cycles, our little scandal will be history.''

Oh, if only it were that easy, Emma thought sarcastically. ''Except we'll be married, Joe.''

Joe lifted his hands, heavenward. ''We're married now.''

Emma curtailed the urge to lunge across the table and grab him by his shirtfront. ''But we didn't *know* we were married until a few hours ago,'' she pointed out sweetly.

Joe twisted his lips into a crooked line then dissented equably, ''That doesn't make it any less true.'' He drummed his fingertips on the table urgently. ''We have to go with reality here, not what we *wish* would have happened. And unless you've got a better strategy, I suggest we go with mine.''

Strategy, smategy. Emma glared at him in exasperation. He was making his plan sound simple and it wasn't, damn it! ''This isn't a game,'' she said, scowling. It wasn't a matter of semantics. They were talking about their lives!

Joe tilted his head back and flashed her a winner's smile. ''*Au contraire,* babe,'' he argued cockily. ''To ratings-greedy newshounds like Tiffany Lamour, it is a game, albeit a very high-stakes one. And I'm telling you right now that I have no intention of letting her win.''

His stubborn competitiveness again. Emma shook her head in withering censure. ''No matter how many people you take down with you?'' she confirmed in a low voice dripping with sarcasm. She had never resented his relentless drive and ambition for ''greatness'' more than she did at that moment.

Emma started to rise, the session, as far as she was concerned, over.

Her hips had barely cleared the seat when Joe reached over and clamped down on both her wrists. His preemptory action caught her off guard and forced her off balance. Her buttocks hit the seat again as Joe continued to glare at her indomitably.

"Let's recap for a minute here, shall we?" he suggested emotionally. "And remember exactly whose fault it is we are in this mess in the first place. Because had you told me who your father was, or how he felt about you being involved with hockey players period, I never would have even been dating you, never mind asking you to run away and marry me. You would have been safe in your little girls-only dorm at Brown. And I would never have had my own rep trashed to other owners, or have been tossed back to the minors or had to work my way up to the NHL all over again. The bottom line is you owe me, sweetheart." He released his possessive grip on her wrists and sat back. "You owe me big."

Guilt swept through Emma. Much as she wanted to, she couldn't disagree, her inability to be honest with him had cost them both a tremendous amount of hurt. But that did not mean his cockeyed plan was going to work. Every inch of her throbbing with built-up tension, she countered passionately, "My father will never go for it."

This time it was Joe who was up out of his seat. But instead of leaving the table, he leaned over it, caged her with his arms and lowered his head, until their faces were mere inches apart. Until she could feel the heat emanating from his body, the strength in his sinewy frame.

"Well, then we're going to *have* to make him go for it," Joe growled fiercely. He paused for a moment, ensuring she understood the depth of his determination, "because it's the only way I can stay on the team!" He straightened abruptly, moved away.

Trying not to feel as bereft by his abrupt absence as she had been stunned by the way he physically invaded her space, Emma pushed back her chair, stood ever so gracefully and purposefully, and straightened the hem of her business suit. She turned a level, patient gaze Joe's way.

Joe turned back to her, his gaze roving her upturned face

dismissively. Noting the strength of her resolve, he seemed to calm down a little bit. "Besides," Joe said offhandedly after a moment, "it's not as if either of us are seriously involved with anyone else."

Emma tried—and failed—to be completely immune to the news he was not romantically connected to anyone else right now. "How do you know?" Emma challenged right back, irked by his presumption that she was as "romantically alone" as he apparently was.

He regarded her smugly, a sense of purpose glittering in his eyes. "One, because when we were caught in a compromising position, no one came over to punch me out afterward or said in absolute horror at the time, 'Omigosh, what will so-and-so think?' And two, I talked to Janey about you the other night before I went camping and she said you are every bit as famous for your 'one and dones' as I am."

Emma's heart gave a nervous kick against her ribs. "One and dones?" she repeated, confused by the unfamiliar slang.

He settled against the opposite wall, arms folded against his chest, and continued playing King of the Mountain— or in this case, conference room. "One date and you're done and you never want to see the other person again. You're completely disinterested."

Okay, so that was true. But it wasn't for lack of trying, Emma conceded temperamentally, irked that "her husband in name only" could still get her so riled up, so fast. Wasn't she supposed to be over Joe? Way over him? As for the rest of her romantic life… During the past seven years, Emma had tried to find someone compatible whom she was attracted to, but it just never worked. The chemistry wasn't there, or their values were so far apart it was ridiculous, or the guy had no sense of humor, or just wanted to get into her pants. It was always something. Always, Emma thought fiercely. And it had nothing to do with the fact that whenever she did let someone else kiss her, all she could see—or think about—was Joe Hart's face.

"And as for me, well we both know, I only have one real love," Joe continued arrogantly. "Hockey."

The sport that had turned into the bane of her existence. "And no woman is getting in the way of that," Emma ascertained sarcastically.

"Right." An edge of belligerence crept into his voice.

Emma smiled, glad she wasn't the only one in the room prone to emotions she couldn't quite control. Maybe this wasn't as dangerous as she'd thought. If Joe wasn't at all interested in having emotional feelings for her, she would not have to worry about falling in love with him all over again. She'd be too darn ticked off at the complete lack of romance in his professional sports-oriented soul.

Sensing a crack in her emotional armor, Joe straightened and continued persuasively as he slowly, patiently closed the distance between them. "All I'm talking about, Emma, is a year," he told her softly, taking both her hands in his. "Maybe two. All we have to do is stay married long enough for the scandal to die down and people to think we gave it our best effort—and for me to establish myself with the Storm, to the point that no matter what happens with us your father won't want to do his level best to destroy my career again."

Emma let out a shuddering breath as she tilted her face up to his. "My father would expect a lot of you if you were my husband." She couldn't believe they were really talking about this!

"I know that," Joe replied, just as seriously. His grip tightened protectively. "And I wouldn't let him—or you—down. I'd treat you right, from day one. Come on, Emma. We were friends once. More than friends."

They had loved each other. Or a least she thought they had.

"We can do this," Joe promised.

Emma swallowed as her thoughts turned unexpectedly

amorous and erotic. "Live together?" she croaked. *As husband and wife?*

"I admit we were awfully young back then, but the physical side of our relationship never seemed to be the problem. You know that."

His kisses had the power to turn her world upside down.

"Besides, it's not as if you're still a virgin," Joe said, continuing his argument sagely.

Actually, although she would prefer he not know it, she was.

"We're seven years older now. A lot more sophisticated."

Emma knew Joe was. And so, she admitted reluctantly, was she. Albeit not in the bedroom. In the bedroom, she was still as innocent as she had ever been.

"We could have a friendship and an affair. And if we were married at the same time, well, so much the better. It's not as if we were never likely to do this. We tried to do it once. We just...failed."

And Joe, Emma knew, did not like to fail. Not on the ice, not in life. Had their abruptly ended marriage haunted him as much as it had her? Was their unexplored love at the root of his crazy problem-solving proposal to her? Was it possible? Would doing this ultimately help her to move on, too? Put her misguided love for Joe behind her once and for all? After all, they were both adults. And adults had sex for all sorts of reasons....

"Look, I'm not saying we'll ever have sex." Or even ever sleep together again, Emma amended silently. "But if we do," Emma continued stubbornly, looking him right in the eye, "I want it to be on my terms."

Behaving as if they were in the midst of very serious business negotiations, Joe considered her demand thoughtfully, then countered with one of his own. "I'll agree to that—if you agree that while we are married we're exclusive. Physically involved only with each other, no one else."

The thought of Joe being hers—all hers—gave her a thrill. Resolutely, Emma pushed it away. Thoughts like that would get her heart broken, all over again.

SIX HOURS LATER, EMMA AND JOE were in her Raleigh apartment, waiting for their guests to arrive. She was in a tailored cream-colored silk sheath with matching jacket. He was in a charcoal-gray suit and tie. He looked fabulous except for one thing. He still hadn't shaved, and his jaw was lined with a good two-and-a-half-days' growth of beard. Catching her glance, he smiled at her mischievously and said, "This bothering you?"

Emma watched as he stroked the golden-brown stubble lining his handsome jaw. "Not at all," she fibbed.

She knew their mothers weren't going to be too happy about him neglecting to use his razor.

But she figured it was his one act of rebellion.

She had hers, too. Though it was her wedding day, she had nothing borrowed, nothing blue, nothing old and nothing new on her person.

If that wasn't enough to jinx their nuptials and prevent any real emotional involvement on either side, she didn't know what was.

Not that she was all that superstitious in any case.

The doorbell rang and she went to let the guests in. Her father and mother were first. Joe's mother, Helen, was second. Attorney Ross Dempsey and Storm Coach Thad Lantz brought up the rear. All were dressed as they had been directed, in semiformal clothing.

Saul Donovan gazed at the flowers around the room, the stands of candles on either side of her hearth. He arched his brow in disapproval at both of them. "What's going on here, Emma?" he asked gruffly.

Show time! Emma linked hands with Joe in solidarity. "Joe and I are saying our vows again."

Everyone blinked in stunned amazement. The room fell silent.

Joe squeezed her hand encouragingly and Emma continued, as if it were the most natural thing in the world, "We know you weren't present the last time, but we wanted you all to witness our vows. The photographer and minister will be here in about—" she consulted her watch "—fifteen minutes." Which gave them, in her and Joe's estimation, enough time to let their parents in on their game plans, and not enough time to argue the validity of their proposed solution. As Joe's siblings surely would have, had they been invited.

Saul's eyebrows slammed together as he glared at Joe. "This is your solution?" he demanded, his gaze roving Joe's stubbly chin.

Relief flowed through Emma as Joe stubbornly held his ground, instead of running off to shave.

"Sir, with all due respect," Joe told her father, as he wrapped an arm reassuringly around Emma's waist, "your daughter's reputation, personally and professionally, has been tarnished by her association with me. Marrying her is the only honorable thing to do, and it's the fastest and surest way the two of us can think to get the gossip to die down, so people just forget what has happened the last few days."

Helen Hart looked at them both a long, assessing moment before she interjected quietly, "But you two don't love each other, Joe."

My thoughts exactly, Emma thought, even as she espoused the argument she and Joe had carefully laid out to justify their actions. "We did once, years ago. And had I not lied to Joe about who I was we might still be married today." Seeing those gathered around them were still highly skeptical, Emma continued persuasively, "We're hoping those feelings will come back to us if we spend any time together."

"And if they don't?" Margaret Donovan asked, acting less like a public relations exec and more like a fiercely protective mom.

Emma shrugged off her mother's emotional concern. She and Joe had promised each other they wouldn't let feelings—theirs or anyone else's—get in the way of what they both knew they had to do. "Then we'll know for sure it never would have worked out and we'll both be free to move on."

No one could argue that.

It didn't mean Saul approved, or was simply going to let it happen.

"Emma, a word with you, please." Her father took her by the arm and led her into the adjacent bedroom. He guided her to sit down on the romantic white eyelet comforter on her antique four-poster bed.

"I know what you're going to say—" Emma held up a staying palm.

Saul plowed on, anyway, "You don't have what it takes to be a hockey player's wife."

Braced for an attack on Joe's character—not her own—Emma blinked. Her lower lip slid out in a dissenting pout. "Really."

Her father gripped the poster nearest him and leaned into it. "I'm not trying to be cruel here, honey—just honest. You've had a very pampered and sheltered upbringing. You're used to having everything and anything your heart desires. Having the attention totally on you."

Emma knew that. But she had never asked for any of that. And in fact, had often wished her parents hadn't become multimillionaires while she was growing up. She would have much rather had their attention, than all the money they'd provided her. Like fancy boarding schools and an even more prestigious university. "And whose fault is that?" Emma prodded dryly.

Her father ignored her attempt to draw their attention to his actions. "Being married to a hockey player is anything but glamorous."

It didn't look that way to Emma.

"First of all, you're stuck in the limelight, while your

star husband's life revolves around one thing and one thing only—his sport. He's gone all the time, tempted by groupies at every turn, and obsessed by whatever happened or didn't happen that day on the ice. Not to mention prone to injury and career fortunes that can turn on a dime and turn your lives upside down.''

''That's a pretty bleak picture you're painting,'' Joe said from the doorway. The look on his face said he had heard—and openly resented—everything Saul had just said.

''Albeit a true one,'' Saul replied grimly as Emma sighed.

JOE KNEW HE COULD SIDE WITH Emma's overbearing father, and possibly win some points with Saul, bettering his current position with the team, but he was less concerned with that than giving Emma the moral support she so badly needed.

''And furthermore, when I told you to fix this situation with Emma this wasn't what I meant,'' Saul continued angrily.

''Oh, I know what you had in mind, sir.'' Joe moved to Emma's side. He stood next to her, positioning himself so close their knees were touching. ''You were hoping I'd just throw in the towel, quit hockey and go away for good,'' Joe continued sternly, aware that beside him, Emma was trembling, upset, as he continued to square off with her father, who was ruining what should have been at the very least, a scolding-free occasion. ''Barring that, ask to be put on waivers and be traded again to another team before the season started, maybe even at a reduced salary. The damage from this debacle to be borne solely by me and my career.'' Thereby bringing back the ''nothing but trouble rep'' Saul had branded Joe with early in his career.

''Obviously, you're not as dense as I thought,'' Saul remarked, something akin to respect coming into his penetrating gaze. "Although you could do a lot more in the grateful category."

"Why should Joe be grateful to you?" Emma demanded, leaping to her feet and moving deliberately away from both men.

Saul turned to face her. "Because," Saul explained with grating patience, "I was good enough to overlook what happened before—with you—and give Joe a second chance to make it with the Storm. Because I thought— erroneously, it now seems—that Joe was mature enough to handle being around you without getting himself and you into trouble."

"Oh, baloney!" Emma said. "You wanted Joe because he's the best up-and-coming right winger in the NHL. You don't give a hoot about Joe personally or his future and his prospects as a player. You knew from the get-go that you'd just get rid of him if he stepped over the line, toward me."

Joe marveled at Emma's passionate defense of him.

Saul frowned. "I made no secret of that when I talked to Joe Friday night. His deal with our team was predicated on his steering clear of you, Emma."

"Only it didn't happen, Dad. We did run into each other that night, and stuff happens, and now we are where we are! End of story!"

"You can either stay and be part of it, or not," Joe told Saul, speaking for both of them. "It's your choice. But if you're leaving, Emma and I would prefer you do it before the press and the minister arrives."

To Emma's relief, her father made no effort to leave nor did anyone else, and two minutes later, the doorbell rang again.

Joe had convinced Emma it would be a good idea if they asked the W-MOL news team to carry exclusive video of their vows. They both hoped the scoop would get the tenacious local organization out of their hair. The local

Raleigh, Durham and Holly Springs newspapers were also represented.

Although they'd had none of the accoutrements the first time they had said their vows to each other, Emma thought it had still been wildly romantic.

This time they had all the trappings, and it was only nerve-racking. At least that was what Emma told herself as they repeated their individual promises to love, honor and cherish each other, and slipped exquisite platinum rings on each other's fingers.

"What God has joined together, let no man put asunder. Joe, you may kiss your bride."

Emma expected Joe to give her a sweet, chaste kiss.

She should have known better.

A reckless hellion on ice, he was no less daring in the first few seconds as her "husband." The amorous glint in his eyes letting her know he planned to make it as realistic and convincing as possible for the audience of doubting Thomases around them, he took her in his arms, bent her backward from the waist and planted one on her.

Shifted off balance that way, Emma had no choice but to wreathe her arms around his neck and hold on for dear life as his lips moved surely, sensually over hers. She swore to herself she wasn't going to play his game, wasn't going to kiss him back, but instead let the hotly possessive kiss be all one-sided and strictly for show.

It was a good plan. A very safe, intelligent way of resisting him. And to her chagrin, it didn't work. Before even a second had gone by, her lips parted under the pressure of his. Her knees weakened. Her heart sped up. And, breasts pearling beneath the fabric of her dress, she melted against him. By the time, the possessive kiss came to a halt, she was tingling from head to toe, and so dizzy with barely contained desire that she barely heard the obligatory laughter and clapping and cheers around them.

Emma's father had a smile plastered on his lips and

poker eyes. Emma wasn't fooled. She knew Saul Donovan was furious, with her and with Joe.

Their mothers, however, had a completely different view of the impetuous display of passion.

Margaret and Helen were regarding them with awe and pleasure, the smiles on their faces seeming to speculate that maybe…just maybe…this crazy relationship of Joe and Emma's could work after all.

IT WAS ANOTHER TWO HOURS before Joe and Emma were able to get the apartment cleared of their guests. First, there was champagne, and then the cake—which the reporters were invited to eat—and more pictures. A few brief statements, words for the camera. Acceptances of well-wishes and a subtly worded message from her father that only Joe and Emma could hear, telling Joe that he had better make Saul Donovan's only daughter happy—or else. A message Joe seemed to take in stride. As if said task were going to be the easiest thing in the world.

Until finally…finally, they were done. And they were alone again.

Joe shut the door behind him, unfastened the first two buttons on his shirt and removed his tie.

Suddenly nervous, not sure why, since their marriage vows had more or less been a way out of trouble and nothing more, Emma began to clean up. "Sorry about the warning from my father."

Joe helped her collect empty glasses and plates and take them to the kitchen sink. "Nothing I wouldn't have done for my own daughter," he told her confidently as he shrugged out of his suit coat.

"Besides," he continued lazily over his shoulder as he made another foray into the living room, "I intend to make you happy. I plan to make us both happy. Otherwise," he finished, coming back to her side, "the next two years or so would be miserable, and there's no point in that."

No kidding, Emma commiserated as she quickly slid the dishes into her dishwasher.

Noting that Joe—who was rummaging around in her fridge, checking out the contents—was beginning to make himself very at home in what was still her apartment, Emma decided to lay out even more ground rules for their cohabitation. She turned to him. "About tonight…?"

Joe shut the refrigerator door and turned to give her his full attention. "What about it?"

Emma smiled at him efficiently. "We need to decide where we're going to sleep."

Joe shrugged his broad shoulders amiably. Amusement twinkled in his golden brown eyes. "The bedroom?"

There was a slight problem with that. "There's only one bed."

He grinned wolfishly. *No doubt about what was on his mind!* "I think we'll both fit," he said.

Emma flushed, despite herself. Time to get serious here. "We can't sleep together," she warned.

Some of the laughter left his eyes, but none of the desire. "Those rings on our left hands say differently."

"Can't you just sneak off somewhere else to sleep?" she asked plaintively. Wouldn't that be so much easier? For both of them? Apparently not, in Joe's view.

He quirked his brow in a way that seemed to indicate she had lost her mind. "On what everyone thinks is our wedding night?"

"No one would have to know but you and me," Emma persisted.

He regarded her skeptically. "What if someone found out? What then?" Joe returned, just as practically. Like he didn't really care, either. Except for the impact on his career and his standing with Saul and the team.

But Emma did care. For reasons that were a lot more personal than professional. "Well, what are we going to do?" she demanded, her senses swirling as he closed the distance between them to mere inches, once again. "We can't share a bed!"

His gaze drifted over her like a sweet, warm breeze. She flushed and stepped back, her waist grazing the dishwasher.

"Why not?" he inquired innocently.

"Because..." Emma swallowed, wishing she didn't recall quite so well how sweet and sensual his lips felt mating with hers.

He took a lock of her hair, tucked it behind her ear. "We might accidentally touch each other?"

Emma shrugged off his touch, stepped even farther away. She reassured herself she did not want him, not at all. She drew a bolstering breath. "Because sharing space that way is just too intimate." Too endearing. Too sexual.

To her surprise, Joe did not point out the fact that when they were dating they had slept wrapped in each other's arms whenever they could manage, without taking it to the next step and actually making love. They had wanted to save that for their actual wedding night.

Which was, Emma realized, now tonight...

He simply moved to the window overlooking the parking lot next to the building. He stared out through the still-open blinds into the dusky summer light, looking unsurprised by whatever it was he saw. He crooked a finger over his shoulder, beckoning. "Come here. I want to show you something."

Reluctantly, Emma crossed to his side, saw the W-MOL Action News van still parked outside in the lot. Immediately, a lot of very unladylike words came to mind.

"What are they doing?" she asked, fearing she already knew.

Joe's lips took on a cynical tilt. "My guess is they are waiting to see if what just happened here was a scam, or possibly get some 'action' footage of us leaving for our honeymoon or whatever it is we have planned for the rest of the evening."

"But we're not going on a honeymoon."

"We know that." Joe aimed a thumb at the center of his chest. "They don't."

"Well, you're going to have to go out there and tell them that and ask them to leave."

Her husband did not budge.

"And raise their suspicions about the validity of our union even more?" Joe asked as the phone rang.

Emma went to answer it, saw from the caller ID it was Gigi Snow. As Emma had hoped, her client had heard about Emma's marriage to the hockey star on a W-MOL news break, and she wanted Emma back on her daughter Michelle's wedding again.

Emma agreed bygones should be just that and promised she would meet Gigi and Michelle at the Wedding Inn the following morning, to continue with preparations.

She hung up the phone to find Joe watching her. Emma sighed. "I've got so much work left to do on that wedding it is unreal." But her hectic schedule the rest of the week would keep her from dwelling on her precipitous marriage to Joe. And that was a good thing, in Emma's view, a very good thing.

"If that's the case, then you need a good night's sleep." Joe shut the blinds, tugged his shirttails out of the waistband of his slacks and finished unbuttoning his shirt. Ignoring her stated wishes to the contrary, he headed for her bedroom. When she made no move to follow him and, instead, just continued looking at him in mutinous silence, he sighed. "Come on, Emma, we can do this, it's only for one night. Tomorrow we'll both move to my place, anyway."

Emma blinked, caught off guard by his nonstop one-sided plans for them. "Your place," she repeated. Did he even have a place?

Joe sighed in exasperation, as if already weary of having to explain himself and the reasons behind his actions to her. "I bought a house in Holly Springs last fall, so I'd have somewhere to crash when I came home to visit my mom, but I haven't had time to fix it up. We'll give your notice here and move all your stuff there tomorrow.''

That was some decision he had just made. ''Why would I want to do that?'' Emma countered belligerently. ''I like my apartment, Joe.'' It was convenient. And fixed up just the way she wanted in southern belle chic.

Ignoring her protests, he came over to take her hand. ''You have to do it because we have to make this marriage of ours look as real as possible. People are just waiting to pounce.''

''Well I'm not going to do it.'' Emma jerked her hand away from his.

''Yes.'' Joe braced both of his hands on his waist. ''You are.''

Emma tossed her head. ''You are not the boss of me.''

A challenging light glimmered in his amber eyes. ''I am, however, your husband,'' he pointed out, just as sagely.

Her heart began to speed. Emma stubbornly refused to give ground. ''So?'' *You're my husband? So what?*

''So I'm too tired to argue this any more, Emma.'' Without warning, Joe scooped her up in his arms and held her against his chest.

''What are you doing?'' Emma demanded, incensed.

''Exactly what you think,'' Joe said, turning sideways to go through the bedroom doorway. He looked down at her determinedly. ''I'm taking you to bed.''

Chapter Six

Joe set her down gently next to the foot of the bed and then finished stripping off his shirt. Disappointment swept through Emma, potent as the chill winter wind, as she realized this was as far as the romantic gesture was going to go. Joe looked as disinterested in making wedding night love with her as she promised herself she was with him.

Aware her feet were hurting from so many hours of standing, Emma did her best to steady her trembling knees and slipped out of her high-heeled shoes. She went to put them in the closet. When she turned back around, he had already stripped down to his boxers, was turning back the covers and climbing into her bed.

She stood there, stunned. Not sure what to say or do next. The evening was becoming so surreal.

He folded his hands behind his head and continued to regard her nonchalantly. "Do you need help getting into your—whatever it is you wear to bed these days?" he asked pleasantly.

"No. Thank you." Aware she had half a mind to sleep in the satin sheath and jacket that had served as her "wedding dress," just to spite him, Emma disappeared into the closet. She grabbed a pair of cotton pajama pants off a hanger, then shut the door, blocking his view.

"I'm very good at unzipping," Joe called from the other side.

Emma rolled her eyes as she shimmied out of her panty hose, shucked her bra and pulled a rib-knit cotton tank top over her head. "I'll bet."

Finished, she opened the door and stalked back out into the bedroom. Head high, she moved past him into the adjacent bath and busied herself brushing her teeth and washing her face. When she emerged again, Joe was still lying there, in her bed, looking as relaxed as could be. Almost ready for sleep.

Was it her imagination, or had her queen-size bed shrunk?

Or was it simply the fact that his broad-shouldered, two-hundred-pound, six-foot-two-frame was taking up so much room?

"I still think it would be better if you slept on the living room sofa." When he didn't budge, Emma looked down her nose at him. "It would be the gentlemanly thing to do."

He snuggled even more deeply into her sheets. "I earn my living with my physical agility, Emma. No way am I going to mess up my perfectly conditioned muscles to try to curve my body like a slithering snake to fit on that trendy red sofa you've got out there, just so your feminine sensibilities are appeased."

As much as she was reluctant to admit it, he had a point. Emma had accidentally fallen asleep on the oddly shaped piece of furniture that served as dramatic counterpoint to all her chintz-and-classic antiques, and awakened a half hour later, stiff, sore and out of sorts. "So sleep on the floor," she urged him unsympathetically. "I'll give you some pillows and a blanket."

"No thanks." He flashed her another sexy grin. "I'm cozy right where I am."

Emma stood with her legs braced apart, and planted her hands on her hips. "I don't see why you're being so difficult about this," she said as her toes curled into the soft ivory carpet.

"Hey." Joe palmed his nicely suntanned chest. "I'm not the one still standing there arguing about what should be a very simple, very safe and platonic thing."

Irritated he was making her feel like she had something to prove, when she absolutely didn't, Emma sashayed primly around to the other side and climbed beneath the covers. Although Joe was strictly on his half of the mattress, she still felt cramped and uncomfortable. Nevertheless, she lay back against the pillows and folded her hands over the top of the coverlet. Stared straight up at the ceiling.

Sighing in satisfaction—or was that triumph?—Joe reached over and turned out the bedside lamp. A mixture of moonlight and the yellow glow of the street lamps poured through the sheer white drapes. For several minutes, they continued lying there in the semidarkness, not moving or speaking. Yet Emma could tell by the tenseness of his body and the meter of his breathing that he was no more inclined to go to sleep than she was.

"There is one thing I'd like to know," he said conversationally after a while.

Which made them even, sort of, because there were a zillion things she'd like to know. She didn't want this situation to be any more intimate than it was. Which was not an easy thing, when she was all too aware of the masculine scent of his soap and skin. "It just kills you to lie there and be quiet, doesn't it?" she said, feeling even more irritated with—and aware of—him.

"Just like it kills you to have to engage in a real conversation with me instead of a witty exchange of insults?" Joe drawled right back.

Emma sighed and turned on her side, so she was facing him. She could do this. She just had to remind herself he didn't matter to her. Not the way everyone now thought, anyway. She propped her head on her upraised palm. "What is it?" she demanded with a beleaguered sigh.

"What exactly did you say to your dad that night, after I left the dorm?"

Emma flashed back to her father's angry face as Saul told Joe Hart to get lost, that he and the Storm coaches and attorneys would deal with him later.

"'Cause he sure looked awfully surprised this morning, to find out we had been to see a justice of the peace," Joe continued amiably.

Emma knew Joe probably didn't care either way, he was just asking the question as a diversion, a way to keep things from turning...sexual, while they waited to fall asleep. So she didn't need to let him know how hard she had tried to protect Joe, back then, from her father's wrath. Even if it meant her father thought worse of her.

She rubbed her fingertips across the embroidered edge of eyelet lace on the coverlet, aware Joe was waiting for her answer. "That's because I didn't tell my parents about us going to the chapel." Not even after it had become clear Joe was not going to change his mind and come after her again.

Joe rolled onto his side, too, so they were lying there, face-to-face. "What did you tell them, then?" he asked softly.

Emma shrugged and turned her gaze from the powerful muscles of his chest. "The truth. That I wanted to drop out of college and run away with you, and you didn't want to run away with me." She paused to look into his eyes. "And when you failed to make me see things your way, you broke up with me."

"And broke your heart." Joe recollected what else had been said in hurt and fury, in the hall outside her dormitory room, while her father listened on the other side of the portal.

Emma nodded, wishing she could take back those oh-so-revealing words, because it would make her so much less vulnerable to him now.

Joe frowned, perplexed. "Then why was your dad

so mad at me for so long—if he thought I had saved you from doing something really stupid?''

Emma released a pent-up breath. ''He was ticked off because you had dared to come near me. Same as now. Because he knows how a lot of the hockey players are, Joe. He's been in many a locker room. He knows all about the groupies and the easy sex and the egos and tunnel vision on the game itself, how that tends to work against a happily ever after and he and my mother both wanted a happily ever after for me.'' It just hadn't happened, Emma realized sadly. With or without Joe.

''I'm not promiscuous, Emma. Getting a piece of…just for the sake of doing it…never appealed to me.''

''That's good to know,'' Emma retorted in a low muffled voice as she rolled onto her other side, away from him.

He hooked an arm around her waist and pulled her back, until her back was pressed against the unyielding hardness of his chest, her bottom nestled against his powerful abdomen and thighs. His lips brushed the curve of her neck as he peered over her shoulder into her face. ''You don't believe me.''

Emma shut her eyes and told herself that was not desire she was feeling. She hugged her arms to her chest, insisting, ''I don't care whether it's true or not.''

''Bull.'' Hand to her shoulder, he turned her so she was lying flat against the mattress once again. He draped a leg over hers, propped his head up on his hand and continued staring down into her face. ''The truth is, you've never gotten over me, Emma Donovan-Hart, any more than I've gotten over you.''

JOE HAD SAID THAT JUST TO get her goat. Or at least he thought he had. Now, hearing her small intake of breath, seeing the look on her face, he was surprised to note that he had indeed hit the nail on the head with his presumption.

More disturbing still was the fact that there was some truth in his assertion where his own feelings were concerned, too.

Not that she was about to concede to being vulnerable, where he was concerned.

"Dream on," Emma scoffed. "And while you're at it, you keep your hands to yourself." She pushed his leg away from hers. "And your lips, too."

How had she known he was thinking about kissing her just now? Just to see where it would lead? He sent her a sexy, sidelong glance. "Scared you'll succumb?" he taunted softly.

Emma regarded him grumpily and refused to answer. "I don't know how in the heck I ever let you talk me into this."

"Probably," Joe predicted complacently, "because you still have a secret hankering for my body."

"You wish!" Emma rolled back onto her side, away from him.

They drifted into silence once again.

What a hell of a way to spend a wedding night, Joe thought. But short of forcing the issue, or taking Emma where she clearly was not ready to go, all they could do was lie here, thinking, waiting to drift off to sleep even when he knew it was going to be impossible. Just one minute of her soft body nestled against his had his muscles tightening, the blood rushing to his groin. And that coupled with the deeply held yearning to make her his…and only his…. Well, suffice it to say, it was going to be a long night. A hell of a long night.

Joe closed his eyes and tried not to think how much he wanted to kiss her soft lips again, or feel the silken heat of her skin, pressed up against his.

The next thing Joe knew it was 5:00 a.m. and the alarm was going off on the nightstand. Emma reached over top of him, her breasts brushing against his chest, as she punched the shut-off button.

Joe rubbed his eyes as she moved away, rubbing up against him once again. Then she was leaping out of bed gathering up her things and heading for the shower. Joe lazed in bed, waiting for his turn in the bathroom, and idly hoping for a tantalizing glimpse of Emma's lively, feminine curves. To his disappointment, though, instead of walking out in a towel or a robe, she was already fully dressed when she emerged some fifteen minutes later.

"You're in a big hurry this morning," he noted, disappointed he hadn't been able to watch her put her lipstick on or brush her glossy brown hair, or even slip on her sling-back heels.

"No surprise there," she retorted in a low, clipped tone. "I've got a lot to do today."

So did he. So reluctantly he hauled his body out of bed and went to find the gym bag he had brought with him the afternoon before with his workout clothes and running shoes, while Emma headed on down to the kitchen.

"Listen, I'm going to arrange to have your lease broken and all your stuff moved over to my place today," he said as Emma was standing at the counter, waiting for the coffee to finish brewing so she could take off.

She turned to him, clearly annoyed. Joe didn't care. Someone had to take charge here. Make some decisions. And it was damn well going to be him.

"Why would I want to give up my place?" she demanded impatiently.

Realizing this was one woman who was not going to be easy to tame, never mind merge lives with, Joe shot back, "Because for it to look as if this marriage is as real as the fates of our careers need it to be, we both have to live in the same place."

A little of the fight went out of Emma's dark green eyes. "So why not here?" she said a little more quietly, as she poured steaming coffee into her stainless steel travel mug bearing the Carolina Storm insignia.

Trying hard not to notice how fresh and pretty she

looked in her work clothes, when he had yet to shower, Joe drew on all his patience and explained, "This apartment is too far from the Storm practice rink in Holly Springs." He paused to pour coffee into a regular stoneware mug. "My place is only five minutes from there. And you work in Holly Springs, too. So it just makes sense."

"Except for one thing." Emma tossed him a sassy smile over the rim of her coffee cup as she paused to take a drink. "Both our families live in Holly Springs."

"So?" Joe shrugged as he added sugar to his coffee.

"So," Emma continued, "having them a half an hour or so away limits the opportunities to run into them and so on."

"I hate to break it to you, Emma, but if either of our families want to see us, they will. Commute into Raleigh or not."

"Fine. Do whatever," Emma said, glancing at her watch. She was obviously in a hurry to get to work. "I don't have time to argue about it."

EMMA ARRIVED AT WORK half an hour before she was expected. Five minutes later, the Snows showed up, with Michelle's fiancé, Benjamin Posen, in tow. "I was just over at the Flower Mart and I have to tell you, none of those flowers are going to be acceptable," Gigi Snow told Emma the moment they were all settled in her office. "I want our orchids flown in from Hawaii."

Out of the corner of her eye, Emma saw the groom flinch. His bride-to-be noticed, too. "That's going to be very expensive," Emma said, getting out her calculator.

Too expensive, obviously, for Benjamin Posen, who was still being expected to foot half the bill of this extravaganza.

"Yes, Mother," Michelle Snow said as she reached over and took Benjamin Posen's hand. "Can't we just rein in the budget a little bit? After all, two months from now, no one is going to remember where the floral arrangements came from.''

''Oh, yes they will,'' Gigi Snow huffed, her reed-thin figure stiff with tension as she paced back and forth. ''And you know why? Because this is going to be the wedding of the year in North Carolina!''

A knock sounded on the door frame. They all turned to see Joe standing in the open portal. He was dressed in athletic shorts, T-shirt and running shoes. He still hadn't shaved and his light brown hair was rumpled and standing on end in much the same way it had been that very morning, when he had rolled out of bed. So why did he look so delectably sexy to her?

''Hey.'' Joe issued the standard southern greeting as he nodded at the group.

They all smiled back, enthralled. Joe, exuding the supremely male confidence of a professional athlete, appeared as if he had expected as much. But then, Emma told herself, she shouldn't be surprised. Being publicly adored—by complete strangers, no less—came with Joe's territory.

Joe extended the index finger on his right hand and beckoned Emma to join him in the hall. ''I need to see you.''

Benjamin Posen looked alert, and interested to see the hockey star. Gigi Snow, on the other hand, began to look annoyed.

Aware she was already on shaky ground with the Raleigh socialite, Emma smiled back at Joe in a crisp, professional way. ''I'm busy here,'' Emma said.

Joe was undeterred. ''This'll just take a minute.'' Joe winked. He came on into the room, grabbed Emma by the hand and tugged her gently but firmly to her feet. ''Excuse us, you all.''

The next thing Emma knew she was out in the hall and Joe had shut the door to her office behind her, insuring them some privacy.

Annoyed by his presumptuousness, Emma dug in her feet before he could lead her any farther away from her work. "What in the world do you think you're do...?"

"Your key." He pressed it into her hand, his fingers lingering warmly against hers. "To my house," he said, looking deep into her eyes. "You're going to need it to get in tonight."

Emma ignored the faintly possessive expression on his face and the thrill that coursed through her at his warm touch. "Where are you going to be?"

Joe shrugged his broad shoulders aimlessly. "Out and about. I've got to go over to the practice arena for some physical-agility tests and meet with my conditioning coach for the off-season."

Finally, a diversion. Emma smiled. "Great." That would keep him out of her hair.

Helen Hart started down the corridor, toward them, just as Gigi Snow opened the door to Emma's office and stuck her head out. Obviously, she was looking for Emma. Gigi looked none too pleased to see her still standing there with Joe.

"Hey, Mom." Joe lifted a hand in greeting.

"Joe. Don't leave here without taking those boxes of memorabilia," Helen instructed sternly. "They've been here long enough. I know how valuable they are and I really don't want to be responsible for them any longer. Okay? If they mean that much to you, you've got to be responsible for taking care of them."

"Sure." Joe shrugged. "I'll get 'em and lug them over to my house right now."

"They're in the storeroom," Helen continued. She handed over her keys.

"All right." Joe reluctantly let go of Emma's hand. "I'll get 'em right now, Mom."

Joe turned and looked Emma in the eye. "I'll see you at home tonight," he murmured, his words heavy with meaning.

Aware all eyes were upon her, Emma pretended to be inundated with newlywed bliss. "I can't wait," she murmured back, wondering what her bossy new husband had in mind for her next.

Helen smiled at Emma.

Out of the corner of her eye, Emma noted everyone in the office was all ears. "How are things going, dear?" Helen asked, nodding at Emma's office as Joe strode off.

Emma sighed and, tearing her eyes from the retreating figure of her handsome husband, motioned for Helen to join their clients.

"Apparently, we've got a problem with the flowers," she said.

JOE BACKED HIS SPORTS CAR up to the service entrance and went back inside to the storeroom. No sooner had he unlocked the door, switched on the overhead light and stepped inside, than his mother appeared. Joe took one look at the expression on her face and knew her demand he immediately retrieve the cherished memorabilia collection he'd started when he was a kid had been nothing but an excuse to get him alone. Pronto.

Joe, however, was not in any mood for a parental "talk." Especially as one-sided as this one was likely to be. "I can get this, Mom," he assured her lazily, pretending not to know she was there to deliver one of her velvet-gloved lectures on his deportment.

"It can wait." Helen shut the door behind her, ensuring them privacy. Her polite smile faded. "Sit down, Joseph."

Abruptly, he felt all of about sixteen. Joe rubbed a hand across his stubbly jaw, knowing his continuing refusal to shave was irritating his mom almost as much as it was Emma. "Look." He swallowed around the knot of emotion in his throat. "I have an idea what you want to say—"

"Do you, now?"

Joe sighed. That holier-than-thou tone. He set his jaw,

slanted her a glance. "Must we talk about this?" he said, just as impatiently.

Helen perched on the top rung of a step stool. Looked him straight in the eye and didn't glance away. "You're the one who undertook such a serious commitment."

It wasn't all that serious, Joe disagreed silently. He and Emma were just doing what they had to do for the next couple of years, for the sake of both their reputations and careers. Sensing his morality-minded mother would not be pleased to hear that however, Joe merely shrugged, and defended himself as best he could under the circumstances. "It's not like I committed a crime here, Mom."

"You did if you married Emma without loving her with all your heart."

Geesh. Hit him where it hurts, why don't you? "Not everyone has or ever will have what you and Dad had, Mom," Joe retorted, stepping past the shelves of starched damask tablecloths and leaning up against the cedar-planked wall.

Helen sobered, her anger and disapproval fading marginally. "They can if they want to, Joe. Love isn't something that just magically happens to you. It's a *decision* you make. Every single day."

What the heck was she talking about? Joe frowned. "I don't get it," he grumbled impatiently.

Helen's expression gentled but her voice held a touch of steel, "The chemistry is there between you and Emma. Everyone sees that. Bottom line, it's why neither her parents nor I stopped you from saying your wedding vows again yesterday."

His sense of dread increasing, Joe found himself getting a little testy, too. "Not to quibble over details, Mom, but you can't stop me from doing what I want—" *or need to do,* Joe amended silently "—at this point in my life."

"That may be true, Joseph," Helen volleyed right back with the legendary Hart confidence. She looked deep into his eyes. "But I can sure as heck hound you like the devil to make sure you follow through on your responsibilities."

Out of respect, and the desire not to make this dressing-down any longer than it was already going to be, Joe bit back a sigh. "Which are?" he queried with feigned politeness.

His mother was not fooled. Not in the slightest.

"To be a good husband to Emma."

"Hey." Feeling the need to defend himself, Joe aimed a thumb at the center of his chest. "I'm providing her with a place to live, food in the fridge." Or he would when he had a chance to go to the grocery. "She already has her own car to drive and an ample salary." Not to mention an heiress-size fortune and wealthy parents to fall back on, if and when necessary. Not that Joe could really see Emma asking Saul and Margaret Donovan for anything. She was much too stubborn and independent. "What more do you want?" Joe demanded of Helen. His mom was acting as if Emma were a poor, unfortunate soul, now she was married to him. It wasn't as if Emma wanted for anything, from what he could see.

His mother gave him the look that was even worse than her use of his given name. "I want you to be her partner, Joe." She spoke as if underlining every word. "Her soul mate. For real."

To be honest, all that sounded a little suffocating to Joe. He gestured in frustration. "Isn't that what a husband and wife are?" he demanded right back.

Helen ignored Joe's mounting exasperation. "I want you to take care of her emotionally as well as physically."

His mother might as well have been speaking Greek for all the sense it was making to him. Joe narrowed his gaze. "How am I supposed to do that?" Joe huffed. When his lovely wife didn't appear to want for anything!

Helen gave him a cryptic smile, more guilt-inspiring than any three-hour lecture on the gravity of his sins. She stood, brushing imaginary lint off her skirt. "You're a team player, Joe, and a remarkably fine one at that. You figure it out."

EMMA STAYED AT WORK as long as she could, but eventually exhaustion, and the need to remove herself from Helen Hart's thoughtful, sympathetic regard, sent her out the door of the Wedding Inn, in search of her new abode, new address in hand.

To her relief, it looked as if she was going to be comfortable, anyway. Joe's house was situated at the end of a quiet cul-de-sac in a newer part of town. The one-acre yard was beautifully landscaped, and obviously had a sprinkler system. As Emma walked up to the house at 8:00 p.m., her dress sticking to her in the muggy June heat, she could hear country-and-western music pouring out of the open windows.

Heart skittering at the thought of what the evening might hold for them, she used the key he had given her earlier and walked inside. And then and there, her impressed attitude faded.

It was quite frankly a disaster. The kind she didn't need. The oak-floored foyer and formal living and dining rooms were filled with boxes, stacked two and three high. Most of the air-express boxes had Joe's name on them, although a few of the moving boxes were marked simply "Emma."

Trying not to think how long it was going to take to restore order to the mess, she kept going down the hall, toward the rear of the house, where a two-story family room and spacious country kitchen were located.

Joe was clad in a pair of bright blue beach shorts. His hair was damp. He smelled of soap and shampoo. And, Emma noted, he still hadn't shaved.

Trying not to notice how tanned, buff and powerful his upper body was, she threaded her way through another maze of boxes, stacked two high, and made her way to his side. He was bent over the back of the television set, connecting cables. "Hey," he said cheerfully, giving her barely a glance, so intent was he on his task. "I was wondering when you'd get home."

Emma looked around. Her serpentine-curved red velvet sofa was against one wall, as were the end tables and console from her apartment. Next to the fireplace and directly facing the TV was a tobacco-brown leather recliner and oversize leather sofa, coffee table, end table and lamp. All still had price tags on them that indicated they had been purchased locally. Probably today. "Why don't you have the air-conditioning on?" Emma asked irritably. She hoped it wasn't broken. It was eighty-nine degrees outside and very humid. And about that inside.

"I like the fresh air."

And going shirtless and shoeless, obviously.

Emma tugged at the collar of her jacket, plucking it away from her skin. She'd only been in here a few seconds and already sweat was trickling between her breasts, welling up between her thighs. "It's hot, Joe." *I'm hot.*

"Hot feels good after the last couple years in Canada." He looked her up and down, taking in the trim silhouette of her business suit. "Put some shorts and a T-shirt on, kick off those high heels and peel off those stockings, and I guarantee it'll feel good to you, too."

Emma fanned herself with her handbag. "Assuming I could find my clothes."

He grinned, one step ahead of her there, too. "I had the movers put all your clothes in the bedroom next to the master. I figured you'd want to put them away."

Not really. But Emma supposed she would have to if she wanted to be able to get dressed for work the following day.

"Hard day?" Joe shot her a brief, sympathetic glance, then went back to what he was doing.

"Impossible." Emma lifted the length of her hair off the nape of her neck.

"Gigi Snow is a royal pill, huh?"

"And then some."

"Yeah, my mother thinks the same thing." Joe paused and looked at her as if trying to find a way to comfort her.

Not sure she wanted him to comfort her, Emma turned on her heel and changed the subject. "Did you move your stuff here?" she asked.

"I had planned to, initially, but it was going to take too long, so I told the super in my apartment building in Montreal to sell all the furniture and pack up everything else and send it air express. So he did. And then I went to a furniture store and bought the essentials and had all that delivered today, too."

"So basically this—" Emma gestured broadly "—is everything you own?"

"Yep." Joe smiled, enthusiastic as ever, when it came to getting things done. He regarded her with bemusement. "I figured the sooner we get settled, the better."

Emma couldn't argue with him there. This mess was very…unrestful.

Finished with the TV, he popped in a tape, picked up a clipboard and pen and sat down in the center of the big leather sofa. "Listen, if you don't mind—" he waved her away like a pesky fly "—I've got work to do."

"Sure." Trying to feel relieved instead of hurt by his abrupt dismissal, Emma changed out of her work clothes, moseyed on into the kitchen and, figuring it wouldn't hurt her to relax a little, took a beer from the fridge. She looked in the cupboard for a glass, found none. Twisting off the top, she headed toward the living room. Joe was leaning forward, watching the tape intently. It was a tape of a game he had played the previous season in Vancouver.

Emma put the bottle to her mouth and drank deeply, while she watched Joe skate to the net, nearly put the puck in, get cross-checked, tripped and shoved into the crease in front of the goal. Joe put out a gloved hand to stop himself and barely missed conking his head with concussion-giving force on the hard metal posts. The fight that ensued was priceless, and, Emma thought, vintage Joe

Hart. He didn't throw the first punch, but when hit, he swung right back.

Just watching the tape, Joe looked furious at the other player all over again.

Emma took another sip as she watched the film of Joe and the other combatant being escorted over to the penalty box by the black-and-white-shirted referees. Joe's head was turned away from the camera, but it was clear Joe and the other player were trading heated insults, as well as ready to go at it all over again.

"What were you two saying to each other?" Emma asked curiously as she sat down beside him. She might not like the mess she and Joe were in, but she loved the passion he exuded when he played hockey. Always had. It was what had kept her going back to the AHL arena in Providence again and again. Well, that, and the passion he had exhibited for her.

"Nothing your ladylike ears should hear," Joe answered in a low, disinterested tone as he made a few notes on the pad in front of him.

Emma watched, fascinated, as the tape showed a furious Joe in the box, dripping sweat, and turning to continue to yell something at the other player in the opposite box. She slid across the butter-soft leather cushions to get a better look at the TV. "Think I can't take it?" she taunted, even as she made out a few of the words: "Yeah, you wish you—" it looked as if he had taunted the other player. You wish you what? Emma wondered.

Joe sent Emma a sidelong glance as her bare thigh brushed his. "I think you shouldn't have to hear that…uh…whatever," he said, deliberately censoring himself.

Again, for her protection.

If there was anything Emma didn't need at this stage of the game, it was to be sheltered unnecessarily by Joe, her father or any other man. Never mind be told she couldn't take a few bad words or heated insults, just as she didn't have the inner grit it took to be married to a professional hockey player. His treating her like a delicate flower irking her beyond measure, Emma plucked the VCR remote from the coffee table in front of them and hit the reverse button. "I'll just figure it out for myself, then."

Emma pushed Play on the VCR remote.

Joe pushed stop on the TV remote.

The TV screen went blank.

Thwarted, Emma turned to him. Joe grinned, clearly realizing—and enjoying, Emma noted cantankerously—he was getting under her skin by refusing to cooperate with her. And suddenly she knew this battle was about much, much more than whatever had or had not been said at that particular hockey game.

He lifted a censoring brow in her direction. "Are you going to let me watch my game tapes undisturbed? Or not?" he asked plainly. If the answer was no, there was clearly going to be hell to pay.

"Not," Emma clarified defiantly, holding the challenge in his eyes, even as she reached across his lap to wrestle the TV remote from his hand, "until you either tell me what I want to know or let me see for myself."

Joe shook his head in wordless amusement even as he let the electronic device go with surprisingly little quarrel. "Then you've no one to blame but yourself," he surmised victoriously as he put two fingers in his mouth and let out a startlingly loud whistle. Fists closed, he crossed his arms in front of his chest and held them there. "Two minutes for interference!" he declared, grabbing her wrist and pulling her over onto his lap.

Trying not to laugh at his unexpected morph into hockey referee, she kept her hold on the remote and tried without much success to scramble off the hard cradle of his thighs. A playful light in his eyes, he wrapped one strong arm around her waist and used his other to divest her of the remote and toss it aside, well out of reach. "Into the penalty box you go."

Feeling his immediate arousal, as well as her own tingling response as their bare legs rubbed up against each other, Emma flushed and shoved at his chest. She wished it wasn't so hot in here, so intimate. And more than that, she wished she had remembered sooner that Joe Hart was a man who worked hard and played hard, and when he wasn't doing one, he was diligently doing the other. "Stop that!" she commanded, even though she knew it was too late—she had interrupted his work—and now that he had switched gears, she was going to have to "play," too.

"Ah-ah-ah!" Still holding on to her with one arm, he made yet another "call"—via a punching motion to the side, his arm extending downward from the shoulder. "Another two for roughing!" Tightening his grip on her possessively, he ignored her unsuccessful attempts to wiggle out of his grip and shook his head at her in mock dismay. "Shame on you, Mrs. Hart!"

Being called by her married name sent another shimmer of awareness through her. Aware all her struggling was doing was increasing the friction between their already overheated bodies, she stopped and regarded him warily.

To her dismay, he had the same look of utter concentration and ruthless determination he had in his eyes when he was playing a game. The breath stalled in her chest, even as anticipation swept through her body, as she thought about what it was going to be like to be in a clinch with him again—without an audience chaperoning them this time.

If his kiss at the wedding had been sexy and exciting, she could only imagine what his kiss *now* would be. "Joe—" she warned, doing her best to remain imperious as she splayed her hands flat against the hard, bare surface of his chest and angled her chin up at him.

"I know you're new at this, so I'll give you a helpful hint," he offered with mock gallantry, her attempt to simultaneously calm him down and extricate herself only adding fuel to the fire. "You don't want to add unsportsmanlike conduct to the mix," he told her gravely, bending his head to kiss the nape of her neck, as one hand slid beneath the hem of her cotton blouse to caress the skin just above her waist. "That might get you sent to the locker room for the rest of the game."

If the penalty box was his lap, Emma didn't want to even think where the locker room might be.

Aware she wanted nothing more than to call a halt to the game and kiss him, really kiss him, without an audience or a reason this time, and that her heart would be in real jeopardy if she did, she simultaneously stomped on his instep and elbowed him in the chest.

His startled grunt of dismay ringing in her ears, she vaulted off his lap. Only to feel his foot come up, just as deliberately and sneakily, beneath her ankles. She went flying—he caught her around the middle and flipped her. The next thing she knew she was lying prone on the sofa, looking up into the very satisfied expression on his face. His body was draped along the length of her, blocking any thought or hope of exit. "I'm afraid I'm going to have to add another five minutes for that little display," he informed her with mock severity. "Fisticuffs are not tolerated in this game."

"It wasn't fisticuffs," Emma argued, even as she tried unsuccessfully to bring her knee up. Rookie or not, she was not going down without a fight.

"Oh, I beg to differ on that," he drawled, capturing her wrists and bringing them above her head and anchoring them there even as he parted her knees with his and sank his weight into the cradle of her thighs.

"It felt very…oh, I don't know—" he paused playfully, his ardent gaze lingering on the curves of her breasts before returning to her face "—down and dirty to me. And frankly, I have to tell you, Mrs. Hart, I was shocked," he murmured as he brushed his lips over hers. He continued to regard her mournfully. "I can see I underestimated you as an opponent, something I try never to do."

But she did not for one second want to be his opponent. Reason coming quickly back, she shook her head at him in slow, deliberate warning. "Joe, you are not going to kiss me," she stated plainly. Not this way. Not without love.

But his sexy grin only widened. "Want to bet?"

Chapter Seven

Joe knew Emma didn't want them getting close again. Until he had kissed her at the wedding yesterday afternoon, and shared a bed with her—albeit platonically—he hadn't wanted that, either. But now that they were married, and destined to stay together for at least a year or two, he saw no reason why they should deprive themselves of sexual comfort and satisfaction. And he figured Emma would eventually come to that conclusion, too. Sooner, if he took the time to demonstrate the pleasure they could have in store, given the time and opportunity and relatively little effort.

So he took her chin gently in hand and lowered his lips to hers. She murmured a soft, sexy sound of protest and clamped her lips tightly shut. He grinned. He always had liked a challenge.

When the kiss she'd been expecting didn't come, she opened her eyes again. He kissed the other corner of her mouth. "Expecting something else?" he drawled, and thought he saw something—disappointment maybe?—flicker in her pretty eyes. "Something slower?" He pressed his kiss to her cheek. "Or hotter?" He brushed a caress across her temple. "Or wetter?" He stroked the shell of her ear with his tongue.

This time she did moan and buck against him, her

breasts brushing the hardness of his chest. Lower still, he felt the blood rush into his groin.

"You're going to pay for this," she swore emotionally.

"Because I kissed you?" Joe planted another one on her chin, enjoying the feel of her, so warm and close and feisty, almost as much as the raw desire reflected in her eyes. "Or because I didn't?" he taunted, even more softly. *Not the way she wanted, anyway.*

Her chest rose and fell with the quickness of her breaths. She struggled against his grip. He held fast. "I mean it, Joe."

"So do I." He tunneled his free hand through her hair, tilting her face up to his, her lips to his. "So make me pay, Emma," he urged her softly as he slowly, deliberately lowered his lips to hers. "Make me pay for everything and anything I've done to you."

He knew she didn't mean to kiss him back—any more than he had meant to be kissing her this evening—and somehow that made the culmination of their long-denied desire all the sweeter. Groaning, he deepened the kiss, exploring the soft, sweet cavern of her mouth, and the silky give and play of her lips against his. Never passive, she took the lead and kept right on kissing him, long and hard and deep, soft and sweet. Until Joe's heartbeat hammered in his ears and he was so aroused he could barely think. He didn't know how or why or when, but suddenly she was every bit as needy and in control of the situation as he.

Emma hadn't meant to give in to him, to the pressure of his lips and the plundering sweep of his tongue, but the moment he had begun to kiss her—really kiss her—her heart had soared and every ounce of her restraint had fled. Making her want only one thing. To be close to him again. As close as they had once been meant to be, closer than they had ever been before.

He let go of her wrists and she wreathed her arms around his strong, broad shoulders, melting against him in boneless pleasure. And still Joe kissed her, as if he meant to have her and make her his.

Completely caught up in the moment, Emma smoothed her hands down the warm solid muscles of his back. Lower still, to the waistband of his shorts. She moaned again, loving the warm, hard, masculine feel of him. The pressure and weight of his body draped over hers. Never before had she been so tempted to let go of caution, and just feel, want, need. Take each moment as it came, without thought or worry over the future. And that was when he broke off the kiss and lifted his head, looked deep into her eyes. "Let's go to the bedroom, Emma."

The words were soft, matter-of-fact, and they acted like a cold bucket of water on her overheated senses. They were talking about sex here. Not the love she needed, wanted, had to have. "No." Emma struggled to sit up halfway, and this time he let her. "We can't." She shoved the hair from her eyes.

Joe sat up, too. Moved so they could both swing their legs over the side of the sofa. He looked at her. To her frustration, whatever he was feeling was well hidden.

"I don't get it." His voice was low, carefully neutral.

Emma swallowed, wishing that she was as well versed as her husband in curtailing her innermost emotions and desires at the instant a time-out was called. Feeling like she had just been called over to the bench by an unhappy coach, Emma stood. Embarrassed she had behaved so wantonly, so fast, she turned to him, determined to make him see this wasn't a game they were playing. "It's not that I don't want you," she said in a low, strangled tone. "I do."

He lifted his palms. "Then what's the problem?" he asked in a low, gruff, kick-butt athlete's tone.

The problem was she knew if they made love, or took their kisses any further, the passionate tryst would end up involving her heart, and she couldn't let that happen. Joe had hurt her enough before when he walked out on her—and their marriage—because he had been afraid his hasty marriage to her would damage his standing with the team. She couldn't let it happen again. Couldn't let him make her fall in love with him all over again. This time, to secure his position on the Storm. Because that, in her mind, was just as bad, as what had happened before. "Because if we let ourselves make love it's going to seem like a real marriage," she said flatly.

Joe got to his feet, too. Her heart raced as he squared off with her once again. "It is a real marriage."

"Legally," Emma conceded, jerking away from him. "Not in here." She pointed to her heart.

HER OPINION STATED, EMMA said a strained good-night and went off to sleep alone in the guest room.

Unable to sleep, Joe settled back down on the sofa and turned on the television. But no matter how much he tried, he was unable to concentrate on the game tape he had been studying.

Frustrated because it wasn't like him to think of anything but hockey twenty-four hours a day, seven days a week, Joe hit the pause button on his VCR and went out to the kitchen for a light-carbohydrate beer.

He'd thought he could handle living here with Emma. That it would be like having a roommate again, albeit one of the opposite sex, instead of a teammate.

He had figured they could reside under the same roof.

Make joint appearances when required.

And pretty much go their own separate ways the rest of the time.

He realized now that was going to be impossible.

He was as physically attracted to Emma as ever. He couldn't be anywhere near her without wanting to hold her in his arms and kiss her passionately, without wanting to tumble her into bed and really make her his. It was territorial. Male. Instinctive. He wanted her to be his woman and his alone. Unfortunately, Joe realized as he twisted off the cap and took a long thirsty drink, Emma did not want to be tied to him in that way.

The way he had hurt her in the past made her afraid to trust him.

And though that wasn't all his fault, he knew he was responsible for some of it. And that in turn left him riddled with guilt.

He had known from the beginning that her sheltered life had left her both inexperienced with the opposite sex, and hence, vulnerable, to the potent come-ons of guys like himself. Just as he had realized that she was as sexually attracted to him as he was to her. And that sleeping with him would signify the kind of lifelong commitment he had *not* been—at the reckless age of nineteen—afraid of making.

Who knew what might have happened if she had told him the whole truth about her identity and family connections from the get-go—and they had stayed married that first year and actually consummated their relationship…? But they hadn't. And the two of them had both moved on. To the point he hadn't figured the two of them making love now would be any big deal.

He had been wrong. As usual. Joe sighed. And now they had yet another misstep to deal with.

"I CAN'T LIVE LIKE THIS."

Joe looked up from his morning newspaper to see Emma standing in the portal of the breakfast room. She was dressed in a pretty pale yellow business suit that molded her slender curves, and high heels that made the most of her spectacular legs. She smelled like perfume and shampoo. Just like that, his pulse was off and running….

Joe swallowed the bite of PowerBar he had in his mouth and took a drink of juice, trying all the while to appear a lot more nonchalant than he felt.

Trying hard not to notice how soft and glossy her hair looked, he regarded her cautiously. "What do you mean?"

Was she talking about the fact they'd flirted with the idea of having sex last night? 'Cause he had been awake most of the night, body aching, his mind filled with lustful—and luscious—thoughts, even as he wished in retrospect he had used a little more finesse to get her from the sofa to the bed.

Emma gestured around her broadly before striding through the sunlit kitchen to the family room beyond. "It looks like a dorm room exploded in here, Joe."

And it felt a little too homey having her here with him first thing in the morning, before he could even wolf down some breakfast. Aware it was suddenly a little hard to breathe, Joe looked over at her. Whatever it took to get her off his case... "You're saying you want me to cart my boxes to another area of the house?"

"No," Emma explained as if he were particularly dense, "I want you to unpack them."

Joe frowned. He had gotten kind of used to living out of boxes. It made it easier when he had to move on to the next place.

Emma strode past him in a whiff of tantalizing floral perfume. Looking particularly feisty with agitated color staining her high, elegantly shaped cheekbones, she plucked up a neon beer sign from the top of one of the boxes and scowled at it.

Joe tipped his chair up on two legs and leaned back thoughtfully. He knew where she thought that belonged. "I guess I could mount that above the fireplace," he drawled, just to irritate her.

Her mouth dropped into a round O of surprise. Her eyes narrowed to slits. "Tell me you're joking."

He had been. Until he had seen her reaction. "Think it would look better above the sofa, huh?" He stood and began rummaging around his toolbox for the hammer and nails he knew were there somewhere.

Her glance traveled over the T-shirt-and-athletic-shorts-clad body before returning, with cool fury, to his face. "I think it would look better in a tavern."

Joe nodded enthusiastically. "Exactly the theme—or is it decor—I was going for in here."

"Seriously, Joe—" She was suddenly right next to him, trying to keep him from picking up the hammer.

Pretending the feel of her soft hands on his skin wasn't causing a swift, hot reaction elsewhere in his body, Joe straightened up and turned to face her. "I know what you're thinking, but no way am I putting this in the master bedroom, above our bed. That's where my picture of dogs playing poker goes."

She ignored his bluff to concentrate on the most meaningful thing he had said.

"Our bed?" she repeated, in mocking disbelief.

"Well…" He shrugged, using every opportunity to lobby for what he had decided during the long lonely night that he wanted, as soon as humanly possible. "We are married, sweetheart. And that brings with it certain… perks."

Perks, Joe noted, Emma had no intention of enjoying today, tonight or any other time in the near future.

Emma dropped her hand and rolled her eyes. Looking suddenly as if she couldn't get far enough away from him, she strode past him, arms clamped across her waist in a way that drew—and kept—his attention on the softly rounded curves of her breasts. She stopped next to the boxes of his hockey memorabilia, which were set next to the big glass-fronted, mahogany display case Joe had bought the previous day.

Ignoring what she could not dispute, she stated firmly, "At least put this stuff away today."

Joe had been planning to—in fact, that had been on his agenda during the midday break between the dual practices he had scheduled at the arena. Until she had tried to tell him to do just that, anyway. "I don't know." He braced his hands on his waist, considering. "Maybe I will. And then again, maybe I won't."

Temper flared in her emerald-green eyes. Emma released a long, slow breath, then told him, "I mean it, Joe. I need order in my life."

Order was the least of what she required, as far as Joe was concerned. "And I—" he clasped his hands around her waist and drew her flush against him "—need you."

"Joe—"

He cut off whatever she was going to say with a soft, persuasive kiss that quickly had her fully pressed against him, melting in his arms. She had used a peppermint-flavored mouthwash, and the taste of it mingled with the sweetness that was her. Knowing it was likely his only chance to have her before they both headed off to work, he foraged her mouth. When she moaned, he drew her even more flush against him, so she could feel his hardness. He wanted her to know how much she excited him, and he wanted to arouse her, too. Raw longing swept through him as the continued thrust and parry of their tongues sent a wake-up call to every inch of his body. And Joe knew, when they did make love—and they would, soon—it was going to be hotter, wilder and more exciting than anything either of them had ever experienced.

Knowing, however, that he did not intend to make love to her for the very first time and then rush off—anywhere—he let the kiss come to a lazy close and drew back reluctantly. Her eyes were misty, her lips damp and parted. To his immense satisfaction, she looked every bit as carried away on the tide of passion as he. "You're not playing fair," Emma whispered shakily.

Fair had nothing to do with it, as far as Joe was concerned. There was only reality and fantasy, and damned if Emma Donovan-Hart wasn't a mixture of both. His body taut with need for her, he told her gruffly, "I play to win. Always have, always will."

"Isn't that the truth," a low feminine voice said from the patio off the family room.

Joe cursed inwardly as he realized they weren't alone. Then he and Emma looked over to see none other than CSN TV host Tiffany Lamour standing on the other side of the open screen door.

HER HEART STILL RACING from Joe's passionate kiss, Emma watched as Tiffany Lamour slid open the screen door and walked in like she owned the place. Tiffany's glance slid over to the boxes containing the hockey memorabilia, the Gordie Howe practice jersey atop of one of the boxes. "I'd heard rumors about your collection," Tiffany murmured, stepping nearer. She paused to finger the fabric before turning back to Joe. "But I had no idea you'd have it here. At the house. Out in the open like this. Especially given what happened in Holly Springs last night."

Emma had to agree with Tiffany about that. Anything that had belonged to the Detroit Red Wings Hall of Famer who had played major league hockey in five different decades was incredibly valuable. Anything with his name on it that bore the wear and tear of lots of use, even more so. As for the rest... "What happened last night?" Emma asked curiously. Unlike Joe, she hadn't read the paper, or thought to listen to the news on her bedside radio-alarm clock.

He turned back to Emma. "The thieves stole some golf clubs from a pro shop," Joe said in a low, bored tone.

"At the Holly Springs Country Club five miles from here! And there were twenty-five sets of them, all either pure titanium or a titanium-graphite mix, as well as a cache of custom-made drivers. And they also took some memorabilia that had been under lock and key, including a signed ball used to win the U.S. Open several years ago."

Whoa, Emma thought. She knew how much her dad's clubs cost. Clubs of that quality, in that number, easily totaled in the tens of thousands of dollars.

"How do you know all this?" Emma asked, not only annoyed Tiffany had interrupted her and Joe, but witnessed them kissing so passionately to boot.

Joe left Emma's side long enough to retrieve the Raleigh newspaper. He found the City and State section, and brought it back to her.

At the top, a bold black banner proclaimed, Golf Club Bandits Strike It Rich at Local Pro Shop!

Tiffany continued espousing her knowledge while Emma scanned the article herself. "The article quotes your brother, Mac, the Holly Springs sheriff, as saying this was the eighth robbery in the Holly Springs area this spring. And he is theorizing the hits are being orchestrated by someone with an insider's knowledge of the local golf scene, because thus far only places with really valuable clubs are being hit, and no one has been home when any of the stuff was taken from the private residences."

"So?" Joe challenged Tiffany.

"So, that being the case, I think you would be worried about having your hockey memorabilia like this since everyone knows about this collection and you don't appear to have a security system installed," Tiffany said.

Geesh, she was nosy and overbearing, Emma thought, belatedly aware she had noticed no such security system herself. Emma considered Tiffany Lamour to have an irritating amount of concern for someone she did not even have a friendship with. Unless she was trying to use this issue to get closer to Joe...

"Thanks for the concern, but—" Joe moved as if to escort Tiffany to the door.

Tiffany put up a palm to keep him from taking her elbow. "I didn't come over here to talk to you about your lack of foresight in that regard," she said.

"Do tell," Joe remarked dryly, his face devoid of expression.

"And," Tiffany continued before either Joe or Emma

could say anything else, "I had no idea she would still be here, either."

Well, that was witchy, Emma thought. And unfortunately, all too true. Usually, she was at her office at the Wedding Inn by seven-thirty in the morning, and here it was nearly eight-fifteen and she was still standing around talking.

"Speaking of which…" Emma looked around in an attempt to locate her shoulder bag and keys. Gigi Snow was probably already waiting for her, with a list of new and unreasonable demands.

Joe pulled Emma back into the curve of his arm, using her like a shield against their early-morning interloper. "What can we do for you, Ms. Lamour?" he asked, stiffly.

"Now, Joe." Tiffany beamed an openly seductive smile at him. "There's no need to stand on formality. Particularly after all we've been to each other."

Been to each other? Had there been something more between them, something Joe had yet to mention? Emma wondered jealously. She turned to Joe uneasily.

Joe looked at Tiffany as if he had never seen her before and didn't even know her name. An awkward silence fell that he made no effort to bridge. Tiffany flushed at Joe's rudeness, but continued on as if he had welcomed her warmly into their home, anyway. "I would like you to be on my show, Joe. I want you to do an in-depth interview about your move to the Carolina Storm."

"Too early for that."

If, Emma thought caustically, he ever agreed to it at all. Somehow, she didn't see him doing so. And neither apparently did Tiffany, judging by the petulant slide of her lower lip.

"I disagree, Joe," Tiffany persisted in a low, sultry voice as she looked Joe right in the eye. "I think, given the enormous amount of interest in your personal life right now, that it is the perfect time for you to bare your soul on TV."

Joe didn't look away. "I don't discuss my personal life," he said.

Something shifted in Tiffany's expression, became ruthless as she warned, in the same silken tone, "You can't afford not to do this, Joe."

Or what? Emma wondered, as animosity flowed between the two. "I'll be the judge of what I can and won't do," Joe returned in a cool, neutral voice. He stepped forward and gripped Tiffany Lamour's elbow the way he would have taken hold of something smelly and disgusting that needed to be taken out to the garbage.

"Now, if you'll excuse us, Ms. Lamour, I'm driving my wife to work this morning, and we really have to go."

Joe walked their uninvited guest through the rest of the house and practically pushed Tiffany out the front door. Tiffany pretended it was a courtesy. They all knew it was not.

"Smooth," Emma said as Joe shut the door behind her.

He braced his hands on his waist and looked down at her. "You about ready to go?" he demanded briskly.

Emma made a face. "You're really going to drive me to work?"

His lips formed a grim line. "Yes."

"Why?" Emma persisted.

Joe shrugged. "I want her to see us leave together."

"Because…?" Emma prodded.

Joe snorted impatiently. "Because she obviously suspects our marriage is a sham. This, plus the fact that we are actually living together, will prove it's not."

Emma tensed, even as she told herself she shouldn't be surprised that this—like everything else about their renewing their wedding vows—was just a publicity ploy, meant to keep them out of trouble. With the press. And her father, and hence the team. Hadn't Joe made it perfectly clear to her, time and time again, that hockey was his first—his only—true love? Why then did she keep expecting him to transfer some of that heartfelt devotion to her and their marriage?

"Is that the only reason?" It was not really the question she wanted to ask him, but it was the only one that came out.

Joe blinked. "What do you mean?"

Speak now or forever hold your peace.

"Tiffany Lamour seems...awfully interested in you," Emma managed to say finally. Too interested, as it happened, for Emma's comfort. What was it her father had said, when he had tried to explain to her why he didn't ever want her involved with a hockey player? *"You have no idea what kind of temptation players face, Emma, the things some women do, the way they throw themselves at the men.... And it's a temptation that never ends, not as long as a player has his name on the roster...."*

Joe slanted her a haphazard glance. "So what if she is?"

This wasn't news to him. Nor was it, apparently, cause for concern. At least in his view. Emma swallowed. *I have no reason to be jealous here,* she warned herself silently. *Just because Tiffany is beautiful—in that brittle, slim, blond way—and powerful enough to substantially help or hinder Joe's career. And is pursuing him openly in the light of the scandal of our marriage.*

None of that meant Joe was vulnerable to Tiffany's machinations. He certainly hadn't looked susceptible just now.

And as for her father, he had been thinking she didn't have what it took to be the wife of a professional athlete. She could handle Tiffany and more. All she had to do was be honest with Joe, and encourage him to be just as forthright with her. "So I couldn't help but notice that Tiffany seems to get under your skin," Emma noted. In a way few others do.

"It's because she's got that whole spoiled-heiress thing going for her," Joe said as he located his socks and running shoes and sat down to put them on.

Emma went over and shut and locked the sliding doors. "You resent the fact that she comes from a wealthy family?"

Joe got up to help her close and lock the windows on the first floor. "I resent the fact that she uses her father's power and prestige to land herself a talk show on the cable network that her daddy owns, and then leverages that to throw what amounts to an on-air temper tantrum-revenge session whenever she doesn't get exactly what she wants. I can't stand women like that. Who grew up having everything they ever wanted, never at any cost to themselves."

Emma'd had her fill of spoiled heiresses, too. At boarding school. College. Even now. "You sound like you really know the type," she said sympathetically, hoping he wasn't lumping her in there, too.

"I ought to," Joe said with a beleaguered frown as he scooped up his keys and, with a hand on her shoulder, directed her toward the front door. "I watched my mother deal with enough of them at the Wedding Inn over the years."

Emma walked out with Joe. She saw Tiffany Lamour sitting in a rented Cadillac, the engine running. Tiffany had her gaze directed at the sheaf of papers she was rifling through. Joe had been right, Emma noted, when he figured Tiffany would dawdle until Emma left. Hoping, perhaps, to get another shot at Joe? Alone this time?

Behaving a lot more gentlemanly than usual, Joe pretended not to see Tiffany still parked at the curb as he opened the car door for Emma and waited while she got in.

Emma figured if he could do it, she could, too. So she picked up the threads of their conversation as he slid behind the wheel. "A lot of the brides who get married at the Wedding Inn are from very wealthy families," Emma mused.

Joe nodded as he slid the key in the ignition, started the

car and backed it out of the driveway. He rested his right arm along the top of the seat, so it brushed Emma's shoulders possessively. "And the majority of them are spoiled shallow, and apt to run at the first sign of trouble or when they don't get their way," he continued with feeling as they drove away. "Not to mention lie and manipulate and do whatever seems expedient to get what they want."

Aware he was getting a little carried away with his generalizations, and that those assumptions were now broad enough—and unfair enough—to include her, Emma rolled her eyes. "Speak freely, why don't you, about the young and privileged?"

"Hey." Joe sent her a quelling glance. "I'm not lumping you in with the likes of those."

"Good thing," Emma said with relief. Because if he ever did decide that just because her family was now wealthy that she was automatically morally bankrupt or a "lightweight" in the emotional-endurance department, the writing was plainly on the wall. It would be all over between the two of them. No marriage, no flirtation, no renewal of their love. Just Joe, once again going his own merry way...

Emma fell silent and was still quiet five minutes later as they arrived at the Wedding Inn. Telling herself it was good she was no longer going to be alone with him, she regarded him out of the corner of her eye. "You coming in with me?"

"Nope." Joe parked in front of the entrance and kept the car running as he fixed her with the full intensity of his amber gaze. "Got to get to the arena to meet with the team trainer who is going to supervise my summer conditioning."

Emma knew the trainers drew up personal programs for each athlete on the team. It was important for them to get as strong and fit as they could in the off-season, before their preseason practices began later in the summer. She didn't know why, but she was pleased Joe was going to be very busy, too. Too busy for Tiffany to bug…at least that was Emma's hope.

"What time are you going to be done tonight?" Joe asked her casually.

Emma tried not to read too much into the question as she unfastened her seat belt. From the parking area she could see that the Snows were already here, waiting for her, some forty-five minutes in advance of their actual appointment. That did not bode well for the rest of her day. "I don't know." She shrugged her shoulders casually, already wondering what Joe had on tap for tonight. "Whenever I get done." Was he going to be home, waiting for her? With the house hot as a tropical paradise and himself in a state of undress? Would he put the moves on her? *Did she want him to put the moves on her again?*

"Well, call my cell and leave a message, and let me know your plans," he told her authoritatively.

Emma hadn't answered to anyone about her moment-to-moment whereabouts in years. It was a disconcerting feeling, having him do so. Kind of thrilling, too. Though Emma didn't begin to know why. "What if you're working out?" she asked. All the athletes on her father's team had two practices a day during the off-season to keep them in top physical condition.

"You don't need to worry about that," Joe told her cheerfully. "I'll make sure you get a ride home," he reassured her with a wink and a pat to her knee.

For a moment, she thought he was going to lean over and kiss her cheek, like any other husband dropping off his spouse, but he didn't. So Emma smiled and got out of the car.

As soon as she shut the door and stepped back, he drove off.

So much for the "perks" of matrimony, Emma thought.

Chapter Eight

Still lamenting the lack of a goodbye kiss, and chastising herself for lamenting the lack of another heated liplock, Emma headed inside the Wedding Inn. And was promptly lambasted by Gigi Snow, who had taken up residence in the lobby.

"There you are!" Gigi stormed toward Emma. "What are you going to do about the latest catastrophe?"

"What catastrophe?" Emma asked warily.

Beside Gigi, Michelle burst into tears. Emma noted the poor young woman not only looked like she had just tumbled out of bed, she appeared not to have had any sleep.

"It's all my fault!" Michelle burst into tears.

Her heart going out to her—weddings were enough stress without a hypercritical mother—Emma wrapped an arm around the young girl's shoulders and soothed gently, "Let's all go into my office, where we can discuss this more comfortably." Not to mention out of earshot of any other potential guests who might come in.

Michelle was still sobbing as Emma guided her into a comfortable upholstered wing chair on the other side of her desk. Emma handed her a box of tissues and knelt in front of the distraught bride.

Michelle pressed a balled-up tissue to her mouth. Eyes brimming, she looked at Emma and confessed, "I l-l-lost the flowers at the airport."

"What do you mean?" Emma asked Michelle. "I thought Lily Madsen, the florist, was driving in to pick them up."

Michelle's lower lip trembled as she sought to save herself from her mother's wrath. "There was a fee for that. And Benjamin thought we should save money and do it ourselves."

"You mean he thought you should do it!" Gigi Snow fumed, looking like she wanted to smash something against a wall.

"He was going to help me, Mother, but then they had that robbery over at the country club last night and they called all the club management in to help with the inventory of just what had been stolen and be interviewed by the sheriff's department."

Gigi huffed. "Benjamin doesn't have anything to do with the pro shop! He's a marketing manager, in charge of membership applications."

Michelle shrugged. "The police think it might have been engineered by someone who came to a see about a membership and received a full tour—and all sorts of information about the club—but didn't actually end up joining. Anyway, Benjamin had to be there, to give Sheriff Hart the information he needed. So I went to the Raleigh-Durham airport alone when the red-eye flight came in from Hawaii, at 5:00 a.m." Michelle began to tear up again. "I didn't realize how big the boxes were going to be. It took two carts to load them. And then I had to go to the bathroom, and…" She bit her lip again. "When I came out of the ladies' room, they were gone." She burst into sobs all over again.

"You mean you left them unattended." Emma patted her on the shoulder.

Michelle nodded emotionally. She pivoted away from her mother's lethal glare. "I parked it right beside the door. I didn't think anyone would steal them. I mean, I was just in there for a second!"

Emma knew how foolish Michelle's actions had been—now. But there had been a time just seven years ago when she had first met Joe and had been that sheltered and hopelessly naive, too. And for that, her heart went out to the young heiress.

"Well, we will just have to order them again," Gigi said, throwing up her hands in disgust.

"I have to warn you," Emma interjected gently. "You'll have to pay for a new shipment." The shipper was not going to be held responsible for this since Michelle had accepted delivery before the theft.

"That's fine!" Gigi said.

Michelle turned on her mother, all the more upset. "I can't ask Benjamin to do that!" she wailed, fresh tears falling. "He hit the ceiling the first time, over what we—he—was going to have to pay for those flowers! To ask him to do it again…" Michelle gulped, clearly not willing.

"This is his fault," Gigi Snow lectured her daughter stonily. "I expect him to take care of it. Now, if you'll excuse me, I have a fitting of my own." Gigi looked at Emma. "I presume you will handle reordering the flowers?" Emma nodded her assent. Gigi departed in a waft of perfume.

As soon as her mother was gone, Michelle began to sob in earnest. Emma slipped across the hall to get two bottles of chilled spring water. She came back and sat down beside Michelle, waiting for the storm to pass.

"I wish I had never agreed to this big wedding," Michelle said. "Everything is so out of control!"

"Maybe you should tell your mother and father how you feel," Emma suggested, holding out the wastebasket.

Michelle tossed her damp tissues into the can with a vengeance. "Mother will never listen to me, and Father is too disinterested. All he cares about is his business. He doesn't want to hear anything about the wedding! He never has! He just thinks the same as Benjamin, that the whole thing is costing way too much! And I know we can't afford it, either. I heard Daddy tell Mother that if she didn't start putting the brakes on her spending, he didn't know what they were going to do! That's why Mother is pushing so hard for Benjamin to pay for half of it. She says she doesn't care what she has to do—I'm going to get the wedding of my dreams. Only it isn't my dream. It's hers! And it always has been. Because if you want to know the truth, I think the whole thing is costing way too much, too.''

Emma concurred. A quarter of a million dollars on a single weekend's social event was way too much. Even if the memories did last a lifetime.

Michelle sipped the water Emma had brought her. ''And you know what the worst of it is?'' she asked Emma wearily. Without waiting for a response, Michelle continued, ''I can feel Benjamin's doubts and regrets every time we're together. I mean, I know he loves me. But does he love me enough to endure all the grief he is getting from my family and will no doubt continue to get in the future?''

Joe hadn't when the two of them were initially together, Emma thought. The moment Emma told Joe she wanted to keep their marriage secret, and why, the moment he had found out who her father really was, and calculated just how much trouble that would likely bring him professionally, he had dumped her so fast he'd made her head spin.

Now, of course, events had conspired to force him to take another tack to save both their reputations and careers. As long as their plan worked, well, of course he would stay with it. But if it didn't...if this somehow backfired on them in the end, as Emma secretly feared, then what? Would Joe be able or even willing to endure the grim pressure coming from her father indefinitely, or would Joe once again be looking for a way out?

''HEY, EMMA!'' HANNAH REID breezed into the Inn shortly after seven-thirty that evening. The owner and chief mechanic of Classic Car Auto Repair, Hannah appeared as if she were fresh from work. She had a smudge of grease on one cheek and was still clad in the jeans and T-shirt she typically wore beneath her grimy coveralls, emblazoned with the name of her business.

"Joe sent me over to pick you up. He said I didn't have to bring the limo or wear a uniform, though." Hannah paused, taking in the stunned look Emma knew was on her face. "That okay with you?"

"Sure, but I thought Joe was picking me up from work," Emma told Hannah, as the two of them headed out the door to the red Aston Martin convertible Hannah had idling at the curb.

Hannah hopped in behind the wheel. "He said you'd say that. But I was to bring you over to the practice arena, anyway."

Emma frowned as she settled into the passenger seat and fastened her safety harness around her. "I don't want to go to the arena. I want to go home."

"He said you'd say that, too." Hannah started the car and took off down the long, tree-lined driveway, her wavy auburn hair blowing in the wind. "And I should ignore you."

Typical, Emma thought. It never seemed to occur to Joe that there was any way to do things but his. "What if I refuse?" she asked dryly as the breeze ruffled her hair, too.

Hannah shrugged, looking unperturbed as always as she slanted Emma a teasing glance. "Then I'll catch heck from Joe and he'll come looking for you, and probably cart you off to the rink, anyway."

Emma thought about what that might be like. Only one word aptly described it. *Exciting.* "What's going on over there, anyway?" she asked as she struggled to keep her pulse from racing ahead with her unexpectedly amorous thoughts.

"Beats me." Hannah adjusted her sunglasses on the

bridge of her nose as the hot, summery air wafted over them. "Joe just said he had somethin' a little special planned for his new bride, and he'd appreciate it if I'd help him out."

They arrived at the arena where the Storm players held practices and worked out. Hannah let her off beside the door. Aware there were no other cars in the lot except Joe's, Emma walked inside. Able to see they were dark and unoccupied, she bypassed the weight and locker rooms, and the gymnasium where the fitness equipment was kept. The bright overhead lights in the windowless arena had been turned off. The rink was lit by the wall torches along the perimeter in the soft, semiromantic way that reminded Emma of the skating rinks she had patronized as a kid.

Joe was already on the ice. He was clad in a pair of form-fitting jeans and a sweatshirt. Trying not to notice how gracefully and easily he moved across the ice, even when just messing around, Emma shivered in her summer-weight suit from the frigid air around the rink. She made her way carefully down the cement steps through the half-dozen rows of spectator bleachers to his side. Doing her best to keep her defenses up—under the circumstances she could feel them fading fast—she folded her arms in at her waist. "What's going on?" she asked in the most casual tone she could manage.

Joe gave her a look of choirboy innocence as he worked his way lazily over to where she was standing. His skates made a whooshing sound as he turned his blades sideways and skidded expertly to a halt. As they came face-to-face, he waggled his eyebrows at her. "Figured you might want to take a few turns around the ice with me tonight, for fun."

Emma studied him. As enticing as his offer was, Joe never did anything without a reason. "And your ulterior motive is...?"

His amber eyes twinkled mischievously. "Do I need one?"

The sizzle she felt whenever she was close to him both irritated and disturbed her. Pretending she wasn't oh-so-aware of every masculine inch of him, she shrugged. "I've never known you not to have a game plan of some sort. So why here, Joe?" she persisted softly. "Why tonight?"

For a moment, Emma thought he wasn't going to answer. At least not candidly. Finally, he rubbed his beard-stubbled jaw and confessed in amused chagrin, "Oh, I expect it might have something to do with the fact that if I got you home any earlier tonight than I'm planning to get you home that you'll have me unpacking those boxes."

"Which means what?" Emma guessed dryly, her pulse picking up yet another notch. "You didn't make any progress on them?"

"I wouldn't say that." Joe rocked back on his heels. "Exactly."

Emma rolled her eyes.

"Anyway…" Joe skated close enough she could smell the sandalwood-and-leather cologne he favored. And maybe a little of her peppermint mouthwash, too. "I thought it would be nice to just skate around for a while, and then have a little supper." He inclined his head to the left.

For the first time, Emma noted the portable stereo, picnic basket and folded gingham tablecloth several bleacher sections down.

"We've got the whole place to ourselves tonight," Joe continued, looking as happy and relaxed as she wished she could feel. "All the workouts are finished. The custodial crew has already been here and left."

Emma had had such a stressful day. She could use the exercise. And truth was, she didn't want to go home to the moving-in mess they had left that morning any more than he apparently did. There was only one problem with his plan. "I don't have any skates," she lamented.

Joe grinned, confident as always. He skated a short distance away, then came back with a small duffel bag and handed it to her. "I'm way ahead of you. I even brought you some clothes from your closet, so you're all set."

Emma unzipped the bag and saw a brand new pair of lace-up skates, thick wool socks, as well as her favorite pair of old jeans and a red turtleneck sweater made of soft, warm polar fleece. "How did you know what size skates to get?" she asked curiously.

Easy, his look said. "I just took the shoes you had on yesterday over to the skate shop, and had them sell me a pair in a similar size. I'll help you lace them up if you want."

"I think I can manage," Emma said.

Joe pointed. "There's a ladies' room through that door. I'll be waiting for you on the ice."

When Emma emerged from the dressing room, Joe had turned the portable stereo on and was skating around in lazy circles, frontward, backward, left to right. He smiled when he saw her and came right over to her.

One hand on the half wall that circled the ice, she bent and snapped off the thick rubber strips that protected the blades on her skates. She set them aside, then stepped out onto the ice. To Emma's chagrin, her ankles felt a lot more wobbly than she'd anticipated.

Noticing, Joe laced a steadying arm around her waist and adjusted his strides to hers. "Been a while, huh?" he asked as they skated slowly but surely around the perimeter of the rink.

For so many things, Emma thought. Trying hard not to notice how good it felt to be ensconced against him this way, or the fact that the songs that were playing were upbeat, lively Kenny Chesney tunes perfect for working out, Emma shrugged her shoulders and tossed him a nonchalant smile. "I haven't been on the ice since the year we dated."

Joe's eyes darkened. His lip took on a troubled curl. "How come?"

Because it reminded me of you and I was trying so hard to forget. "I don't know," she fibbed. "I guess I've been busy."

"You used to skate competitively as a kid, didn't you?" Joe recited a fact he apparently recalled from their dating days.

Emma nodded. She tripped slightly going around the curve, and Joe kept her from falling. "Yes, but I quit when I was twelve."

"Why?" Joe asked, the look he gave her reminding her that she had never really filled him in on that portion of her life. She'd been too focused on the then and there, and the completely overwhelming physical passion she felt for him.

"Because one, it wasn't my dream—it was my mother's," Emma said, her legs wobbling slightly.

Noticing, Joe positioned her even more securely against him.

"And two, there was way too much pressure on me to win," Emma continued, a little more breathlessly than was warranted as she leaned into his steadying grip and tried not to think about how good it might feel to kiss him again. "It took all the joy out of it."

Joe frowned as he struggled to understand. "Pressure from whom?"

As she began to get her on-ice balance back, Emma relaxed. "The coach and the choreographer and the professional seamstress my parents hired. They all wanted to make it to the big time. It didn't behoove them to be associated with a skater who kept losing."

"Oh." Joe skated on ahead of her, and without letting go of her hand, turned, so he was skating backward while she skated toward him.

Emma took his other hand, too, as they began to jitterbug a little. "You're not really familiar with that, are you?" she said, studying his face.

Joe appeared perplexed as they glided over the ice as smoothly and sexily as if they had spent years ice dancing. "What?"

"Having a parent trying to force you to be something or someone you're not," Emma said as Joe caught her against him, slow-dance close. *Whereas Emma's whole life had been like that.*

"Maybe not now." Joe slowed their pace accordingly as the music took on a slow, sultry beat. Emma rested her face against the solidness of his shoulder for a moment, loving his warmth and his strength.

"But there was a time when I fought tooth and nail with my mother over becoming a pro hockey player."

Emma drew back, amazed. "Get out of here! She's crazy about the way you play! Always bragging about you." To the point it had started to drive Emma a little crazy, even before Joe had burst back into her life.

"Now she does," Joe said emotionally. "But back when I was fourteen and flunking all my classes 'cause I spent all my spare time skating, rustling up games and working out, she was not happy with me at all. It took every ounce of persuasiveness I possess to get her to let me go up to Canada, live with a host family and play junior hockey up there as soon as I turned sixteen."

"I never knew that."

Joe shrugged in a way that let her know it wasn't something he usually talked about.

Pleased he had confided in her, Emma asked, "Why didn't you tell me this back when we first got involved?"

"A couple of reasons." He paused and tried to make her understand. "One, I was embarrassed that my mother cared more about the possibility of me getting hurt than realizing my dreams. And two, her lack of faith—that I really could make it to the pros—hurt. It's enough to deal with the doubts of the coaches and scouts and other players, without feeling it from your own kin, too. Especially when a lot of the other hopefuls had huge family cheering sections behind them.''

''And that wasn't the case with you,'' Emma realized sadly.

''Nope. Not then, anyway.'' Annoyance rang in his voice. ''Once I made it to the NHL that all began to change. But before then, all my mother could think was that she had let me shortchange my education for something that might not ever pan out, and could end up scarring my psyche and body forever.''

Emma took a deep breath. ''Yikes.''

''Yeah.''

Joe let her move away from him again and they skated in silence. Having found her ''skating legs'' again, Emma swirled around, behind, and in front of him, from side to side, until he finally grabbed hold of her again. And grasping both his hands, she skated backward in a lazy serpentine pattern. ''I'm glad you made it to the pros,'' Emma said finally.

''Me, too.''

They looked at each other and smiled. ''I just wish you had told me some of this stuff when we were dating,'' Emma said finally. She might have understood him better. And she wanted to understand him, she was beginning to realize. So much.

Joe wasn't about to apologize. ''I was still in the AHL then. I hadn't yet made it to the big time.'' He shook his head, recollecting in all seriousness, ''Putting voice to the doubts others had about me might have messed up my chances.''

''You hockey players are a superstitious bunch.''

Joe grinned and didn't pretend otherwise.

Emma smiled back and dug in the toe of her skate, so she came to an abrupt standstill. ''And speaking of superstitions, what is it with not shaving, Joseph Hart?'' She reached up to touch his face, rubbing the flat of her palm across the light brown stubble that got a little softer and longer every day. He was incredibly handsome and masculine to begin with. No doubt. But the beard lining his face gave him a faintly dangerous, very sexy look. Emma—who'd never liked facial hair on men, period— was beginning to like it. Maybe too much.

Her use of his given name brought a sexy shimmer to his eyes. "What do you mean?"

If she moved a little closer, she could kiss him. "You haven't used a razor since we literally ran into each other at my parent's estate." And though he looked ruggedly handsome as all get out, she was curious about the reasons behind his actions.

His mouth was so close to her head, she could feel the heat of his breath on her forehead. "It's only been a couple of days."

"Five and a half," Emma corrected him, tingling all over. And already her life had been turned upside down. Changed irrevocably.

"Why?" Joe wrapped both his arms around her middle. "Do my whiskers bother you?" he asked in a low, sensual voice.

Unbidden, the image of kissing him again, here and now, flashed in Emma's mind. In an effort to distract herself, she ran her hands playfully over the bristles. "I just want to make sure it's not a 'play-off beard' type of thing," she teased. "You know, the kind of beard you start as soon as the play-offs begin and keep growing until you either win or are eliminated."

Joe chuckled, the sound of his husky male laughter warming her heart. "You're right," he murmured, rubbing his thumb across her lower lip, tracing its shape. "Because if it were that type of beard, and it were related to our marriage, I could be growing this beard for a very long time, couldn't I?"

A few more slides of his skates and hers, and suddenly her back was to the boards around the side of the rink.

Play the

Lucky Hearts Game

and get...

2 FREE BOOKS
and a **FREE MYSTERY GIFT...**
YES! YOURS to KEEP!

I have scratched off the silver card.
Please send me my *2 FREE BOOKS* and
FREE mystery GIFT. I understand that I am
under no obligation to purchase any books as
explained on the back of this card.

Scratch Here!
then look below to see
what your cards get you...
2 Free Books & a Free
Mystery Gift!

354 HDL DU6Y   **154 HDL DU7G**

FIRST NAME   LAST NAME

ADDRESS

APT.#   CITY

STATE/PROV.   ZIP/POSTAL CODE   (H-AR-09/03)

Twenty-one gets you
2 FREE BOOKS
and a **FREE MYSTERY GIFT!**

Twenty gets you
2 FREE BOOKS!

Nineteen gets you
1 FREE BOOK!

TRY AGAIN!

Offer limited to one per household and not valid to current Harlequin American Romance® subscribers. All orders subject to approval.

© 2002 HARLEQUIN ENTERPRISES LTD.
® and ™ are trademarks owned by Harlequin Enterprises Ltd.

◀ DETACH AND MAIL CARD TODAY! ▶

The Harlequin Reader Service® — Here's how it works:

Accepting your 2 free books and mystery gift places you under no obligation to buy anything. You may keep the books and gift and return the shipping statement marked "cancel." If you do not cancel, about a month later we'll send you 4 additional books and bill you just $3.99 each in the U.S., or $4.74 each in Canada, plus 25¢ shipping & handling per book and applicable taxes if any.* That's the complete price and — compared to cover prices of $4.75 each in the U.S. and $5.75 each in Canada — it's quite a bargain! You may cancel at any time, but if you choose to continue, every month we'll send you 4 more books, which you may either purchase at the discount price or return to us and cancel your subscription.

*Terms and prices subject to change without notice. Sales tax applicable in N.Y. Canadian residents will be charged applicable provincial taxes and GST. Credit or debit balances in a customer's account(s) may be offset by any other outstanding balance owed by or to the customer.

If offer card is missing write to: Harlequin Reader Service, 3010 Walden Ave., P.O. Box 1867, Buffalo NY 14240-1867

BUSINESS REPLY MAIL
FIRST-CLASS MAIL   PERMIT NO. 717-003   BUFFALO, NY

POSTAGE WILL BE PAID BY ADDRESSEE

HARLEQUIN READER SERVICE
3010 WALDEN AVE
PO BOX 1867
BUFFALO NY 14240-9952

NO POSTAGE
NECESSARY
IF MAILED
IN THE
UNITED STATES

"Joe," Emma breathed as she settled against the half wall that separated the rink from the spectators' bleachers.

Joe tunneled his hands through her hair. Lifted her face to his. "Just one kiss, Emma. That's all I'm asking."

When he looked at her like that, Emma couldn't deny him the request, and the truth was she didn't want to deny him anything. Unable to help herself, she wrapped her arms around his neck, pressed her breasts against his chest. Time ground to a halt, and nothing mattered but Joe, and this moment between them. He used the gentle pressure of his lips to coax her mouth open. Taking his time about it, he kissed her slowly and deeply, then hotly and passionately, until heat pooled in the pit of her stomach and her knees grew weak. Suddenly she was kissing him back, with all the wonder and affection in her heart.

She moaned as he kissed her even more fiercely, one hand slipping beneath the hem of her sweater, past her ribs, to her breasts. He explored the tautness of her nipple, his thumb caressing the aching bud through the silk and lace of her bra, until the sensation, the need, was almost unbearable. Lower still, she felt the answering hardness of his body. And knew he was aching, he was wanting, as much as she. Just as she knew, as he slowly, reluctantly, lifted his lips from hers, that this was not where it would happen, when he made love to her for the first time. Joe wanted it to be special. Just as she did. Smiling, he took her into his arms again and kissed her thoroughly, all over again.

By the time the sexy, tender, romantic kiss came to a halt, Emma realized the impossible was happening. Reservations be damned. She was falling in love with Joe Hart all over again.

And he knew it.

JOE SWORE AS HE PULLED INTO the driveway of their home.

"What?" Emma turned to him. It had been such a lovely-low-key evening, she hated to ruin it. But he looked irritated about something.

Joe scowled. "I was going to go to the supermarket and get some stuff for breakfast tomorrow and I forgot. Now that I'm working out again I need to start eating better."

"You want me to go with you?" Emma glanced at her watch, saw it was only eleven. "The grocery on Main Street is open until midnight."

"Nah. I'll go." Joe waved off her offer to help, then looked deep into her eyes. "Anything you want while I'm there?" he asked cheerfully.

Emma nodded, even as she thought about how nice it was to have someone watching over her, or how easily she could get used to such tender loving care. "Lowfat yogurt with fruit in it."

Joe made a face and regarded her skeptically. "You really eat that?"

"For breakfast, every morning," Emma affirmed, laughing at the expression on his face. At least she had when she was living alone. "It's good for you," she persisted, even though she could see he wasn't buying it.

"Yeah. I'll keep to my scrambled eggs and whole-wheat toast, if you don't mind."

Emma shook her head. There were still a lot of differences between them. But somehow she didn't mind. "Whatever floats your boat."

He laughed at the corny adage. Leaned over and pressed a light kiss to her brow. "I won't be long."

Emma slipped out of the car. She didn't want to think about what was going to happen next. What she wanted to happen next. "Take your time," she advised.

She needed to think about this.

Did she want to make love tonight? Emma asked herself as she headed for the door. She knew he did. But was she ready to take such a big step after waiting years for the right man, the right time?

Behind her, Joe waited, car idling in the drive, until she

had unlocked the door, hit the light switches and stepped safely inside. She turned and waved, and he drove off.

The house was blissfully quiet. And at first, as Emma walked into the kitchen, stepping around boxes stacked here and there, she noticed nothing amiss. It was only when she walked into the family room to see how much progress—if any—Joe had actually made putting things in order that she did a double take.

Chapter Nine

"I thought you were kidding me about unpacking some o
the boxes," Emma drawled when Joe returned from the
store, groceries in tow. Already in a pair of azure-blue satin
pajamas, she was in the kitchen having a glass of milk.

"What are you talking about?" Joe asked, trying hard—
and failing mightily—not to notice how unbelievably
pretty she looked in the Orient-inspired nightclothes. The
tunic top was sleeveless, high-collared and had a keyhole
opening with a cloth-covered button at her collarbone that
showed just a hint of cleavage. The pants were snug
around her hips, showing off the flatness of her abdomen
and the enticing curve of her derriere, then flared out nicely
at the thigh and ending just above her slender ankles. She
didn't seem to be wearing a bra. The thought of slipping
his hand beneath her top and touching her, without encum-
brance, was unbearably exciting. She had brushed her dark
wavy hair and pinned it loosely to the back of her head in
a way that had him wanting to take it back down. And as
if that alone wasn't enough to turn him on completely,
she'd just had a bath. He could see that, from her flushed
cheeks and the damp hair curling at the nape of her neck.
And she smelled so good, like soap and perfume and
woman. All woman.

Testosterone flooded his system.

To hell with putting away the groceries. Joe wanted to sweep her up in his arms and head for the bedroom. Now.

Emma, however, wasn't thinking the same way. Oblivious to the lusty nature of his thoughts, Emma gestured toward the family room that had been filled with boxes just that morning.

Joe shook his head and, recalling his responsibility to take care of his wife emotionally as well as physically, struggled to follow the laid-back conversation she was trying without much success to have with him.

"I can't believe how much you accomplished today," Emma said.

Belatedly, Joe looked where she was pointing and realized there were only three left of the dozen or so cartons that had been stacked around the room. Which was strange.

"Tell me you didn't move those all by yourself," he said.

Emma's dark brows knit together. "I thought you moved them out of here," she said, perplexed.

Joe slowly set the grocery sacks onto the kitchen counter. His pulse jumping, he strode past her, toward the glass-fronted trophy cabinet. It was as empty, as it had been the last time he had seen it. A feeling of dread spiraled through him. "Where's the hockey memorabilia?"

"That's what I'm trying to ask you." Emma paused. She looked up at him, some of the pink leaving her cheeks. "You're telling me you didn't put it elsewhere?" she ascertained slowly.

"No," Joe said. He hadn't.

"Then where could it be?" Emma asked plaintively.

Good question. And one they were unable to answer, even when Joe's brother, Mac, showed up to make a police report.

"Anything else missing?" Mac asked, pad and pen in hand. As was typical when he was on duty and wearing his Holly Springs sheriff's uniform, he was all business.

Emma came back down the stairs. She looked upset. "My jewelry box," Emma said.

Mac pushed back the brim of his hat. "Was there anything valuable in that?"

Emma nodded glumly, as she moved to stand next to Joe. She tucked her hand in his. "Sapphire earrings. An emerald ring. A garnet necklace. Plus several gold chains and a hammered silver necklace."

Mac kept writing. "Any of it insured?" he asked briskly.

"All of it," Emma said, moving a little closer to Joe. Feeling unbelievably protective—and stupid and foolish—for letting Emma possibly walk in on the end of a home burglary, he wrapped his arm around her waist and held her tight.

Mac turned to Joe. Joe's protectiveness toward his wife did not go unnoticed. "What about the memorabilia?" Mac asked.

Feeling guiltier than ever, Joe admitted reluctantly, "I never got around to it." And he knew that his homeowner's insurance wouldn't cover it—the value of the memorabilia required a special rider to the policy and an additional fee.

Mac shook his head in wordless censure.

That swiftly, Joe was reduced to the reckless baby brother once again. At least in his ultra-responsible eldest brother's eyes. And this time, Joe thought, the perennial do-gooding Mac would be right.

"I can't believe someone came in here and took it all," Joe muttered beneath his breath, knowing full well he had no one to blame for this but himself. If he hadn't been so set on arranging a date to romance Emma that evening, he would have been home to thwart the burglary.

"Any idea how—or when—they got in?" Emma asked, pacing back and forth nervously.

Mac looked to Joe.

"I was here from four until six this afternoon. Everything was as it should have been then. As for how they got in—''

One of Mac's deputies sauntered in. ''Through the garage, apparently. One of your neighbors saw a white panel van—the kind workmen use—with a ladder on the top, pull up in front of the house around six-thirty this evening. She thinks but isn't sure that there were two men in it. Wearing some sort of white painters' coveralls and caps. She didn't pay much attention. She was making dinner at the time. And she figured you were just having some work done on the house, you just moving in and all. But she said they used some sort of electronic device to open the garage door, backed the vehicle in and let themselves into the house.''

''I haven't been locking the door from the garage to the family room,'' Joe said. Which was something else to feel guilty about.

''Then I suggest you start,'' Mac said. He looked back at his deputy. ''How long were they here? Did the neighbor say?''

''She indicated it couldn't have been more than fifteen minutes because the next time she went to the window they were gone and the garage door was shut again.''

''Which means they came in, took the memorabilia and the jewelry and got out,'' Emma murmured, clearly upset.

Mac pulled a couple of typed pages off his clipboard. He handed one set to Emma, another to Joe. ''Fill these out for me and then drop them by the sheriff's office tomorrow.''

Joe scanned the pages, surprised by the intrusive nature of the questions. He frowned. ''Why do you want to know where I get my hair cut and take my dry cleaning? What does any of that have to do with what happened here tonight?''

''Professional burglars—like the ones that hit this place tonight—usually have contacts in the area they operate who tell them when people are going to be on vacation or out of the house. They also know where the most valuable belongings are likely to be, in any given community. So, chances are, this was orchestrated by someone one of you knows, at least vaguely.''

"How will you figure it out?" Emma asked.

"By comparing your questionnaires with the surveys given to us by other recent robbery victims. Chances are, they all have something in common. It's up to us to figure out what that is and work from there."

"Oh," Emma said.

"In the meantime—" Mac continued.

Joe held up a hand. He knew what Mac was going to say. "I'm going to get a security system installed, right away," he promised. He didn't care how or why this marriage had "resumed." His job as Emma's husband was to protect her. From this moment on, he was damn well going to do it.

EMMA AND JOE FILLED OUT their sheriff's department robbery victim worksheets, then headed to bed. Emma in the guest room, Joe the master bedroom. Once again, Emma thought, depressed, it was business as usual in their marriage-in-name-only. Joe had even turned the central AC on, instead of leaving the windows open as he had the previous night, but Emma couldn't sleep. Every noise, every little movement outside her bedroom window and in other parts of the house had her starting in fear. Finally, she got up, turned on her bedroom light and wandered downstairs to the kitchen. Joe followed soon after.

"What is it?" he asked, coming over to stand next to Emma.

Emma shut the refrigerator door, feeling more restless than ever. More disappointed. Their evening together had started out so promising. She had hoped the romantic mood that had existed at the practice arena could be continued at home. Indefinitely. The robbery and the visit from the sheriff's department and Joe's obvious guilt—about not seeing her safely all the way inside the house—had taken care of that.

He was grim. Withdrawn. Cranky. And so was she.

She sighed, looked over at him, wondered if their timing would ever be right. "I can't sleep."

Joe leaned against the counter. He was clad in a pair of gray boxer briefs that rode just below his navel and delineated the muscles in his thighs, the flatness of his abdomen, the abundant nature of his sex. The desire that had been simmering inside her ever since their earlier kisses went straight to boil. She wondered what it would feel like if Joe held her against him now. With so little in the way of clothing between them...

"Me, neither," he said.

Silence fell between them. Emma wondered what Joe would do if she initiated that first kiss. Would he be shocked?

Joe folded his arms across his chest and looked over at her calmly. "There's no chance the burglars will come back," he soothed her calmly. "This was a very targeted hit. And they already got what they wanted."

Emma nodded and averted her eyes from the solidly delineated muscles of his upper body. His skin looked so smooth. She knew it would be warm to the touch. She was glad he hadn't shaved his chest. She liked the mat of dark brown curls, a shade or two darker than his hair, spreading across his pecs, then arrowing downward and disappearing into the top of his boxer briefs.

"So you don't have to worry," Joe continued to reassure her as he looked deep into her eyes.

"I know." Unless, Emma thought, you decide never ever to kiss me again. Unless you decide our kissing and fooling around was what got us into this mess...

Joe edged closer. He had showered before hitting the sheets, too, and he smelled of soap and the unique masculine scent of his skin and hair that was more arousing and enticing than any cologne. He looked down at her intently, the growth of beard on his face giving him a ruggedly sexy look. "Then?"

"I'm still jumpy." Emma shivered, though the air was not overly cool, and edged closer to Joe. It was foolish, she knew, but she wanted—needed—his protection. Emma tilted her head back, looked up into his face. "Why can't you sleep?" Emma asked, just as curiously. He didn't look anxious. Not in the slightest. Just ticked off that their place had been broken into and that there was no insurance on the memorabilia.

For a moment, she thought he wasn't going to answer. Finally, he frowned and said with a certain weary sadness that tore at her soul, "I'm not ever going to be able to replace the memorabilia. If it were just—" He stopped, didn't go on.

Compassion welling up inside her, Emma touched his arm. "What?" she demanded. Now was not the time for him to shut down on her.

Joe shrugged. His handsome features tightened with regret. "If it were just stuff that I had purchased—say for an investment, it would be one thing. But the stuff that belonged to Gordie Howe, for instance, was given to me by my dad when I was six. It was the last present I had from him before he died." Joe's jaw hardened. Moisture glistened in his eyes.

Emma felt her throat closing up, too.

Joe shook off the momentary weakness. Straightened. Moved away. "It's all my fault," he muttered guiltily. "I've been warned, countless times, not to leave the stuff lying around. I should have rented a vault or something."

Emma touched his hand. "Why didn't you?"

He was quiet for a moment, then said, almost reverently, "Because I always felt what was the point of having it if I couldn't look at it whenever I wanted?"

Emma understood. "That's the reason I left my jewelry in the case," Emma said as she linked fingers with him. "I know it would have been wiser to put it in a safety deposit box at a bank and only get it out when I had a special occasion and wanted to wear it. But that always seemed like so much trouble.''

Joe's mouth curved wryly. He lifted her hand to his lips, kissed the back of it, then let it go, as gently as he had taken it. ''Guess we learned something, didn't we?'' He ambled over to the empty display cases, stood looking at them.

Feeling the need to comfort him, even if he didn't particularly want to be comforted, Emma walked over to join him. She touched his arm, felt the curve of his bicep tense beneath her fingertips. ''Mac will find the stuff,'' she promised gently.

Joe's shoulders tensed even more. ''He's a good sheriff. Always has been.'' He turned to look at her with hard eyes. ''But I don't think any of my memorabilia will be showing up at the local flea market.''

''You never know,'' Emma said stubbornly. ''Sometimes thieves are foolish. They run ads in the newspaper. Or take things to local pawn shops.'' Joe looked unconvinced. Emma persisted in trying to lighten the mood, engender some hope. ''Come on. How many authentic Gordie Howe's practice jerseys can there be? If someone advertises the one your dad gave you is for sale, someone will know. All we have to do is put the word out and go from there.''

Joe nodded, and though he still looked unconvinced that her plan would accomplish much of anything, said nothing more on the subject. He sighed, looked over at the shark-shaped clock above the mantel. It was as hideous as everything else he owned in terms of room accessories, and she knew he had put it there shortly after moving in just to get her goat. And it had annoyed her—then. Now it just seemed so much like Joe it made her smile.

But Joe wasn't smiling.

''It's late,'' he ordered in a voice that brooked no dissent. "We both have to work tomorrow. We better try and get some sleep."

No one had told Emma when to go to bed since…since their wedding night. And look how that had turned out. "You go ahead," Emma said, gesturing toward the front of the house and the stairs. "I think I'll stay up awhile."

Joe edged closer, ignoring her advice as deliberately as she had ignored his. Eyes narrowed, he scanned her face. "You're still afraid to sleep alone, aren't you?"

Maybe, Emma thought defensively, as he sifted a hand through the tousled length of her dark brown hair. "Why does it matter?" she asked, glad she had taken out the pins before she'd gone to bed.

Joe rubbed the silky strands between his fingertips and thumb. "Because you're my wife," he said in a soft voice that had desire welling up inside her all over again. "And it's my job to comfort you."

There was only one kind of comfort Emma wanted. And it wasn't the sexless hug he seemed suddenly prone to give her.

She stepped back. "You've done that."

His lips curved into a sexy grin. "Not well enough if you're roaming the house at two in the morning, too agitated to stay in bed."

She turned away from the too-male censure in his expression. "I'll be fine."

"Damn right you will be—" Joe came up behind her and placed both his hands on her shoulders "—because you're sleeping with me."

"I'M DETECTING A PATTERN HERE," Emma said as Joe took her by the hand, and half coaxed, half propelled her up the stairs, down the hallway, toward the master bedroom and his king-size bed. Despite her protests, he had the feeling she wasn't half as reluctant as she was pretending to be.

"What do you mean?" Joe whipped back the sheets,

guided her down onto them, then scooted in after her. Telling himself this wasn't anything he hadn't done before, and quite platonically at that, he brought the covers back, enveloping them both to the waist.

"I mean this is our third night as man and wife, and the second time you've insisted we sleep in the same bed."

"My mistake," Joe said.

Her brow furrowed as she looked at him in cautious bewilderment.

"I should have done so on all three nights." He reached over and turned off the bedside light, and then turned toward her. She rolled onto her side away from him and started sliding toward the opposite edge, as if to escape to the safety of her own bed. Knowing if she left his bed she wouldn't sleep a wink all night, and that she needed her sleep—they both did—he rolled onto his side, wrapped an arm around her waist and brought her back. She murmured a soft "O" of surprise, then settled against him.

"This really doesn't…" Her voice developed a huskiness that indicated the depth of her upset.

"Mean anything. I know," Joe whispered in her ear as he pressed a kiss against her hair. He wished she hadn't looked so soft and vulnerable and doe-eyed in the seconds before he turned off the light. Because that only made him want to claim her as his all the more. "Go to sleep," he ordered gruffly. Promising himself he was going to take the high road here. And do the noble thing.

Even as Emma went very still in Joe's arms, her breathing sped up. He felt her tremble as she settled more deeply into the mattress, the shifting of her body giving new heat and hardness to his. It was all Joe could do not to moan as he felt the blood rush to his groin. Maybe this wasn't such a good idea after all. On the other hand, he had brought her in here. Offered her sanctuary and peace of mind in his arms. The least he could do was wait until she went to sleep before moving safely away from her.

Only problem was, Joe thought as his lower body continued to heat with stunning speed, Emma wasn't going to sleep. Not nearly. Instead, she was turning toward him, splaying her hands across his chest. Tilting her face to his. Delicately pressing her lips to the bristles lining his jaw, even as her fingertips found and traced the contours of his pecs.

Calling on every ounce of gallantry he possessed, Joe remained very still. Maybe if he pretended he was asleep, he had a prayer of not ruthlessly taking advantage of a woman who—he was still pretty damn sure—was still naively innocent in so many ways....

Her lips moved across the dimple on his chin. Her hands lower still. There were limits, Joe thought, on how noble he could be. Especially when he wanted her so damn much. He barely contained another groan as he realized he was fully aroused. "Emma...for goodness' sake—"

"Hmm?" Her fingertips tucked inside the waistband of his boxer briefs.

Joe took them right back out. "We can't play around here." The kisses at the practice arena had been one thing. Though alone, they had still been in a public place. Public places carried with them a certain amount of risk. Demanded, due to the lack of privacy that, say—his own bedroom in his own home guaranteed—a certain discretion. Although it was never easy to put on the brakes with Emma, period, it was a heck of a lot easier there than here.

"Why not?" Joe heard the pout in her voice.

Because I don't think I can stop. "Because you had a shock tonight," he said eventually.

Emma sat up and clasped her arms around her bent knees. She looked over at him, her slender body vibrating with impatience. "So did you."

Joe played professional sports—he was used to lots more pressure and stress. "I seem to be handling it better," he said.

Emma lay back down and stretched out beside him, so they were lying face-to-face. "If that were true, you wouldn't be reacting any differently to me right now than you have been since you put that wedding ring on my finger. If that were true,'' Emma continued, tracing the springy hairs on his chest, ''you would still be doing whatever you could to get me to make love with you.''

''Believe me,'' Joe said as he kissed her hand and pushed her away again, ''the complete and utter irony of this situation is not lost on me.'' He was finally getting what he had wanted from the first moment he had laid eyes on Emma and could not—would not—take advantage of said opportunity. He rolled onto his back and rested his forearm over his eyes. ''I waited until now to develop a selfless streak.''

''You've always been noble. That was in fact the problem. Had you not been noble you would not have refused to stay married to me when you found out who my dad was or that my parents would not approve of my even dating you, never mind becoming your wife! Instead, you would have taken my virginity that night and consummated our marriage, and used that fact as leverage to keep your spot on my father's NHL team. But you didn't, and because of that we both suffered.''

No quarrel there, Joe thought. When it came to Emma, he had a history of making the wrong moves at the wrong time. And for the life of him he couldn't understand why. Usually, he was all business, focused only on his goals. Unfortunately for both of them, when he was around Emma he had a habit of getting sidetracked, to the point he was no longer thinking with his head, but with his heart. And although heart was needed in the game of hockey, and the even-higher-stakes game of life, it was a mistake to think only with your heart the way Emma obviously was now.

''The point is, Emma, I want you,'' Joe countered gruffly, calling on every ounce of self-control he possessed as he reached over to turn on the bedside lamp. ''But I want you when you want me for the right reasons,'' he told her as the room was flooded with light once again. "Not when you're trying to wipe out the memory of our house getting broken into, our peace of mind violated."

EMMA COULDN'T BELIEVE IT. He was turning her down! She was offering to take their relationship to the next level, and he was—once again!—playing Sir Galahad. Okay, so her motives weren't all that pure. She did want to forget. She was using this situation to do something she wasn't sure she would quite have the nerve to do otherwise. At least not so soon into their in-name-only marriage.

On the other hand, she had waited seven long years to be with Joe again. Seven long years to find out if making love with her husband would be as spectacularly satisfying and wonderful and yes, romantic, as she had always hoped. She didn't care how this whatever-it-was-of-theirs turned out in the end—she wanted him to be her first lover. And she would be damned if she was going to let a little thing like a completely uncalled for attack of conscience on his part deter her!

Emma unfastened the cloth-covered button at her collarbone. She sat up and, taking hold of the hem, slid the silk tunic over her head and tossed it aside. She'd never let him see her naked before, and she thrilled at the excitement in his eyes.

Stubbornly, she kept her gaze locked with his, even as her heart raced in her chest. "We can do this and be friends, Joe."

Joe's body tautened, exuding so much heat he could practically have started a forest fire all on his own. A worried light came into his eyes. "That's not what you said last night," he countered roughly, suddenly seeming all of his twenty-six years. And then some.

His gaze slid over her soft curves as she shifted her body over him. Inserting her thighs between his, she settled closer so her bare breasts nestled against the hardness of his chest. He felt so good against her, so warm and strong

and male. Emma shot him a sultry smile as the reckless-
ness she always felt when she was around Joe for any time
at all took control. He might not want to admit it yet, but
he wanted this, too.

He groaned as her budding nipples rubbed against the
mat of hair on his chest. He tangled his fingers in her hair.
"Last night you were completely against this."

"I know." Emma pressed a kiss on his collarbone,
shoulder, jaw. "But I've had time to think, and I've
changed my mind," she said as his lower half sprang to
life. "We've agreed to stay married for the next season or
two. We're becoming friends. We might as well be lovers,
too."

Giving him no chance to argue, Emma lowered her lips
to his. He kissed her back, with the fierce longing she
recalled from all those years ago. Need sprang up inside
her as their tongues tangled, searching, tasting, giving, taking. Her heart beat hard in her chest as his arms tightened
around her. And then they were shifting again, so he was
over her. His body hard, demanding as he pressed against
her.

"Damn, Emma," he muttered as he slipped lower, so
his weight was positioned between her thighs. He cupped
her breasts with both hands, lifting the softness to his
mouth. He stroked the nipples with the pads of his thumbs,
then laved them both in turn. Pleasure flooding her in
great, hot waves, Emma arched her back and let out a
whimper she couldn't seem to stop. Her fingers fell to the
waistband of his briefs, but he was sliding lower still,
hooking his fingers in the waistband of her pajama pants
and dragging them down over the flatness of her abdomen,
to the tops of her thighs. "Beautiful," he murmured, "so
beautiful." And then his lips moved down there, too.
Aware this was the fulfillment of every fantasy she had
ever had, she hitched in a trembling breath and caught his
head in her hands, tangling her fingers in his hair.

"Oh… Joe," she whispered, and this time it was an

entreaty, a plea. Knowing exactly what she needed, he took her pajama pants the rest of the way off and pulled her over to the edge of the bed. He knelt on the floor next to her, and then his hands swept back up, to her tender flesh. She shivered as he parted and stroked her moist, womanly folds as if she were the most precious thing in the world to him. New sensations blossomed and then exploded inside her. Her head fell back and then she came apart in his hands, pleasure trembling inside her.

Joe joined her on the bed and held her close, after the aftershocks had subsided. Aware she was naked, sated but still throbbing, and he was rock hard, straining the front of his boxers, Emma turned to him with a sultry sigh. "Now," she whispered, stroking his face, even as her heart filled with a depth of love and tenderness she hadn't known she possessed, "what are we going to do about you?"

Joe grinned at her in a way that filled Emma with feminine confidence. "That," he assured her, kissing the back of her hand, "is all up to you. If you still want—"

"Oh, yes," Emma said, aware that the pleasure he had just given her had simply fired up her need to have him deep inside her. The depth of his desire for her giving her the confidence to be aggressive, too, she rolled him onto his back, climbed on top of him and lowered her mouth to his. "I want. You better believe I still want, Joe Hart."

JOE HADN'T EXPECTED EMMA to let him this close, this soon. He'd expected to have to work for it, the way he'd had to work for everything he'd ever really wanted in this life. Yet here she was—in his arms, in his bed, her lips fastened on his. And it was everything he had ever dreamed. Everything he had ever wanted.

She was pressed full against him, her hands already sliding down beneath the waistband of his briefs, and this time when she moved to slip them off and find out just how much he yearned to make her his, he let her. The look on her face as she saw him, as she cupped him in her hands for the very first time, drove him to the brink even as the ridge of his arousal grew harder. She slid downward, wanting to explore him, the intimate way he had explored her, but Joe knew they'd never make it to the culmination if he allowed her to kiss and touch him that way right now. So he stretched out over top of her, lowered his mouth to hers and let her lead him where she wanted him to go. He groaned as their tongues twined urgently and her body took up the same primitive rhythm as his, and there was no doubt, where they wanted this to lead. He edged her knees farther apart, lifted her up and eased into her.

Or he tried to. There was a lot more resistance than he expected.

Emma's eyes widened in surprise even as she tried to accommodate him. And Joe knew, as he gently moved past that first fragile barrier, that this wasn't just their first time, it was *her* first time. Stunned by the fierce possessiveness welling up inside him, Joe slowed himself down with effort, giving her the time she needed to adjust to the size of him and the feel of him inside her.

Emma didn't think she could take much more. He was so big, so hard, so hot. And she was so tight. But as Joe held her against him so tenderly, encircling her with his heat and strength, and kept right on kissing her, her whole body began to relax again. Quivering with sensations unlike any she had ever felt, she moaned as his hand swept between them. Touching, caressing, until desire trembled inside her tummy, making her feel weightless, soft. Her heart pounded in her chest as he tunneled his hands through her hair and lifted her mouth to his.

"Nothing," Joe murmured as he kissed her again and again, his body taking up the same, slow, timeless rhythm as his tongue, "has ever felt so right."

Emma knew exactly what he meant.

I love you, she thought, feeling that this was where she belonged—where she had always belonged. And then she was moaning again, moving against him, with him, arching her body up to his, able to hear the soft, helpless sounds in the back of her throat and the fiercer, lower sounds of his own voice in concert with hers. Her spirits soared as he pressed into her as deeply as he could, and then, just that quickly, she was awash in pleasure, shuddering. He followed, free-falling into a pleasure that shimmered between them, seeming to go on and on. And Emma knew at long last what it was to be a part of a man and to have him be part of her.

LONG MOMENTS PASSED AS JOE held her in his arms. Emma knew what he was going to ask her. And the question wasn't all that long in coming.

"Why didn't you tell me?"

Emma would have liked the cover of darkness at that particular moment. Unfortunately, the bedside lamp was still on. And Joe wasn't about to let her hide, in any case. She shrugged. "I didn't see the point."

"Didn't see the point or didn't want me to know?"

"You know now."

"Yes. I do."

Silence fell between them. Emma could see the guilt welling up in that handsome head of his. She didn't want to be anything more he had to regret. Their lovemaking had been too special, meant too much to her, for her to let it be reduced to that. She scowled at him impatiently. "Let's not dwell on the loss of my virginity, shall we?" She sat up, looking for her pajamas. To her frustration, they weren't in the tangle of his bedcovers. At least not that she could see. "It had to happen sometime. With someone," she fibbed with as much face-saving grace as she could muster.

"Is that so." His face now bore the same determination he had on game days, as when he took the ice. The kind that made him win, no matter whom he faced or what the obstacles.

Emma didn't want to feel like they were in the midst of a high-stakes play-off game, but that was exactly how she felt as they faced each other and he waited for a more detailed explanation of her actions. As if Joe was the star shooter, bearing down on her, and she was the goalie trying to defend the net. She shrugged as if it were the most natural thing in the world, when she knew darn well it was not. "Well, unless I wanted to head to the Great Beyond without ever...you know...and I don't. Didn't. Whatever." So she had encouraged him to make love to her! All the way! So what?

His eyes began to sparkle. "So that's all this was," he guessed dryly. "A learning-experience thing."

Emma flushed. Leave it to her *husband* to put her on the spot with all sorts of inquires she did not want to answer. "I think..."

"What?"

"That what we just did defies categorization."

"Not really," he disagreed.

Emma quirked a brow.

"We just consummated our marriage," he explained with exaggerated patience.

"So?"

"So now it's real," Joe informed her with a great deal of distinctly male satisfaction.

Emma was beginning to feel as if she was not only in the midst of a game being played, but a goal scored. "It's been real in the legal sense all along. That's how we got in our current mess, remember?" she reminded him as she found the edge of the sheet, pulled it up over her nakedness and tucked it in around her.

Joe sat back against the headboard, perfectly content to be gloriously, handsomely naked. "Not this real," he pointed out in a low, relaxed tone. "Not this way."

Emma tore her eyes from the sinewy splendor of his body. If she kept looking, she'd start wanting. If she started wanting, she'd start feeling tempted. And they knew where temptation had led them. She folded her arms in front of her defiantly. "What are you saying?"

"That I like it real," Joe told her with a sexy grin as he brought her back down on the bed and stretched out beside her. The passion in his low voice fueled her own. "And that I like you." He tugged her up against his nakedness so there was no doubting, no ignoring his considerable arousal. "And I like making love to you. So much, in fact," he whispered as he unwrapped the edges of the sheet, parted her knees with his and moved in, pressing hardness to softness, "that I'm going to make love to you all over again."

Emma meant to protest. She really did. But the moment Joe took her in his arms again and began kissing and caressing her, she couldn't for the life of her remember why she had been meaning to resist.

Everything she thought she needed—the passionate declarations of love, the real heart-and-soul marriage of wills and minds—paled in comparison with the tenderness in his touch and the way he looked at her.

It wasn't what he said.

It was how he made her feel.

Safe. Protected. Cared for. Desired. To the point that Emma knew, as Joe began to make mad, passionate love to her all over again, commanding everything she had to give and bestowing on her everything in return, that not only was this the only marriage she was ever going to have, but that Joe was the only man.

Chapter Ten

"My, don't you look happy this morning," Helen Hart said when Emma walked into the Wedding Inn, briefcase in hand.

Emma entered her office and Helen followed her inside. As Emma opened the lush velvet draperies and white sheers, sunlight bathed the room in a cheerful glow. "That obvious, hmm?"

"Maybe it's just the honeymoon glow that all newly-weds have."

Emma certainly felt like she was on her honeymoon. She and Joe had made love twice during the night, and again this morning before showering and heading for work. Had they not had professional responsibilities to attend to, they would still be there now.

Aware she was tingling, just thinking about the depth of their passion, Emma thumbed through the stack of un-opened mail on her desk.

"You know, when you and Joe repeated your vows on Monday I admit to being pretty skeptical this would ever work. Then I saw you two kiss each other at the end of the ceremony and thought, well maybe. But I still wasn't sure. Especially after I tried to have a conversation with Joe about the sanctity of marriage. But now…" Helen's voice trailed off approvingly. "Seeing you this way…"

"Has changed your mind?" Emma guessed.

Helen nodded slowly. "You look like you're head over heels in love with him."

If Emma'd had any doubt about that, it had been cleared up last night. The question was, how did Helen's youngest son feel about her? Joe hadn't said. And though his kisses were certainly full of tenderness and passion, that did not mean he loved her, too. Or would ever love her in the way she wanted and needed to be loved.

On the other hand, Emma mused as she continued to flip through her mail, how much did Joe saying the words really matter if the two of them continued to have fun together, understand each other and offer each other pleasure in bed?

"Oh, dear," Helen said softly.

For a moment, Emma thought Helen was talking about the slight but problematic shift in her own mood. Then Emma noticed Helen's attention was directed toward the majestic entrance of the Wedding Inn. "What?"

"Michelle Snow is headed this way. And it looks like she's crying." In wedding-business mode, Helen turned back to Emma. "I wonder what Gigi Snow has said or done to that poor bride now."

Emma figured they were about to find out. By the time Michelle reached the wedding-planning office, Emma had the tissues ready. Helen had returned with a bottle of spring water and a crystal glass bearing the Wedding Inn logo.

Michelle pulled a stack of RSVPs out of her purse and thrust them at Emma. "Mother said you all needed these this morning."

Emma nodded. They had to get the final dinner selections and guest numbers done today. "Yes, we do. Thank you for bringing them by."

Helen smiled at Michelle. "I'll be in my office if you need me."

"Thanks, Helen," Emma said.

Helen shut the door behind them. "What's going on?"

Emma said. She pulled up a chair so she and Michelle were sitting face-to-face.

Michelle rubbed her swollen eyes. "Benjamin and I had a horrible fight last night."

Emma reached over to pat her hand. "That's normal. Everyone gets very tense the last few days before a wedding takes place."

Michelle shook her head, the worry in her eyes growing more intense "He's having secret conversations on the phone, Emma. Someone will call him and then he'll go off and call somebody else."

Emma had to admit that didn't sound good. But leery of jumping to unfounded conclusions, she pointed out casually, "Maybe it's just business."

Michelle pressed her lips together. "I've known him for two years, Emma. Ben's never had a problem talking business in front of me. In fact, he used to enjoy showing off his conversations with some of the most elite members of the club."

Emma tried to come up with another reason for the groom's secrecy. "Maybe he's trying to arrange a wedding surprise for the both of you. Or the gift the groom traditionally gives the bride." Both were reasons to want to have private conversations.

Michelle shook her head again. "I know what my wedding gift from Benjamin is—a necklace. We picked it out together at Tiffany's last spring. And purchased it then. He just hasn't officially given it to me yet."

Well, that kind of took the romance out of the gesture, Emma thought, feeling a little disappointed for Michelle. "Well, maybe he decided to add something at the last minute," she countered optimistically.

"I don't think so." Michelle shredded the tissues in her lap. "No, whatever it is that is going on with him has made him tense and awful and unhappy. Plus, he's worried about the extra money my mother is demanding he fork over for the wedding. Just yesterday, she told him he had to pony up another twenty-five grand, and he doesn't have that kind of money.'' Michelle teared up. ''Plus—'' Her voice broke. She seemed unable to go on.

Emma watched as Michelle uncapped the bottle of spring water with hands that shook. ''What?''

Michelle swallowed hard. Took a sip. ''Last night we went out to dinner and two of his credit cards were refused. I finally had to pay, because he didn't have enough cash in his wallet.''

''I'm sure that was embarrassing.'' Emma handed Michelle some fresh tissues.

''I told him it was okay, but I could tell he was upset. Anyway, we went back to my place and we—um—well we sort of made up and I thought everything was fine. But then I caught him sneaking out around two this morning, only to sneak back in around four.''

That really didn't sound good. ''Did he say where he had been?''

''No. Well, he said he had been out running, and he was sort of sweaty and wound up, but who runs at three in the morning?'' Michelle lamented. ''I tell you, Emma, nothing about his behavior is making any sense at all! And as if all that wasn't enough to make me have second thoughts about going through with this, we were supposed to pick up some wedding gifts over at my parents' house and bring them over to the Inn this morning so they would be here for the reception. My mother wants all the gifts displayed in the most ostentatious manner possible, as per usual. And I didn't have room in my SUV for all of them, so I asked him to go over there with me before we went to the country club. I figured we could put some of them in the trunk of his car. And that way I wouldn't have to make two trips. He said no. He already had stuff in his trunk, and he wasn't taking it out. And that's when we really got in a fight.'' Michelle burst into tears all over again. ''He called me all sorts of names, said that my mother and I were ruining his life and he stormed off to work. That's when I came over here.''

Whew! What a twenty-four hours.

Michelle bolted out of her chair and began to pace in an agitated manner. ''If it weren't for my mother—and me not wanting to hear her say I-told-you-so—I would call this wedding off today!'' Giving Emma no chance to respond, Michelle took a deep breath. Pressed the flat of her hand against her diaphragm. ''But I'm not going to call it off. Because I am not going to give my mother—or my husband-to-be—the satisfaction.''

That wasn't much of a reason to get married, Emma thought as she wondered inwardly how long this marriage that was about to take place was going to last. But aware she wasn't paid to advise clients on that, she smiled gently and said with more than a tinge of hope in her voice, ''Maybe things will calm down, if we all just step back and take a deep breath and—''

''Then again maybe they won't,'' Michelle muttered bitterly as she turned back to Emma. A troubled light was in her eyes. ''I swear to you the Benjamin I've been seeing the last few weeks is not the man I fell in love with.''

Neither was Joe, Emma thought, unable to help comparing their two situations just a little bit. The difference was, Joe had changed for the better in the time they had been apart, and was getting sweeter to her every minute of every day. Benjamin Posen did not seem to be doing that, as his engagement to one of the richest debutantes in the Raleigh area wore on.

But that was the least of Emma's problems, and something she could do little about, anyway. Meantime, they had the most elaborate wedding of the year to put on and many, many practical things to be done. First on the agenda was making peace between the bride and her groom. ''I know tonight is your bachelorette party and Benjamin's bachelor party. I think the two of you should get together here beforehand. Say around four? I'll arrange a romantic high tea for the both of you on the balcony upstairs. It'll give you a chance to catch your breath and think about what's really important here, which is the two of you.''

"Well…" Michelle hedged, clearly tempted.

Emma wrapped a comforting arm around the bride's shoulders. "This will give the two of you a chance to make up and reaffirm your love for each other before things get any more crazy."

"I would like that," Michelle murmured. Her eyes sparkled with tears, but this time Emma noted that they were of the sentimental variety.

Inwardly, Emma began to breathe a sigh of relief. Maybe she could pull this wedding off after all.

"NEED SOME HELP?" Joe asked.

Her heart filling with joy at the sound of her husband's low, sexy voice, Emma looked up from the pile of response cards for the Snow-Posen wedding she had stacked on her desk. She had been going on high-speed all morning, checking the weather for the next two days, talking to Lily the florist about the arrangements and the construction crew about the tents, which were going up in the morning. The twenty-seven-piece orchestra conductor had been in to go over the list of songs they were expected to play at the reception, and the Inn's head chef was waiting for the final breakdown on how many wanted the Maine lobster entrée, and how many wanted filet of beef for the dinner.

Emma rose from behind her desk and moved gracefully around to join him. The smile in his amber eyes matched the feeling deep inside her. "I didn't expect to see you," Emma said, brushing her lips against his stubbly jaw. Nevertheless, she was very glad he was here.

Looking ruggedly fit and handsome in a red-and-gray Carolina Storm players T-shirt, gray running shorts and sneakers, Joe wrapped an arm about her waist and pulled her against him for a brief hug. He pressed his lips against her hair. "I had some space between workouts and figured it might be a good time for us to grab some lunch. So what do you say we find ourselves something good to eat in the Inn kitchen?" He took her by the hand.

The next thing Emma knew she was leaving the confines of her office and walking toward the rear of the building, her hand tucked in his larger, callused palm. "Then if you want, I'll help you finish whatever it was you were doing there," he promised.

Aware how easily they were becoming a couple again, Emma matched her steps to his. "I was doing the final totals on the entrées for the Snow-Posen wedding supper."

Joe reached over and tucked a lock of her hair behind her ear. "How many people are attending that wedding?"

"Five hundred and six, at last count."

Joe whistled, impressed. "That's close to the maximum guest allowance for the Inn."

Emma nodded.

Joe's glance traveled over her features with lazy male appreciation before returning to her eyes. His expression became even more intent. "Something's wrong, isn't it? Something's worrying you."

Once again, he had read her so easily. Glad she had him to confide in, Emma gripped Joe's hand all the tighter. "Michelle Snow is having cold feet."

Joe looked stunned. "You don't really think she'll back out?"

"I'm hoping not," Emma said honestly. Because if Michelle did, and the reason was at least partially due to arguments over the wedding details and cost, it would not only mean heartbreak and humiliation for Michelle and Benjamin, it would be a black mark on Emma's professional reputation as well. People hired wedding planners to make their nuptials go smoothly. And right now, thanks to Gigi Snow's constant mind-changing, general witchiness and overbearing demands, the Snow-Posen wedding was not proceeding anywhere near as blissfully as it should, given how much work Emma had put into it. "I've arranged for them to have a private tête-à-tête this afternoon."

"So maybe that will do the trick?" Joe guessed.

"If luck—and common sense—are on our side," Emma affirmed as they reached the Inn's kitchen. It was bustling with activity as a dozen prep chefs slaved away on the next day's wedding feast, as well as that evening's rehearsal dinner.

Joe walked in and bussed the Inn's head chef, Vonda Gilbert, on the cheek. The fifty-year-old woman broke into a smile as she hugged Joe right back. Although married and the mother of her own brood, she had worked at the Inn for twenty years and loved the Hart kids as much as if they were her own.

"Got somethin' you can spare us for lunch on the patio?" Joe asked.

Vonda nodded, looking neat and professional as always in her white double-breasted chef's jacket and slacks. Instead of a hat, she had tied a jaunty red bandanna over her springy gray curls. "Soup's on the stove, and there are plates of finger sandwiches in the fridge."

"Mmm. My fave." Joe winked, already getting two bowls down from the shelves.

Vonda shook her head, exasperated at Joe's manly reaction to such delicate fare. "They aren't all cucumber or cream cheese—some are chicken and deviled ham," Vonda said as she heaped crustless sandwich squares onto plates.

"I'll take the ones with meat," Joe said, abruptly looking as famished as Emma felt. "What are you going to have?"

"Whatever you've got there is fine," Emma said. She knew it would be delicious.

As familiar with where everything was as the kitchen staff, Emma got out a serving platter. She and Joe loaded it up with the soup, utensils and napkins, plates of sandwiches and iced tea, and some of the tea cakes and cookies Michelle and Benjamin were going to be served later. Then Joe—who'd had years experience busing tables there while growing up—hoisted it onto his shoulder and carried it outside to one of the wrought-iron tables overlooking the rolling green back lawn where the billowy white tents would be erected the following day.

They had just settled down when Mac Hart charged out of the kitchen. He was wearing his sheriff's uniform. A Stetson shaded his handsome brow. Mac grinned as he caught sight of them and strode purposefully over to join them. "Got some good news for you. Two guys were caught breaking into a pro shop in Durham around four this morning. They had a list with them that included two homes that were also broken into overnight, as well as your street address."

"Did the police retrieve the stolen goods?" Joe asked, leaning forward urgently.

Mac frowned. He took a ladder-back chair, turned it around backward and sank down onto the seat, folding his arms across the top. "No," he admitted in obvious regret. "All the crooks had in their white painter's van was two sets of very expensive golf clubs. And some booth-rental paperwork for a golf show in Charleston, South Carolina, this weekend. The Raleigh police have already searched their homes. They found a cache of the clubs that had been stolen in the last few months—all marked for sale at the upcoming show—but no hockey stuff."

Joe's face fell, and Emma shared his disappointment.

"What do they have to say about what they did?" Joe asked.

Mac frowned. "Not much so far. I was just over to the jail to see them a little while ago." Mac paused to pluck a tea sandwich from the plate on the center of the table. "The Raleigh police think the thieves have been acting on someone else's information or direction, but thus far we don't know who that might be. Anyway, I was hoping maybe you could help us. So here's my question. Do you know of anyone who could have directed the thieves to your home, and your memorabilia, last night?''

Perplexed, Joe shrugged, and shook his head. He looked over at Emma.

''I have no idea, either,'' she admitted unhappily.

Still, Mac persisted, trying to crack the case. ''Think, little brother. Is there anyone who either knows or suspects how much this stuff is worth to you, someone who saw it recently and commented on it? Or someone who might want to make you pay by taking it? Because the theft of your stuff is the only piece of this puzzle that doesn't fit. But it's the one clue that may lead us to the real mastermind behind this burglary ring, and the recovery of your stuff.''

Joe thought for a moment and finally said, ''The only person who's commented on it recently was Tiffany Lamour. She was over at the house yesterday morning and saw it just sitting there in boxes in front of the display case in the family room,'' Joe said.

''That woman does have it in for you,'' Cal Hart said, coming around the corner. He was dressed in a shirt, tie and slacks with his physician ID badge clipped to his pocket.

Joe frowned at Cal. ''How do you know?''

Cal helped himself to some lunch, too. ''She was just over at the medical center, nosing around about you. She said she's doing background for a piece she wanted to do on you for her CSN show, but I've got to tell you, baby brother, the questions were pretty personal. And most of them didn't have a damn thing to do with hockey. They were all about your relationship with Emma. Sorry—'' Cal shot an apologetic look at Emma, then turned back to Joe ''—but I thought you both should know what's going on behind your backs.''

Mac lifted a questioning brow in Joe's direction. Begging for more information.

"What can I say?" Joe muttered in obvious frustration as he raked a hand through his tousled light brown hair. "She's ticked off because I won't appear on her show."

"So she's looking for a scandal to try to force you into it?" Emma speculated, unable to completely mask her unhappiness. Why wouldn't the CSN sports show host leave them alone?

"She's still over at the hospital, chatting it up with people as we speak," Cal said.

Joe looked at Cal. "You want me to have a word with her?" Joe asked finally. "Try to get her to stop bothering the staff?"

Cal shook his head and leaned back in his chair. "It's a public hospital. As long as she isn't getting in the way of any work that needs to be done—and she isn't—there's no reason for her not to be there if she wants."

Mac continued to look thoughtful. "Could she have a connection to the thieves?" Mac asked Joe. "Have you ever known Tiffany Lamour to be involved in anything illegal?"

Joe furrowed his brow. "She's underhanded, devious, spoiled, used to getting her own way and capable of some pretty vindictive behavior. But being involved with a couple of common burglars who've been stealing golf clubs? That just doesn't sound like her."

Mac scowled, obviously disappointed. He filched a deviled ham sandwich off the tray, then stood. "Well, I think I'll mosey on over to the hospital and strike up a conversation with her, anyway. See what I can find out—when I turn on the charm." Mac looked at Cal. "Think you can handle an introduction for me?"

Cal smirked and slapped the eldest Hart brother on the back. "Be glad to help you get that woman off our hands."

"In the meantime," Mac warned Joe before he took his leave, "if you do think of something or someone else be sure and give me a call right away. The less time that elapses from the time of the theft until we know where to look, the better our chances of retrieving your stuff. I know how much the memorabilia Dad left you means to you.''

THE PROBLEM WAS, SO DID EMMA. And she couldn't stop thinking about it, even after Joe finished helping her with the last-minute reception details and went over to the printers' to pick up the menu cards and wedding programs.

It didn't make sense for anyone in the pro hockey world to steal Joe's stuff. They could buy their own memorabilia, if they wanted. Tiffany Lamour had reason to want to upset Joe—at least in her own mind—but Emma had to agree that Tiffany probably couldn't have pulled it off in such a short period of time. Nor did Emma think Tiffany would have known how to contact the golf club burglars. The memorabilia had been stored at the Wedding Inn, but Emma couldn't imagine any of Helen's wait or cook staff being disloyal enough to orchestrate a theft from Joe's place. It was possible, of course, that someone who had come into the Inn to arrange a wedding might have happened upon the memorabilia and decided then and there to steal it. But it had been kept in the storeroom off Helen's private office, and aside from Gigi Snow, her daughter Michelle and fiancé Benjamin Posen, Emma couldn't think of anyone outside the employees who had even seen it. Or known it was there.

Neither Gigi nor Michelle had any interest in hockey. That had been demonstrated the first time they had seen the photos of Joe Hart in Helen's office at the Inn. Benjamin, on the other hand, knew a fair amount about the sport. As membership sales-marketing director at the Holly Springs Country Club, he had complimentary tickets to all local sporting events and often attended with people he was trying to entice to join the relatively new, prestigious and very expensive country club.

So Benjamin Posen probably knew the value of Joe's stuff.

Just as he knew the value of titanium golf clubs, and

even who owned them. He also knew when the owners were out of town on business or off on non-golf-related vacations, their houses unwatched.

And, thanks to Gigi Snow's demands, Benjamin needed money. Desperately.

Was it possible that Benjamin Posen was the brains behind the theft ring? Emma wondered nervously. Mac had said someone was tipping the burglars off, directing them. That the theft of the Holly Springs Country Club pro shop was likely an inside job. Maybe the fact the burglaries had stepped up and become more daring in nature as the time drew closer to Benjamin's wedding was no accident.

Michelle had said Benjamin's credit cards were refused at dinner the previous evening, he had disappeared in the middle of last night and would not let her into the trunk of his car this morning.

Emma could call Mac, of course, and he would no doubt bring Benjamin in for questioning. But if Emma was wrong and Benjamin had nothing to do with any of this, she'd be putting him through a horrible ordeal on the eve of what was already a very stressful wedding weekend.

Emma couldn't do that. Not without some proof that she was correct. The question was, how was she going to get it?

"LET ME GET THIS STRAIGHT," Hannah Reid, owner of Classic Car Auto Repair, said several hours later. Finished wiping her hands, she stuck a grease-stained rag in the back pocket of her coveralls. "You want me to go over to the Inn parking lot and lift the hood of your car and pretend there is something wrong with it and it won't start, even though it actually will, and you want me to do this at precisely 4:00 p.m.?"

Emma nodded, wondering if Hannah knew she had a streak of grease on her nose. "Although maybe you should make it three-forty-five?" Benjamin Posen had a tendency to be a little early at times.

"Sure thing." Catching a glimpse of her reflection in the lobby windows, Hannah reached for a tissue and rubbed it across the bridge of her nose. "You want to tell me why I would be doing all this?" Hannah asked, checking to make sure she had indeed gotten all the black off her fair skin.

Aware she was about to undertake some rather risky— if nobly motivated behavior—Emma blushed self-consciously. The less her friend knew, the better. "I'd rather you wouldn't ask."

Hannah raised an inquisitive auburn brow. "Naturally."

"Suffice it to say," Emma continued seriously, attempting to avoid crossing what was a very thin line between well-meant and unethical behavior, "you would be helping me out immensely."

"Of course." Hannah paused, narrowing her pretty green eyes at Emma. "You do know you're losing it?"

Emma uttered a heartfelt sigh, lamenting, "I've felt that way all week."

Hannah smiled, romantic speculation gleaming in her eyes. "Before or after you renewed your wedding vows with Joe Hart?"

Good question. And one Emma didn't have the least trouble answering. "From the first moment I laid eyes on him again, my life has not been the same." And she sensed it never would be again.

"Hmm." Hannah picked up her wrench and returned to the Jaguar she had been working on. "We should all be so lucky."

"So you'll do it for me?" Emma leaned over the engine with Hannah. "I'll pay you for your time, I promise."

"Sure. Why not? I'm always game for a little intrigue." Hannah studied Emma, serious now. "And I'm sure you have your reasons."

"Thanks," Emma said, struggling to keep a lid on her soaring emotions, "I do."

When she returned to the Inn, she found Joe's mother

in one of the dining rooms supervising napkin folding for the big event. Emma motioned her away from the teenage workers, who did many of the menial but very necessary tasks at the Inn. As soon as the two women were out of earshot, Emma said, "Just so you know, I'm planning to conjure up a little wedding snafu for Michelle and Benjamin, then I'm going to ask Ben for a favor and hope that his helping me out ensures that he and Michelle spend at least thirty minutes alone together this afternoon." If all went according to plan, even if the two lovebirds had another spat, Ben wouldn't be able to leave the Inn until Emma completed her sleuthing…and hopefully, vindicated him. "So please, if you happen to come along while this is going on do not under any circumstances volunteer to help," Emma finished seriously.

"Wouldn't think of it," Helen said dryly. She studied Emma thoughtfully, having worked with her on enough nuptials to trust her methods, however unorthodox they sometimes might be. "Is this part of your plan to get the romance back in their relationship before the rehearsal dinner tomorrow evening?" Helen asked, looking as relaxed as Emma wished she could be.

Emma nodded. She wanted Benjamin Posen to be innocent of wrongdoing more than anyone could ever know. The problem was, her gut was telling her it just wasn't so.

"THANKS FOR ARRANGING THIS private tea," Michelle Snow said. Looking pretty and pulled together in a floral sundress, all evidence of her earlier crying jag hidden with skillful application of makeup and probably a number of cold compresses, Michelle smiled at Emma hopefully. "I think it's just what Benjamin and I need."

Emma escorted Michelle across the marble-floored foyer. "Why don't you go up to the second-floor balcony and wait for Benjamin there? I'll watch for him and send him up as soon as he arrives."

Michelle smiled and glided off, looking more relaxed

than she had all week. Which, of course, only made Emma feel all the guiltier.

No sooner had Michelle glided up the sweeping staircase to the second floor, than Emma heard footsteps on the floor behind her. She turned, saw Joe heading straight for her. "Hey, got a minute?" he said.

Emma wished. Her heart skipped a beat as she forced herself to meet his gaze. "Actually, no."

"You don't look busy," Joe said, eyeing Emma with a depth of male speculation Emma found very disturbing.

She swallowed hard around the growing knot of emotion in her throat. Her undercover plan had not included having to lie or misrepresent events to her husband. But here she was... "Well, I am. Busy," she said, a bit too abruptly.

His gaze raked the length of her, before returning to her face. "Doing?"

Emma moved away from him restlessly. Folding her arms in front of her, she glanced out the narrow windowpanes on either side of the imposing front door. "I'm waiting for someone."

Joe's brow furrowed. "I can wait with you," he told her smoothly.

Emma turned and forced an officious smile. "I'd prefer you didn't," she said cheerfully.

He studied her, able to tell as always when something was not quite as it should be. "Did I miss something?" he demanded curiously. Giving her no chance to answer, he took her by the wrist and tugged her gently but inexorably across the lobby, past the staircase. "'Cause I don't remember us having a fight," he drawled in the deep southern accent that stirred her senses. "All I remember," he murmured as he pushed her into an alcove beneath the stairs, blocking the softness of her body with the steel of his, "is the two of us having a nice lunch and making wild passionate love all night."

Emma recalled that, too. So well, she wanted to do it all again. Unfortunately, she couldn't afford to get sidetracked here if she wanted to be able to fully implement her plan to help him recover his treasure. Doing her best to keep a level head, Emma planted a hand against his chest, holding him at bay. "Joe—"

"What?" He looked around behind him and, seeing no one else, wrapped his arms around her and brought her closer yet, so their bodies were touching in one long electrified line. Smiling the way he did when he intended to kiss her, he lowered his lips slowly to hers.

Knowing she would be lost if she experienced the sexy male taste unique to him, Emma jerked in a breath and turned her head to the side. "I can't kiss you here."

She could feel the frustration simmering in his much larger frame. "So let's go home, then," Joe murmured in obvious frustration. "And kiss there." He threaded his fingers through her hair and turned her face back to his.

As Emma gazed up at the handsome lines of his face, she was trembling, too, albeit for an entirely different reason. "I can't," she whispered back, wishing she didn't have to withhold anything from him, but knowing for the moment there was no other way. Because if Joe knew what she was about to do…well, she couldn't really see a straight shooter like him agreeing to it. And she wasn't going to let anyone ruin her plans when she had gone to so much trouble to arrange it.

He lifted his head, still not understanding, and clearly wanting to. "Because you have to work?" he ascertained softly.

Pulse pounding, Emma looked past his broad shoulders and saw with relief that there was still no sign of Benjamin Posen—or Hannah Reid—coming into the lobby. "Yes. I still have things to do here," Emma said firmly, telling herself her deliberate deception would all be worth it in the end.

Joe sighed and, abruptly giving up on trying to steal a kiss from her, stepped back. "Not tonight, though," he said firmly.

"What do you mean?" Emma shot back mutinously. Was he trying to tell her she couldn't work late if she wanted to or needed to?

Joe folded his arms in front of him. "We have somewhere to go," he told her matter-of-factly.

Emma couldn't imagine where. Still holding his eyes and wishing she didn't want to kiss him and make love to him again quite so much, she stated plainly, "I didn't accept any social invitations." Not during such a hectic work week.

"I did." Joe smiled, confident and take charge as ever. "Your parents want us to have dinner with them at seven-thirty." He looked her straight in the eye. "And I said we would."

Chapter Eleven

"You can't be serious," Emma said as she sidestepped past Joe and led the way back into the center of the foyer, making sure they were in full view of anyone who might be coming and going…and vice versa.

"Dead serious, as it happens." Joe rested his forearm on the end of the balustrade. His hot gaze skimmed her upturned face as he revealed in a low, matter-of-fact tone, "I got the invitation from Coach Lantz half an hour ago."

Emma pursed her lips together mutinously. "Why would he ask you?"

Joe shrugged, seeing nothing out of the ordinary by the way the request was handed down. "Coach was just conveying the message from your father, who just happens to be the owner of the team I now play for."

As if Emma had to be reminded of that!

Joe continued resolutely, closing the distance between them to mere inches yet again. "Saul and Margaret want to see me—and my new wife—at their estate at seven-thirty this evening for dinner. Because I am now an employee under contract with the Storm, the option of saying no does not exist."

Emma scoffed, beyond irritated at being summoned for a command performance this way. Parents or no. "Maybe not for you," she sassed back.

"Or you, either, Emma." The last of his patience disappeared from his eyes and a remoteness she hadn't heard before crept into his tone as he laced a possessive arm around her waist. "If I have to go, you have to go. That's what being my wife means."

Didn't this sound like fun. "Fine," Emma said, aware she didn't have time to argue. Out of the corner of her eye, Emma saw Benjamin Posen's car driving past one of the windows, toward the parking spaces at the side of the Inn. Splaying her hands across his chest, she pushed him away. "In the meantime, your mother needs you."

Joe blinked as if he couldn't possibly have heard her correctly. "What?"

"She said it was something important," Emma fibbed, desperate not to let her chance to investigate Benjamin Posen go by. "She's in the ballroom on the second floor." When Joe didn't move, she shooed him away with both hands. "I'm serious. Go!"

Joe stepped back, gave her another long, perplexed look, then took off. But not before muttering, "We're not finished here, Emma."

How well she knew that.

Thanks to her odd behavior, Joe was now full of questions and probably would not rest until she answered every one. But telling herself she would deal with that later— much later—Emma turned her mind to the business at hand and walked briskly out to the parking lot. She paused to say something to Hannah, who was bent over the engine of her car, as requested. "Just shake your head and tell me it looks bad," Emma urged as she closed in.

"Awful," Hannah said as Benjamin Posen walked by, giving Emma a nod and a little wave.

"Just keep it up a while longer," Emma whispered. She hurried after Benjamin. "Ben! Wait up! I'm in a bind and I need a favor."

He turned toward her. Like Michelle, Ben looked as if

he hadn't been sleeping much lately. The only difference was he couldn't hide the dark circles beneath his eyes with skillful application of makeup, like his bride-to-be had.

Wondering if he was as unhappy as Michelle was, Emma continued with a businesslike update of wedding preparations. "The tailor called. The tuxes for you and all your groomsmen are ready to be picked up."

Benjamin frowned and looked even more harried. "Did you need me to do that?" He didn't look as if he felt he had the time.

"No," Emma quickly reassured him. "I'm going to go and get them and bring them back to the Inn so they will be here for you on Saturday, but I've got a problem with my car." Emma pointed toward Hannah, who was still bent over the engine, fiddling. "It won't start, and I was wondering—" she paused, aware of the enormity of the favor from someone she didn't know all that well "—would it be possible for me to borrow your sedan, just for the next fifteen or twenty minutes? I swear. It won't take any longer than that. I wouldn't ask but I'm in such a time crunch."

To Emma's surprise, Benjamin didn't even stop to think about it, he merely reached into his pocket and handed her the keys to his BMW. "No problem. It's the least I can do for you," he said.

"Thanks," Emma said, her heart sinking as she thought about what his willingness might mean.

Benjamin inclined his head toward the Inn. "Michelle inside?" he asked eagerly.

Emma nodded. "She's on the second-floor balcony overlooking the back lawn."

And with that, Emma headed toward Benjamin's car.

She drove the five minutes to the tailor shop where the tuxes had been custom-made, picked them up as previously agreed, and then opened up the trunk to lay them inside. To her dismay, it was completely empty except for one thing. Near the back corner was a plain black hockey puck with no insignia, no writing, no identification of any kind.

"YOU WANT TO TELL ME WHAT'S going on with you, or am I going to have to kiss it out of you?" Joe asked as he emerged from the shower, a towel wrapped around his waist.

Emma tried but couldn't quite suppress a smile at the sexily expressed threat. Struggling hard not to notice how good he looked and smelled, she continued to smooth skin lotion on her legs. "I don't know what you mean," Emma fibbed.

Joe scooted around her and went to the mirror above his bathroom sink. He started to reach for his razor, then pulled away. He swung around so his back was to the mirror, his hips resting on the marble sink. He clamped his arms across his rock-hard chest and studied her towel-clad form, his heated gaze lingering on the swell of her breasts, peeking out of the décolletage formed by the tucked-in corner. His gaze then roamed to her bare thighs and calves, before returning ever so slowly to her eyes. "For starters, why did you send me off on that fool's errand when I arrived at the Inn?"

Emma took one foot down from the rim of the tub, propped her other one up there. Embarrassed at the results of her wild-goose chase, she ducked her head and continued to smooth lotion on her just-shaved legs. "I said it was my mistake."

Abruptly, his eyes glimmered with a cynicism that stung. "And a deliberate one, at that," he said softly, a hint of accusation in his voice. He cocked his head and gave her yet another thorough once-over. "You knew darn well my mother was not looking for me."

She couldn't exactly argue that, so she straightened and said nothing.

She was about to scoot past, when Joe sauntered closer and put his hands on her shoulders, holding her deliberately in place. "And why did you borrow Posen's car, when you could have asked me to go and pick up those tuxes with you?" he persisted.

Emma tried not to think about the warmth of his callused palms on her skin, or the sensual feelings and desires his touch was evoking. She bit her lip as she answered his question, and tension flooded her anew. "It wasn't your responsibility." And that was the truth.

She stepped back; her shoulders grazed the open bathroom door. The next thing she knew, Joe had leaned forward, bracing a hand on the wood on either side of her.

"Keep going," he murmured encouragingly.

Aware her heart was pounding and she was tingling all over, Emma leaned back slightly. She told herself it was nerves causing her body to go haywire and not his proximity. She glowered up at Joe. She could feel the heat rushing to her cheeks, even as she struggled to get a handle on her soaring emotions. "That's it." Emma shrugged, aware the tuck in her towel was beginning to slip. She pressed a hand between her breasts, holding the towel in place. "That's all I have to say."

She could practically see the wheels turning in Joe's head as he weighed her testimony. "I don't think so." His eyes connected with hers and held for several breath-stealing moments. "I had a car there. So did my mother."

Why did he have to be so darn persistent? Why didn't he just walk away from her, as he had at crucial junctures in the past? "Yeah. So?" Emma folded her arms in front of her, being careful not to brush the hands he still had braced on either side of her.

Joe's eyes radiated unchecked interest but no anger. "So why didn't you borrow one of our vehicles?" he persisted.

With a bantering smile meant to disguise the embarrassment she felt, Emma shrugged and said, "Benjamin Posen was handy, and I knew he wasn't going to go anywhere at that moment, and the tuxes were for his wedding.

It made sense.'' Sort of. For a person behaving like an utter, lovesick fool, out to protect the interests of her mate.

''Mmm-hmm.'' Joe grinned as he lifted a hand to gently trace the contours of her face. ''Did you know when you're not telling the truth you have a little pleat right here—'' he delicately painted the area he meant with the tip of his fingertip ''—between your eyebrows?''

Emma flushed, wishing once again he didn't have the ability to read her quite so accurately. Wishing he would stop watching and weighing everything she said and did. Because if he kept it up, he was going to find out what a fool she had been today. And then he might figure out what she wasn't sure she was quite ready for him to know just yet, that she was head over heels, foolishly, recklessly in love with him. ''And do you know,'' she countered in frustration, her lower lip sliding out into a resentful pout, ''that when you're at your bossiest and most demanding— like right now—that I…''

Joe's sexy grin widened. ''You what?''

I want to give you everything you want. And more. And what sense did that make? It wasn't as if anything had really changed between them. Or that their marriage was a true and lasting one. They had made love. Reestablished a casual friendship. That was all. Joe hadn't said he loved her yet, hadn't even come close. The fact his kisses and caresses made her feel loved was irrelevant.

''I hate that you won't confide in me.'' He wrapped both his arms around her waist.

Despite her efforts to keep a protective wall around her heart, Emma found herself leaning into the reassuring solace of his touch, taking comfort in the steady beat of his heart. ''I'll tell you everything eventually, I promise.'' *If and when you ever tell me you love me, too, that is.* She wrapped one arm around his waist and with the tip of her index finger impulsively traced the velvety soft stubble on his dimpled chin. ''But right now I've got a lot on my mind.'' She needed Joe to give her space to figure things out.

Seeming willing to do just that, Joe stroked a hand through her hair and brushed a kiss across her temple. ''About the Snow-Posen wedding?''

Emma nodded. With a determined breath, she stepped back. ''As well as the dinner this evening.'' She looked at Joe seriously, ready to lay all her cards on the table about this much. ''I really don't want to be late. Nothing sets my father off like tardiness.'' And she had the feeling this command performance they were about to put in was condemnation enough on her parents' part. Her father wouldn't have ordered them to appear the way he had, through a third party and another Storm employee, if he didn't intend it to be some sort of a decimating power play on his part.

And Emma sensed Joe knew it, too.

''You're looking well,'' Saul Donovan noted as Emma and Joe joined her father and mother for a glass of wine before going into dinner.

''Thank you,'' Emma said, aware it was all very civil as her mother graciously passed around a plate of hors d'oeuvres. And very tense. She couldn't believe her dad was pulling this overprotective father routine with Joe, but he was. And Joe, poor guy, didn't seem to know whether to react as his son-in-law or a player on Saul's team.

Saul looked at Joe, his company manners on display. Then said, almost too formally, ''I understand from Coach Lantz that your off-season, physical-conditioning sessions have gotten off to a good start, as well.''

Joe nodded and continued to meet her father's gaze, man to man. ''I take the workouts seriously.''

Workouts? Emma thought, gnawing at her lower lip. Try his whole career. Which, of course, was what made this little prearranged tête-à-tête so excruciatingly difficult.

Saul nodded and continued cautiously, "I believe you *want* to be a fine addition to our team."

Uh-oh. Here it comes, Emma thought. The punishment for having the gall to get involved with me.

Saul looked at Joe sternly. "Which is why I'm puzzled about your refusal to be a guest on Tiffany Lamour's CSN TV show."

Beside her, Emma felt Joe stiffen with what had to be resentment but he continued in the same frank vein, "Ms. Lamour doesn't want to talk about hockey. She wants to talk about my personal life."

Saul lifted a brow and continued to play it cool. "And that surprises you."

"It just doesn't interest us," Emma interjected testily, deciding this third degree had gone on long enough.

Her father gave her a long, quelling look and continued in a voice of steel, "Let your husband speak for himself, Emma."

Emma started to rise, figuring if this was the way the evening was going to go then she had no reason to stay. Joe caught her hand before her hips cleared the sofa cushion and pulled her gently but firmly down beside him.

"I was trying to spare Emma the embarrassment," Joe said, planting a firm hand on her knee.

"Too late for that," Margaret Donovan murmured, her own background as a public relations whiz coming into play.

Everyone turned to her in surprise.

Margaret shrugged and continued matter-of-factly. "Emma's reputation as a proper young woman went out the window the moment the two of you were caught on camera, sans clothing. Your decision to become a proper husband to her helped, Joe. But it's not enough. There are questions to be answered. If not on Tiffany's show, then in some venue."

"The more improbably romantic the back story, the better,'' Emma guessed, having some idea where her mother was headed with this.

Margaret looked at Emma steadily. ''You're a very levelheaded woman, Emma. For you to get yourself in the predicaments you have with Joe tells me that there is something special between the two of you. All your father and I are asking is for you two to accept the fact that like it or not you both are very much in the public eye. Joe is a celebrity and a well-known sports figure. And you're married to him. That means you are role models to a lot of young people.''

Emma felt her temper snap. ''Does that mean we are not entitled to a private life?'' she cried. Did it mean that now the sanctity of her marriage had to be sacrificed for the benefit of the darn hockey team?

''Of course you are!'' her mother soothed.

''Good.'' Emma sat back against the cushions. She relaxed only slightly as Joe took her hand in his and gave it a warning squeeze.

''However that doesn't change the way the world works,'' Margaret continued in a voice of steel. ''The simple fact of the matter is that the rather prurient interest in you is not going to die down until some rather difficult questions are asked and answered.''

Emma rolled her eyes. Back to that again. ''And you think Tiffany is the one to ask them?'' she retorted sarcastically.

''I think she'll be merciless, when compared to other sports reporters, yes,'' Saul Donovan conceded, as unremittingly frank as his wife had been. ''But merciless is what you need. When Tiffany is finished, there won't be anything left to ask. Hence, the story will be out there in the sports world where it counts the most.''

And in the process, Emma thought resentfully, Joe would've had to put himself in a position where he was vulnerable to the whims of a vindictive, scandal-hungry heiress.

"Once it's out there for a couple of news cycles, it will be over," Margaret promised, as if it were just that simple. "By the time the new season starts, it'll be such distant history it will never even be mentioned."

"And hence won't hurt the team," Emma said, guessing where this was going.

"Or Joe," Margaret added optimistically. "Or you."

That's what Joe had said about their getting married, Emma thought uneasily. He had said it would end the curiosity, and the gossip. But it hadn't exactly worked out that way, Emma thought. Because Tiffany Lamour was still sniffing around. And her interest in Joe seemed a *lot more* than simply professional....

"All we are asking is that you let the world in on a little of the excitement or happiness or whatever it is you find with each other," Margaret said softly. She reached over and took her husband's hand.

"And that," Saul concluded firmly, "is not too much to ask."

"TIFFANY LAMOUR WILL BE contacting you in the morning," Saul Donovan told Joe as he and his wife walked Joe and Emma to the door, after a dinner filled with what had been—for Emma, anyway—excruciatingly dull small talk about the previous Stanley Cup play-offs, and the prospects of various NHL teams in the upcoming hockey season.

Joe, on the other hand, had really seemed to enjoy himself as long as the subject was hockey. And only hockey. Not that Emma was surprised about that. His sport was, and always had been, the real love of his life. Not even she could compete with that.

"Ms. Lamour wants to tape the interview at her hotel in Raleigh tomorrow evening," Margaret Donovan continued instructing Joe, picking up where her husband had left off. "She will contact you personally about the time you need to be there, what you need to wear, and so on."

Joe nodded. He did not look happy, but to Emma's relief he wasn't about to argue the point with them, either.

Joe was grimly silent, brooding the entire way as he drove them back to their place. Emma couldn't help but wonder if he was already regretting his decision to stay married to her, instead of cutting his losses and leaving her and the Carolina Storm for another team, and a future elsewhere. Given the suspicion and overprotectiveness Joe was facing from her father, she could hardly blame him if he did decide to ask to be released from his contract so he could move on, to a place where none of this would be an issue. It would probably be a relief not to constantly have to worry about making a marital misstep that would get him benched or sent down to the minors.

"What a week, hmm?" Emma said as they got out of the car and walked inside the house.

"No kidding," Joe muttered with feeling. He walked into the family room, switching on lights as he went.

Emma dropped her purse on a chair and kicked off her evening sandals. "He wouldn't be forcing you to go on the show if it weren't for me, if I weren't his daughter."

Joe tore his glance from the empty display case to the floor where the boxes of memorabilia had been. Briefly, sadness flashed in his eyes before he directed his attention to the matter at hand. "Your father is right," Joe said grimly. As his pique faded, he swung around and regarded her with his usual can-do attitude. "As your husband, it's my job to protect you. If I achieve that by getting out there and taking a little heat for what happened between us years ago, as well as last weekend—" he gestured as if it didn't matter to him one way or another "—so be it."

Emma didn't like feeling she was a burden he had to bear. "I just don't see why it has to be Tiffany Lamour's TV show," Emma groused.

Joe's lips thinned despite the fact he was reluctantly resigned to what had to be done. "She's the Barbara Walters of the sports world. She has the most in-depth inter-

views, the highest ratings.'' He paused and gave her the
stony look he used on his on-ice opponents. ''Your mother
is right. If I go on Tiffany's show, I won't have to go on
anything else. It'll be a one-shot deal that will be recapped
lots of other places, way before the season starts, so that
when I do start playing for the Storm it'll be such old news
it will no longer be an issue.''

She hated he had to go through this, when she was just
as much—if not more—at fault than he was for the situation they were now in. ''Then let me appear with you,''
she pleaded. Maybe it wouldn't be so bad if she could feel
they were doing this together.

He shook his head at her and scoffed, ''Get real, Emma.
Players don't take their wives on Tiffany's show.''

She swallowed, watching as he raked his hands through
his hair. ''So we'd be different.''

He clenched his jaw as he leveled the full impact of his
amber gaze on her. ''I'm not hiding behind your skirt.''

Emma frowned as Joe slowly, implacably closed the distance between them.

''Although speaking of skirts,'' he murmured in a sexy
whisper as he wrapped his hands around her waist and
turned that perceptive gaze of his to the slope of her neck.
''I wouldn't mind taking off the one you have on right
now.''

Emma splayed her hands across his chest and did her
best to hold him at bay, even as his lips forged a burning
path to the sensitive area behind her ear. ''I'm serious,
Joe.'' Emma pulled away and headed for the kitchen, well
away from the temptation of the comfortable leather sofa.

She straightened up unnecessarily, putting a glass in the
dishwasher, wiping a spot off the counter. Unable—un-
willing—to look Joe in the eye, she felt so guilty, she
continued practically, ''You've told me what Tiffany is
like. I don't want you put in that position, especially because of me.'' She didn't want Tiffany coming on to Joe
because that would mean Joe would have to turn Tiffany

down, and the TV personality would inevitably become more vindictive than she already was.

She especially didn't want Tiffany coming on to Joe again.

Joe plucked the sponge from her hand and tossed it into the sink. Hands on her shoulders, he turned her around to face him, using his body to keep her prisoner against the waist-high cabinets. Planting a hand on either side of her, he looked down at her soberly. "I can handle her and the interview, Emma. Your father is right. She's not going to go away. If she keeps digging, the controversy could hurt the team."

So it was the team—and his place on it—that he was really worried about, Emma thought, trying not to feel hurt. She swallowed and stared at the knot of his tie and the strong suntanned column of his throat. "So you're going to do what has to be done."

Joe waited until she looked at him again. "And then move on," he said.

With or without me? Emma wondered as a bubble of completely uncalled-for hysteria welled up inside her.

Knowing she should have done a lot more to protect her heart in this situation, she dropped her forehead to his shoulder.

Joe tucked a hand beneath her chin and lifted her face to his. He looked deep into her eyes. "It will be all right. I'll make sure of it," Joe promised her, his determination to come out the winner stronger than ever.

But Emma had been on the losing side, when it came to her love affair with Joe once too often. "And if you can't handle her?" she asked anxiously. "Then what?"

Joe's eyes darkened ominously. "Trust me not to be afraid to do what it takes for us to be together," he said gruffly.

Still caging her with his arms, he lowered his head to hers, waiting patiently until she turned her lips to his. The first touch was so electric Emma moaned and wreathed both her arms around his neck. He stepped in even closer, so his body was pressed to her front, the same way the cabinets were pressed to her back. She was trapped against him, and she reveled in the feeling of hard, indomitable male muscle even as she went up on tiptoe to better return his kiss.

Joe had been thinking about kissing Emma all night. The entire time he had been sitting in the Donovans' living room, enduring the combination cross-examination-lecture from her parents and giving the appropriate responses he had been chomping at the bit, waiting for the moment he could have Emma alone again and make her his. Because the truth was, he had felt—and still felt—even after the first time they'd made love, that she still had one foot, if not half her body, out the door.

It was only times like now, when he was kissing her and she was kissing him back, that he felt like the barriers they'd both erected around their hearts even started to fall away.

Which was why, Joe thought, as he tangled his hands in the silky waves of her hair and tilted her head up to his for better access to the sweet, honeyed heat of her mouth, that he could stand here in the kitchen and do this all night.

Even if Emma was starting to get a little impatient.

He smiled against her mouth as she lifted her hips and pressed them against the hardness of his crotch.

"Let's go to bed," she whispered against his mouth.

Joe knew if they hit the mattress, and Emma opened herself up to him, it would be over all too soon. Not good, when he planned to make love to her in a way that took, oh…an hour. Maybe more. Before starting all over again. He grinned and touched his tongue to the corners of her lips. "Let's not."

She whimpered, soft and low in her throat, as her hands curved around his shoulders. "Joe—"

Reluctantly, he lifted his head and looked down at her, meeting her eyes. Her hair was mussed and it was his fault.

And the same was true for her damp, kiss-swollen lips, flushed cheeks and sparkling emerald-green eyes. She looked so damn radiant and ready for loving he could hardly believe she was his. Which was why, Joe figured, he needed to take his time with her tonight. Make it last. Make it real. Make it so all-fired red hot she would never ever do anything foolish to split them up again. He kissed the back of her hand, the inside of her wrist. "The kitchen is just fine."

And to prove it, Joe lowered his head and kissed her once again. At first slowly, almost lazily, then hotter, harder, deeper. Until she was opening her mouth to the pressure of his, tangling her tongue with his, using the sweet suction of her lips and the roaming ministrations of her hands to drive him wild, too.

Without breaking the kiss, he grabbed hold of the fabric of her skirt and shifted it up, above her hips. She wasn't wearing stockings tonight—so the only thing between him and the most intimate part of her was a tiny triangle of peach silk, the same color as her skirt and top.

He brought it down past her knees and knelt before her, to help her step out of her panties. Hands braced on the counter behind her, she stood, watching as he used the light, sure pressure of his stroking hands to convince her to part her legs for him even more.

She was so beautiful. Soft and feminine. Desire flowed through him as he pushed through the nest of chestnut-curls. Her breath caught, just as he hoped it would, as he found her with the pad of his thumb and eased it back and forth over the slick, sensitive spot. She closed her eyes, let her head fall back, her breath soft and ragged. Reveling at her responsiveness, he moved his thumb back, up, inside. Needing to taste as well as touch her softness, he brought his lips up to her and continued the intimate kiss, stroking, teasing. His fingers were wet with her essence. Heat flowed into the dampening folds of flesh and she began to blossom, quivering all the while. She arched up on her toes, moaning softly, and then climaxed with such mind-blowing intensity it was all Joe could do not to lose control, too.

A satisfaction that was even better than throwing the puck into the net flowing through him, Joe held her until the shudders stopped.

Trembling with the effort to hold back his own response, he rose and clasped her against him. Her skirt was still pooled around her waist. She clung to him, seeming to have all the strength of a rag doll. "You didn't…"

"I will," Joe promised, loving the way she looked, so beautiful, so ravished… "I will."

But not yet. First he had to explore the rest of her.

He brought her against him and kissed her again, hard. She responded hungrily, wrapping her arms around him, crushing her breasts to his chest. Joe plundered her mouth with his tongue, even as he accepted the thrust and parry of hers. She was rocking against him, leaving him absolutely no doubt about what she wanted, and the best thing about it was it was what he wanted, too.

Easing his hands beneath the hem of her sleeveless blouse, he caressed his way up past her waist, over her ribs, to her breasts. Her nipples, already hard, sprang to life in his hands. Needing to see, as well as feel, he pushed her top up, above her breasts. They were lush and full, wrapped in the same kind of sexy-thin peach silk as her panties.

He unfastened the front clasp—the fabric fell free.

All day, Joe had been thinking he had imagined the satiny perfection of her gold-tinged skin, the perfect shape of her breasts and the pouting perfection of her apricot nipples.

The truth was, his memory hadn't done her justice. Not a bit. She was not only as beautiful as he recalled, she was better. And even more enticing, she didn't seem to mind him taking the time to look his fill. She even seemed to shyly encourage it.

He smiled back at her and watched her green eyes darken passionately. Hunger flowing through him in mesmerizing waves, he kissed her again, hotly, thoroughly, his hands caressing her breasts all the while. Body hardening, he rubbed the tender crests until she moaned, then kissed and suckled them until she trembled and moaned.

''Joe—'' Her hands were on his fly.

''I know.'' Savoring the sweetness of her ardor, he let her unfasten, unzip. And then her hands were inside his briefs, caressing his hardness, even as their lips continued the wild mating dance.

Joe stood it as long as he could, but when she pushed his pants down, to mid thigh, and his arousal sprang free, he knew it was time to get down to business. Past time.

He lifted her onto the counter and brought her over to the edge. Parting her thighs, he stepped into the vee. Emma wrapped her arms and legs around him, not caring they were both still half dressed. Only caring, it seemed, that they finally connect.

''Now,'' Emma murmured, pleased when Joe agreed.

He slid inside her, watching her face as he entered her, knowing this night, his marriage, was everything he had ever imagined it could be.

And Emma, heaven help her, couldn't seem to look away, either.

For so long, for so many years, she had dreamed of just this. The erotic reality of being one with Joe was nearly more than she could bear. She clasped the smooth, warm muscles of his back and dug her fingers in.

''Tell me you want me,'' he murmured passionately.

Wanting didn't even begin to cover it. She wet her lips as he penetrated her a little more. ''I want you.''

He rubbed his thumb across her lips, kissed her slowly, thoroughly. ''Tell me you'll always want me,'' he urged hoarsely, guiding her even closer.

''Always,'' Emma promised, her breasts swelling and

pushing against the hair-roughened hardness of his pectorals.

"Good." His voice was rough, filled with the longing for more as he continued to watch her in that reverent, unsettling way. "Because that's the way I feel, too."

He kissed her again, with the same abiding passion she felt. Then he began to thrust inside her, slowly at first, almost leisurely. Then more and more provocatively, until there wasn't an ounce of restraint left between them.

Inundated with sensation as hot and all-enveloping as the Carolina summer, Emma closed her eyes. She had never imagined being with Joe could feel this way. So perfect, so good. Sensation built upon sensations and excitement roared through her. Cupping his hands over her bare bottom, he lifted her a little higher. She tightened around him, pulling him deeper still, until Emma no longer knew just who was possessing whom. She only knew that nothing and no one had ever felt so right. And that she wanted him all the way, with no holds barred this time, no secrets or fears between them. And Joe seemed to want her in exactly the same way. In and up, he moved, the easy friction of their bodies doubling their pleasure, their heat. Emma trembled and whimpered low in the back of her throat as he filled her to overflowing. Then filled her some more, until he was embedded inside her as far as he could be. Until they both soared over the edge, from passion into ecstasy.

"WELL, THAT WAS A SURPRISE," Emma murmured affectionately at last.

Joe knew it had been. He also knew it hadn't just been about laying claim to the heart of the woman who was now his wife. Or bringing about some much-needed physical gratification for the two of them.

It had also been about venting some of the frustration he'd been feeling.

Joe didn't like not being in control of a situation. Didn't

like to be told what to do or what not to do. And he really hated feeling that events beyond their control—or other people—were beginning to come between them once again.

He'd wanted to be in charge of his relationship with Emma. And his marriage. He had wanted to prove to himself that when push came to shove, when it came right down to it, there were only two people in this arena that really mattered—Emma and himself.

Joe grinned as he felt the aftershocks still coursing through the body cuddled up to him. If he'd harbored any doubts about any of their relationship before making love with Emma, he had none now.

She wanted him every bit as much as he wanted her. And as long as they were together, as long as they both felt like this, they didn't have a damn thing to worry about. Except, Joe amended humorously, maybe finding a more comfortable place to recover from their sexual Olympics.

Chuckling at the fact she was still limp and pliable against him, her legs still wrapped around his waist a good five minutes after they had reached completion, he lifted her off the counter, carried her upstairs to his bedroom, past his reading chair in the corner, and tumbled her down onto the bed.

"Now that we've completed the warm-up," he grinned, loving the mounting excitement and pleasure in her eyes, "let's get down to some serious love play."

Emma looked as if she weren't sure he was joking or not. She tugged her skirt down. Joe took it off.

"But w-we just—" Emma stammered.

"Give me ten minutes," Joe urged as he divested her of her blouse and bra, too, before shucking his own tie, shirt and socks. Naked, he joined her on the bed. "I'll be ready to go again."

It took five. Maybe.

AFTER THEY HAD MADE LOVE the second time, Joe fell asleep almost immediately. But Emma was so wired from the excitement of finding the passion she had always dreamed she could have with Joe—at a time when she had long given up hope of ever even seeing him again, never mind being his wife—that she couldn't begin to relax, never mind drift off into slumber so easily.

Plus, Emma admitted reluctantly to herself, she was still upset about the theft that occurred the evening before.

She didn't care about her jewelry. Insurance would replace that.

She *did* care about the memorabilia Joe had received from his father.

She knew how much it meant to him, how heartfelt the loss.

And she felt guilty for not going to the sheriff's office with what she suspected about Benjamin Posen's part in the burglary.

The sooner we figure out who did this, the better our chance of recovering your stuff, Mac had told Joe.

Emma didn't want to wrongfully accuse Benjamin Posen and hence ruin his wedding weekend. But she didn't think she could look the other way to suspected wrongdoing, withhold what could prove to be vital information needed to crack the burglary ring that had been playing havoc in Holly Springs for six months now, either. Never mind ignore the chance to potentially find Joe's cherished mementos. Her efforts to investigate on her own hadn't turned up much. No, she needed professional help. She needed to go to someone she could trust.

And who better than Joe's eldest brother?

Surely Mac Hart would be able to keep this under his hat, so to speak, investigate without disrupting the wedding slated to take place at his mother's place of business this weekend.

Her mind made up, Emma slipped out of bed and went out into the family room. It was nearly midnight. Was it too late to call Mac, who, after working all day, was probably at home?

Under the circumstances, with time of the essence, Emma decided not.

Wary of waking Joe, she went into the laundry room and shut the door behind her. To her relief, the Holly Springs sheriff answered on the second ring. "Mac Hart."

"It's Emma, Mac. And I need your help."

JOE WOKE AND REACHED FOR EMMA. Only Emma wasn't there. The sheets were turned back, the bed beside him empty. He glanced at the clock. Ten minutes after twelve.

Wondering why she wasn't sleeping, too, he got up and went in search of her. The lights were still on in the kitchen and family room. But then, Joe recalled, as he looked around and did not see Emma, they had left them on. He glanced around. No sign of Emma. But he heard the muted sound of her voice, coming from…the laundry room?

What was she doing in there?

And who was she talking to secretly this time of night? he wondered.

As he trod closer, he heard her say, "Thanks so much for handling this for me. You know why I couldn't tell Joe." She paused. "I'd prefer he didn't know. Not unless, well, we have to tell him. All right. Thanks, Mac."

Mac?

His brother? Joe thought jealously.

"Good night."

Joe heard a beep as Emma cut the connection on the phone. Then the door opened. She started and uttered a cry of alarm when she saw him standing there, waiting. Their eyes met. She jerked in another breath, even steadier than the last. And looked guilty as sin.

Chapter Twelve

"Surprised to see me?" Joe asked, already knowing the answer.

"Y-y-yes," Emma said, blushing fiercely.

Guilty as charged, he decided. Now all he had to do was discover the crime. "And why might that be?" he murmured softly, deliberately closing the distance between them.

The air between them crackled with energy as a long second passed, then another, and she regarded him with an innocence he didn't for one red-hot second believe.

She tried to brazen it out, anyway, even as her cheeks flushed a telltale pink. Her glance drifted down his torso, before returning ever so self-consciously to his face. "You're not wearing any clothes," she said, frowning as if greatly perplexed.

Clothes were the least of their problems, in Joe's estimation. "Why were you talking to my brother?" he demanded, not about to let her change the subject on him. "And what is it you don't want me to know?"

Emma glanced back down at his private parts. "Can't you put on some clothes?"

"No," Joe said. He stood facing her, legs braced apart, arms folded across his chest. "Now, answer the question."

She continued to dwell on his nakedness. Not that she was all that clothed herself. She had on a claret-red kimono that exposed a hell of a lot of very good-looking thigh. "You'll catch your death of cold."

"I'm fine, Emma," Joe said, trying hard not to think about what she had or did not have on beneath that flimsy piece of silk. "And I'm waiting."

Apparently realizing she wasn't going anywhere until she had told him what he wanted to know, Emma looked into his eyes again and said finally, "I had an idea about who might have stolen your stuff. Or orchestrated the theft, anyway."

"And didn't tell me?" Joe groused, aware this would have been good news had he not had to drag it out of her, and then only after catching her confiding in someone else. Who, by the way, was not her husband!

Emma shrugged. "I didn't want to accuse anyone unfairly."

Joe studied her face, relaxing as he realized she was telling him the truth. "Is that why you took Posen's car this afternoon?" he asked gently.

Emma nodded reluctantly.

"You were tracking down a thief?"

Emma shrugged, in a way that had the edges of her kimono shifting open slightly. "Trying. It didn't work."

Apparently oblivious to the tantalizing glimpse of décolletage she was giving him, Emma went on to explain what she had tried to do while Joe listened. "The thing is," Emma concluded emotionally, "I'd feel terrible if I accused someone of doing something they didn't do."

"But your gut tells you it was Posen," Joe ascertained, not sure whether he felt relieved they had a lead—or simply angry that Emma hadn't trusted him enough to confide in him until her back was to the wall!

Emma released a long, uneven breath. She shoved her fingers through the tousled waves of her dark brown hair. "Yes," she said finally, looking more temptress now than deliberate deceiver. She looked at him imploringly. "Mac said there's an easy enough way to trace it. All they have to do is look at the country club records and see if there is some connection to everyone who's had stuff stolen. If there is and everyone is a member or, more important, considering becoming a member and thus had some dealings with Benjamin Posen, then they can take that information and go to the guys who are already in jail and see if they won't start spilling their guts about who really masterminded the breaking and entering."

It all sounded good. Except one thing. Trying to curtail his hurt, Joe crossed the distance between them. He sank into a chair and pulled her down onto his lap. "Why didn't you tell me?"

As she shifted over him, he realized she wasn't wearing any panties.

Emma looked down at his chest. She stroked her fingers through the mat of hair on his pecs. She shrugged and continued in a small voice laced with regret, "I didn't want to get your hopes up, in case I was wrong. I was trying to protect you."

Joe frowned, not sure where to start, she was so out of line here. "Emma—"

She lifted her chin and regarded him petulantly. "Well, you protect me!"

Joe laced his hands around her waist. "We can't have secrets between us. I thought we had settled that." Her keeping the fact she was Saul Donovan's daughter from him was what had split them up in the first place!

"I'm sorry." Emma looked down again.

Joe was silent. The desire he felt for her was only growing. He could feel it in the blood diverting steadily to his groin. But his connection to her—the bonds they had been forging—those were a little shaky.

Emma studied him. "I've hurt your feelings."

Joe shrugged. He didn't want to fight with her, but he couldn't see the benefit in not stating what was on his mind, either. "It bugs me that you could go to Mac—a man you hardly know—instead of me,'' he said resentfully.

''Actually,'' Emma revealed, looking as if she felt her actions had been only natural, ''I've had a lot of dealings with Mac since I started working at the Inn. He's always dropping by to check on your mom, or grab something to eat.''

The sibling rivalry Joe hoped had been long buried reared its ugly head. ''Even better. You've spent more time with my brother than me.''

He started to lift her off his lap.

Emma refused to cooperate and stayed put. Smiling now, she looked into his eyes in a way that insisted he could not—would not—remain ticked off at her. ''And Janey—because she bakes the cakes. And your mom.''

To his surprise Joe found he wasn't staying mad at her. ''Not Cal?'' he asked curiously.

Emma drummed a lazy pattern on Joe's chest. ''He's always at the medical center.''

Aware he was beginning to get aroused again, Joe prompted, ''Fletcher?''

Beginning to look as if she were enjoying herself, Emma blew out an exasperated breath. ''I swear the only time that man leaves the vet clinic is to go out to the farms to tend the animals there.''

''Well, at least I'm ahead of two of my brothers,'' Joe said with real feeling.

Emma reached down and untied the belt of her robe. The satin kimono fell open, revealing lush curves and breasts that were already pearling. She looked at him sweetly and revealed in a low, teasing voice that was all temptress, ''You're ahead of all of them, where it counts, in my heart.''

Joe grinned as he felt her shifting, and knew she was aroused, too. ''You wouldn't by any chance be trying to sweet-talk your way out of trouble now, would you, Miss

Emma?'' he said as her silky dampness flowed over his building heat.

Emma shifted a little more, so the tip of his sex was pressing against the widening juncture of her thighs. ''I might.'' She eyed him. ''Will it work?''

Aware he hadn't even kissed her yet and he was already ready to take her, Joe shook his head. ''But I know something that might.''

Picking her up by the waist, he shifted her around so she was facing him. As he set her back down on his lap, she straddled him, her knees on either side of his thighs. Joe didn't think she could be ready. But she was as she opened herself and slid over top of him. For the first time there was no foreplay, no long preliminary kisses, just hot, reckless, incredibly lusty, mind-blowing sex. With neither of them holding back. When she climaxed, which was, for the record, all too soon, he followed, fast and fierce. And as they clung together, shuddering, Joe knew the simple truth.

He loved her.

He didn't know what he was going to do about it, or even if she loved him, but that didn't change a thing.

These feelings he had weren't ever going to go away.

''NOT TOO HARD TO FIGURE WHAT'S been going on here, is it?'' Joe teased Friday morning as they headed downstairs to the kitchen in search of coffee.

Emma stepped over Joe's trousers and a high-heeled sandal. One of Joe's socks. His boxer briefs. Her peach silk panties. And over there, on the chair, her claret-red silk kimono.

She was glad they were already showered, and she, at least, was dressed and ready to go to work. Otherwise she might be tempted to dally.

''Definitely a trail of some sort,'' she murmured, blushing at the memory of their passionate lovemaking the evening before. They exchanged grins that brought to mind a rather wild rest of the night, and early morning. Joe had demonstrated stamina—and an appetite—wilder than Emma's most romantic and outlandish imaginings.

"So what's your schedule like today?" Joe asked as he poured water into the coffeemaker.

Emma measured coffee into a filter. "I won't be home all day or evening."

"Not even to change?"

Emma shook her head in disappointment, even as she relished the homey intimacy of the moment. "The Snow-Posen rehearsal dinner is this evening. Tents are going up on the lawn for the ceremony tomorrow. There's a lot to supervise." She didn't have to explain further. Joe had grown up at the Wedding Inn. He knew all about the business. "What about you?" she asked, thinking how handsome he looked in just a pair of athletic shorts, his golden-brown hair all rumpled, the sexy week's worth of beard on his face.

Joe hit the on button on the coffeemaker, then turned to face her. He lounged against the counter, watching while Emma poured them both a glass of orange juice. "I've got a conditioning session later this morning. Team meeting this afternoon. The interview with Tiffany Lamour sometime this evening."

Emma frowned at the mention of the female piranha.

Joe flashed her a soothing half smile, unabashedly confident as ever. "Don't worry. I'll handle it."

When he talked like that and looked at her like that, she could almost believe it. "Okay." Emma took a deep breath. *Okay.* She swallowed hard around the knot of uneasiness in her throat. Moved on.

Joe closed the distance between them and took her into his arms. He held her near, nuzzling her hair, the shell of her ear and the sensitive place on her neck. "What time will the rehearsal dinner be over with?"

Emma could feel him wanting to make love to her all over again. If only they had the time! She looked into his eyes, wondering all over again at the fateful events that had brought them together again. "It should wrap up around 10:00 p.m.," she said.

Joe smiled, content. "How about I meet you there, then," he suggested gently. "We can head home together."

Emma kissed the U of his collarbone. "I'd like that."

"I'll see you tonight." He gave her a long, lingering kiss that had her spirits soaring.

Emma looked at him, all the love she felt and had yet to hear him lay voice to, in her eyes.

"Until tonight," she said.

JOE HAD JUST DONE THE DISHES and picked up the clothes they had left lying everywhere when the doorbell rang.

Tiffany Lamour was on the other side. "Aren't you going to invite me in?"

Joe frowned. This was the last thing he needed or wanted. "I'm about to leave for the arena," he said brusquely.

Tiffany's shrewd gaze lingered on his bare chest and legs. "Without your shirt or shoes? Come on, Joe," she wheedled softly. "It'll just take a minute. I want to talk about the gist of the interview."

If only Saul and Margaret Donovan weren't forcing him into this, Joe thought. Making no effort to hide his resentment, he opened the door for her. He had to be polite, but that was all. He led the way back to the family room, leaving her to follow at will. "No questions about my marriage or Emma."

Tiffany watched as Joe located his T-shirt and pulled it over his head. "You don't get to call the shots here, Joe."

"The hell I don't." Joe snatched up his socks and sat down to put them on. "I'm doing you a favor appearing on your show."

Tiffany smirked. "Isn't it the other way around?"

Joe knew he was supposed to capitulate, start minding

his manners now, kiss up to Tiffany, but he had no intention of bowing to her demands and instead kept up the don't-mess-with-me attitude. He'd spent his entire hockey career fending off intimidation, both physical and mental. As far as he was concerned, Tiffany Lamour was just another "goon," out there solely to undermine his concentration and his determination. The trouble for rabble-rousers like her was that Joe could not—would not—be bullied. If he had a soft spot at all, and some times he still doubted that, it was Emma.

Tiffany perched on the sofa, showing a helluva lot more leg than Joe had the desire to see. As she rummaged around in her handbag for a pad and pen, she let her knees fall open a tad too far.

Joe turned his glance away. He didn't care what kind of panties she was wearing, or wanted him to see.

"I'm going to ask you whatever I please once the tape starts rolling," Tiffany said as Joe walked around, making sure all the doors and windows were locked.

Joe secured the sliding glass doors to the deck. "Then you better be careful," he retorted, just as slyly. "Because I just might have a few questions of my own, too."

At the edge in his tone, Tiffany cocked a challenging brow. "For instance?"

Joe picked up the pile of clothes on the kitchen counter, carried them into the laundry room, out of Tiffany's view, and dumped them on top of the washing machine. Returning to the family room, he said, "Like exactly what role did you play in Stan Haysbert's divorce?"

Tiffany tensed in a way that let Joe know he had just scored one against her. They both knew her father's money had barely kept her out of court on that one.

Tiffany regained her composure. Standing, she lifted her shoulders in an elegant shrug. "I can edit any way I want, once the taping is over."

"True," Joe agreed just as cordially. "But it helps to have something usable there in the first place. And, oh, by the way, I'm bringing Ross Dempsey, my attorney, with me to the taping this evening. He's looking forward to seeing you in action.''

That quickly, all the fight went out of Tiffany.

Joe didn't trust her sudden capitulation any more than he trusted Tiffany.

''You must really love her,'' she murmured, still searching his face.

Joe did. But he wasn't going to get into that with Tiffany. Or anyone else, for that matter.

The silence between them strung out interminably.

''Fine,'' Tiffany said grudgingly at last. She threw up her hands and put her pen and pad back in her handbag. ''We'll do it your way, Joe, as always. And skip the personal stuff. Although—'' she leveled her cynical gaze on him ''—if you ask me, you're skipping a huge opportunity to tell the world how it really is—and was—with you and Saul Donovan's daughter. As well as how you got forced into this.''

The only thing Joe had been forced into was the interview with Tiffany.

Her manner becoming suddenly matter-of-fact, almost defeated, as if she had given up trying to talk sense into him, Tiffany said, ''You need to be at the hotel at seven. We'll probably go for about two hours, then my producers and I'll whittle the footage down to the twenty-four minutes we'll eventually use. Thirty minutes, minus commercials.''

Joe could have cared less about any of that. He glanced at his watch, then started herding her down the front hall, toward the door.

''Mind if I use your powder room before I leave?'' Tiffany asked.

Joe hesitated. He didn't know why. The request had him on edge.

Tiffany rolled her eyes and looked down her nose at

him. "Honestly, Joe, it'll just take a moment. Unless you would prefer I drive until I find a gas station?"

Actually, Joe would. But manners, and a sense of southern hospitality long ingrained by his mother, had him nodding his assent, however privately grudgingly. "Where— never mind, I'll find it." Tiffany took off up the stairs. "These tract houses are all alike."

Witch.

Joe returned to the family room to grab his cell phone and keys and to make sure the coffeemaker was off. By the time he got back to the front hall, the commode upstairs was flushing. Seconds later she came back down the stairs.

To his relief, this time she avoided his eyes.

"See you tonight." Her manner brisk and businesslike, she departed.

EMMA WAS OVERSEEING THE last of the cleanup from the Snow-Posen rehearsal dinner when Joe arrived to pick her up. He said a brief hello to his mother, gave her a hug, then headed straight for Emma. Still wearing the clothes he had put on for his television interview—a handsome charcoal sport coat and silvery blue shirt and tie—he was at his most appealing. While she, with her heart on her sleeve, was at her most vulnerable. She closed the distance between them, as normally as if they did this every day. Deciding what was the use of being married to one of the most attractive athletes on the planet if you couldn't take advantage of it, she stood on tiptoe and brushed a kiss to his cheek. "How did it go?"

Joe wrapped a possessive arm about her waist and touched his lips to the top of her head. "Fine." He gave her waist another squeeze, then let her go. "What about you?" He searched her eyes. "How was your day?"

Emma sighed just thinking about it. "About as you would expect." She continued collecting the centerpieces from the tables, brass pots filled with an eclectic assortment of wildflowers, flown in specially from the greenhouses at the Lady Bird Johnson Wildflower Center in Texas. "Gigi Snow found fault with everything and let us know about it."

Joe helped her load the centerpieces on the serving cart, while around them the Inn's formally attired wait staff cleared dishes off tablecloths and tossed fine linen tablecloths and napkins into laundry hampers. "Isn't the rehearsal dinner the responsibility of the groom's family?"

"Yes, but since Benjamin's parents live in California, they left all the details to him, and because they aren't financially well off enough to afford what went on here tonight, Benjamin is paying for it."

Joe handed the cart over to one of the help. "Did he have any complaints about the decorations or meal?"

"No. None." In fact, Emma thought, Benjamin Posen had been quite complimentary after he and Michelle had made up over high tea, which in turn had made Emma feel all the more guilty about suspecting the marketing exec of anything illegal.

Joe paused, his thoughts obviously going the same direction as hers. "Did you hear from Mac today?"

"No," Emma admitted reluctantly. "Not a word." She looked at him hopefully. "Did you talk to him?"

Joe shook his head, disappointment shining in his eyes. "He wouldn't discuss an ongoing investigation with me, anyway. It would be unprofessional. He'll listen to what we have to tell him, then take it from there. But until something definite happens to establish Posen's guilt or innocence, he's not likely to tell anyone outside the sheriff's department what is going on."

Emma nodded. As the formal dining room was cleared, two large vacuum cleaners were brought in. She had been hoping Benjamin would have been vindicated by now. The fact he hadn't…well, it just made the whole situation a little more nerve-racking. It was like presiding over a wedding on the deck of the *Titanic*.

Joe frowned as the vacuums were switched on. The noise made it imperative Emma and Joe find somewhere else to talk. He took her by the hand and led her out one of the side doors onto the flagstone sidewalk that encircled the Inn.

Joe nodded at a self-conscious woman in an inexpensive yellow dress, and the tall, thin man beside her in the ill-fitting tan suit. They were standing next to a rental car in the guest parking lot under the lights. "Are those the parents of the groom?"

Emma nodded, her heart going out to Benjamin's mother. "Poor Mrs. Posen. She's had a rough evening. First, Gigi Snow was, well," Emma sighed, "let's just say rather snotty to her, then she sobbed through the entire rehearsal with the minister. I guess it didn't hit her that Benjamin was actually getting married until just now."

Joe clasped Emma's hand consolingly. "How did her husband react?"

"Awkwardly. He didn't seem to know how to comfort her. Anyway, I'm hoping a good night's sleep will help them get through tomorrow."

Joe shot a look at Michelle Snow, who was now climbing into the back of a limousine with her parents. "And the bride and groom?"

Emma shot a look at Benjamin Posen, who was standing at the curb, lifting his hand in an uncertain wave. "They're both very nervous." Very nervous.

Joe studied her in a way that made Emma think he wasn't really thinking about the wedding, but something else, something much more intimate. "Do you think everything will go okay tomorrow?" he asked casually, as the other members of the wedding party and the minister departed, too.

Emma shrugged at the storm clouds gathering overhead, obscuring both moon and the stars. "I hope so, but seeing as how we have a sixty-percent chance of showers overnight, I imagine there will be some snafus."

"The wedding isn't until…?"

"Two o'clock, tomorrow afternoon."

"It may have cleared up by then," Joe soothed.

The way her luck was going, when it came to this wedding, Emma doubted it. And speaking of bad karma…what was *she* doing here? Emma wondered resentfully.

Tiffany Lamour strode briskly toward them, lifting her hand in a joyous wave. "Joe, honey! Glad I caught you!" She dashed up to them breathlessly, coming so close she practically crashed into Joe. "You left the hotel before I could give you a tape. The whole two and a half hours of questions and answers, uncut. I thought you and Emma might want to watch it this evening. Together." Tiffany turned and smiled slyly at Emma. "Your husband did such a great job. Really. You should be so proud."

And why don't I trust that? Emma thought. Why don't I trust you?

"Well, I imagine you all have lots to do, so I'm going to let you go." Tiffany smiled again and sashayed—rather jubilantly, Emma noted—back in the direction of her car.

Emma turned to Joe, who was just standing there, looking a little dumbfounded, videocassette in hand. "What was that all about?" Emma asked suspiciously, her every feminine instinct on full alert.

Joe shook his head. He looked every bit as wary as Emma felt. Grimacing, he said slowly, "I wish to hell I knew."

"WHY DON'T YOU WANT TO WATCH IT?" Emma asked curiously after they arrived home. She was ready to put the interview-tape in the VCR. Joe had other ideas.

Joe reached for the zipper on Emma's dress. "Because there are other things I'd much rather do," he murmured, nuzzling his way down her neck.

Emma put up a hand to stop him.

She didn't know why it was so important she do this right now. Especially when she had already had such a long day and faced an even longer and more problem-fraught one tomorrow. She just knew she was desperate to keep Joe from getting hurt. And her gut told her that despite the show of smug civility that Tiffany Lamour was still out to hurt Joe, and perhaps, Emma, too. "I want to see it," she said quietly.

She wanted to know firsthand just how rough a time Tiffany had given Joe during the interview, and she wanted to discover why Joe was suddenly looking so stressed out. As if he just wanted the world to go away, so he could be alone with Emma and make love to her without dealing with all the complications in their lives that weren't going to go away, no matter how they wished otherwise.

"You heard her," Joe said, not bothering to mask his frustration as he tossed his beautiful sport coat onto the back of the sofa. "It's two and a half hours long."

Wanting to get more comfortable, too, Emma slipped off her heels. "Is there something on it you don't want me to see?"

Joe jerked off his tie and unbuttoned the first two buttons on his shirt. "There's nothing in the interview conducted tonight."

Interesting response. And too cagey for her taste. Emma forced her pulse to slow. "You think the videotape she gave us tonight contains something other than the interview, don't you?" Emma mused after a moment. And if so, what? she wondered uneasily. Had Joe once been caught with his pants down somewhere? Was this a videotape of him and another woman? Or something else equally incriminating?

Joe hedged in a way that made Emma all the more determined to find out what Tiffany was up to now. "I don't know," he said finally. "It shouldn't."

But that didn't mean it didn't.

"All the more reason for us to watch it now," Emma said.

"It's already close to midnight," Joe said.

"I won't sleep until I know what is on it. And my guess is neither will you."

His lips tightening, Joe stared down at her. Probably wishing, Emma thought, that she weren't quite so curious. Finally, he said, "You're not going to rest until you've looked at that, are you?"

"If she is up to something, don't you think we should know what as soon as possible?"

Sighing, Joe popped in the cassette and hit the play button.

An hour into it, Emma turned to him, even more perplexed. "I don't get it, Joe."

Joe stopped the tape.

"These are all softball questions—about hockey. Where's the stuff about your—our—personal life?" Emma asked.

Joe looked edgy again. "She didn't ask anything."

Emma took a moment to consider that. "Nothing?"

"Nada," Joe confirmed flatly.

"Why not?"

His eyes were chilly. "Maybe because I took my sports attorney, Ross Dempsey, with me and specifically asked her not to do so in his presence."

"You think she was intimidated?" One could hope, anyway.

Joe paused a long time and chose his words carefully before answering. "I think I've got the situation under control," he said finally.

"That being the case…" Emma caressed his jaw, deciding as long as they were discussing things Joe did not want to talk about they might as well touch on one more thing that had been nagging at her. "How come you didn't get rid of this—" she stroked his week's worth of beard with the flat of her hand "—for the TV interview?"

Joe's lips took on a roguish tilt and his eyes began to sparkle. "I admit it probably would have looked better had

I done so. And my mom will be the first to lodge a complaint when she sees the interview.''

"Then why didn't you?" Emma persisted, climbing onto his lap.

Joe switched off the TV, via the remote, and didn't answer. "Come on, you." He shifted her off his lap and onto her feet. "Time for bed. You've got a big day tomorrow."

Emma dug in her feet, even as he took her by the hand and began propelling her down the hall. "Tell me why you passed on the razor first."

He paused here and there to switch off the downstairs lights. "Because like most professional athletes I'm superstitious," he admitted as he walked with her through the foyer to the stairs.

A little disappointed he wasn't carrying her or putting the moves on her when desire had clearly been simmering between the two of them all day, Emma followed him up the treads. "So you've been growing this beard ever since you signed with the Storm last Friday night, for luck."

"Actually—" Joe grinned with boyish mischief, lacing an arm about her waist as they headed down the upstairs hall "—I started growing it because I thought it would annoy you."

Emma could believe that, given how they'd acted after initially seeing each other again, and then being forced into renewing their abruptly abandoned marriage vows.

She slanted him a challenging look. "And hence, push me away," she said, recalling at the same time she had wanted nothing more than that, too.

But that was then. This was now.

He nodded soberly.

"But it didn't push me away," Emma remembered, still regarding him closely.

"Right," Joe said, his voice holding a surprising note of tenderness as well as the expected mischief. "And now that our marriage is going better than anyone ever could have imagined, well—" he stopped and brought her to him for a sexy kiss that ended much too soon ''—I guess I'll do whatever I have to do to keep things status quo.''

Sometimes a woman had to do what a woman had to do. ''Even if it means never shaving again?'' Emma teased in the same lighthearted manner, taking him by the hand and leading him toward their bed.

''Even that,'' Joe affirmed.

''Well,'' Emma sighed, prepared to do whatever it was a woman had to do to get things started in the direction she wanted them to go.

As it happened, it didn't take much.

''EMMA, I need to talk to you.''

Emma knew that look on her mother's face. Aware they were at the stage where every second counted, she put up a staying hand. ''Mom, please, we're putting on the Snow-Posen wedding here today. I really don't have time—''

''Then you will make time,'' Margaret Donovan insisted in tried and true steel-magnolia fashion. ''Your father and I saw the tape of Joe's interview for CSN last night. Tiffany Lamour brought one over for us.''

Emma's stomach knotted. She and Joe never had watched the rest of the tape. Instead, they had made love. Rather wonderful love, as it happened...

But her mother didn't know about that. And not about to tell her, Emma decided it best to keep the conversation strictly on the matter that had her mother so upset. ''Tiffany was a regular delivery girl, wasn't she?'' Emma murmured, as she pointed where she wanted the additional tent and the dance floor to go.

Margaret knotted her hands at her sides as raindrops threatened overhead. She stepped back under the covered portico that faced the Inn's back lawn. ''I want to know what happened! Joe was supposed to use that interview for damage control. Instead there wasn't one word about his early secret marriage to you.''

''Thank goodness,'' Emma said. It was hard enough for

her to think about that awful night, without having every hockey fan in America in on the juicy details, too.

Margaret lowered her voice with effort, as uniformed staff pushed a cart loaded with white folding chairs onto the lawn. ''This was supposed to explain your relationship with Joe, quieten gossip.''

''I don't think anything is going to be able to do that except a whole lot of silence on our part.'' And our continued marriage…

Margaret's eyes narrowed. ''I beg to differ,'' she said, savvy as ever. ''As long as there is no reasonable explanation, there will continue to be speculation.''

Emma knew she and Joe were a public relations person's nightmare. She didn't care. ''Then let people speculate all they wish.'' Emma watched as florist Lily Madsen decorated the aisle where chairs had already been set up.

Margaret moved so Emma had no choice but to look at her. ''I called Tiffany this morning. She's willing to add another section of tape to the interview, if Joe is willing.''

Emma shrugged. ''You can ask him.''

Margaret paused, cell phone in hand. ''But?''

Emma figured she might as well be honest. ''I don't imagine he is going to want to get into it now any more than he did last night,'' she said sagely.

Margaret took Emma by the arm and guided her back against the building, well out of earshot of staff scurrying in and out of the service doors. ''What exactly happened at the hotel, where Joe and Tiffany did the interview?'' she demanded.

Something about her usually unflappable mother's hysteria had Emma on edge. ''What do you mean?''

Margaret's eyes were grim. ''Tiffany left our home the other night determined to dig until she uncovered the whole story. Then, less than twenty-four hours later, she's acting as if she never really wanted to know why you and Joe did what you did, anyway.'' Margaret's lips thinned disapprovingly. "Something doesn't make sense here, Emma."

Emma's stomach took another dive. "What exactly are you implying?"

Margaret searched Emma's eyes. "Joe didn't pay her off or something, did he?"

Emma blinked, too distressed for words. "Mother!"

"Well, what other explanation is there?" Margaret demanded, upset.

Emma knew of one. But she couldn't believe. Wouldn't...

"Oh, no." Margaret pressed a hand to her heart. Her face turned white as a sheet.

Emma studied the way her mother suddenly couldn't look her in the eye. And abruptly it all became clear as a bell. She edged closer, fury clawing at her heart. She marched forward. "You know what people say about Tiffany's methods for extracting cooperation from her subjects, don't you? You knew that and sent him to the lion's den, anyway. What is this—some kind of morality test?"

Margaret ignored the question and her eyes gave nothing away. But then her mother didn't have to put it all out in the open, Emma thought, because the answer was clear, anyway. Her parents were testing Joe, trying to find out for themselves exactly what kind of man he was.

"First of all, Emma, for all we know the rumors about Tiffany Lamour are just that—baseless innuendo. Similar to what you and Joe are facing, brought about by entirely innocent—though highly unusual—circumstances. Second, and more important," Margaret continued coolly, lifting one elegantly sculpted brow, "how do you know about any of this?" Margaret knew Emma had never followed the inner workings of the hockey world, not since her relationship with Joe had ended years ago. In fact, at least publicly, she had tried to stay as far away from it as possible. Privately, well, Emma admitted to watching a little of the sport on TV, especially when whatever team Joe had happened to be on at the time was involved in a televised game.

She had always told herself at the time she was just doing it to prove Joe wasn't super human or super handsome or super talented. That she was over him. Now, of course, Emma knew, it had simply been because she couldn't get enough of him.

Not then. And not now. "Joe told me what she is really like," Emma said when she realized her mother was still waiting for an explanation.

Margaret folded her arms in front of her. "Then Tiffany did make a pass at him?"

Emma saw no reason to hide it, now the scandal was out in the open. "Years ago, if you must know. Which is why Tiffany Lamour has never had a nice thing to say about him—or his play—since."

"Except for last night," Margaret observed. "In last night's interview she couldn't say enough sweet things."

Okay, so Emma had noticed that, too. Which had been another reason she'd had no interest in watching the rest of the taped interview, and instead had preferred to go on to bed with Joe and make mad, passionate love to him all over again.

But Emma's mother did not know that. Her mother thought...

"He did not sleep with her to get her to back off, Mom," Emma stated harshly, annoyed she had to defend him. "He would not do that. He is not that kind of guy."

Margaret Donovan bit her lip uncertainly.

Gathering steam, Emma dropped her voice a confidential notch and charged on, "Joe did, however, threaten Tiffany with his lawyer and even took Ross Dempsey to the interview last night, so maybe that's what did it, Joe's determination not to be a victim plus the extra legal scrutiny."

At the additional information, Margaret relaxed, but only slightly. "I hope that's all it is," Margaret said worriedly. "That Tiffany did change her mind, and that this isn't just some sort of temporary ploy on her part to make us think she is doing right by you and Joe, before she actually does an about-face and goes on the attack."

Emma hoped so, too.

"But the fact remains you and Joe have to talk to someone about your marriage. So if not CSN or *Personalities* magazine, maybe we could get W-MOL to do a fluffball interview with you. Since it's a local TV station and we advertise for Storm games on their airwaves, we do have some influence there. Who knows? Maybe if they do a sophisticated-enough job, the network will pick it up, perhaps some of the other cable news channels, as well...."

Here they went again. "No, Mother."

"What?" Margaret stopped, flabbergasted.

Emma knew it was now or never. She had to stand up to her parents some time, draw that proverbial line in the sand. "Joe and I are not changing our minds," she stated emotionally. "Our marriage, and everything else about our relationship, is staying between him and me. End of story. Now, if you'll excuse me," Emma finished, aware she had never felt so simultaneously strong and relieved, "I've got work to do."

JOE WAS HELPING HIS SISTER, Janey, unload the wedding and groom's cakes for the Snow-Posen wedding from her bakery delivery van to the Wedding Inn dining room, where they would be on display. It was no easy task. The cake for five hundred was an enormous, seven-layer confection. The groom's cake was smaller, but because of its sand-trap shape, no less awkward and cumbersome.

"Thanks for helping me with this," Janey said as they centered the heavy metal tray on the rolling cart that would take it to the display table.

"No problem." Joe made sure it was stable, then returned to the van to shut and lock the doors.

"Usually Christopher assists me with deliveries, but he

had a chance to get in some extra time at the Polar Bear ice skating rink this morning—before they open for customers at one—provided he help with the cleanup from last night's birthday parties, so..."

"Still unhappy about him liking hockey so much?" Joe asked as they rolled the wedding cake toward the side entrance service doors.

Janey paused and wedged open the doors, so they could get the cart through. "I wish he'd focus more on his schoolwork."

Joe steered the rolling cart inside.

"Like his father," Janey continued, scowling, "all Christopher can think about is sports."

Joe shrugged. "I'm the same way."

"You're successful. It's a whole different world for wannabes."

"And that's what you think Christopher is going to grow up to be?" An Olympic hopeful, like his father, who never made it, and who became bitter and reckless and resentful ever after.

Janey hesitated. "Maybe we shouldn't discuss this."

"Maybe you're right."

Silence fell between them. Joe tried not to think about it, but he couldn't help it. His older sister's diatribe had brought back shades of Joe's youth, the lack of faith in him, the bitterness and hurt he still felt....

"So how are things going with you and Emma?" Janey helped lift the cake onto the table.

Joe helped center it. "Prying, sis?"

Janey shrugged, not about to apologize for the interest. "She looks happier every time I see her."

To his surprise, Joe felt that way, too. "I don't think Emma was particularly excited about today's wedding, though."

"Tell me about it," Janey muttered as they took the cart back out to get the groom's cake. "That Gigi Snow is one royal pill. She's already called me three times this morning to make sure I get the details right on the cake. And I'm sure as soon as she sees the cakes on display, she'll have even more criticisms to lodge. I only have the cakes, though. Poor Emma. She's got it worse than me. She's going to be exhausted by the time it's all over.''

Joe knew that was true. It had been a grueling week for his wife. Joe knew he had tried to help her get through it. He still had the feeling he hadn't done nearly enough to make them a real ''team.'' But that could change easily enough. Knowing the power of a simple gesture, Joe looked at Janey thoughtfully. ''Emma said the reception will be over around ten.''

Janey agreed. ''If we're lucky.''

Joe played it cool as he paused beside the van. ''I was thinking maybe I would surprise her tonight.''

Janey glanced at him as if he were a space alien. ''With…?''

''I don't know.'' Joe studied his sister, still gauging her reaction.

Janey took the keys and unlocked the door. ''If she's anything like me, she'll probably be too tired to go out.''

Probably right. ''Then I should do something at home?'' Joe helped slide the groom's cake out onto the cart.

Janey made sure her confection was stable before turning to him with a sly glance. ''You're really getting into this husband stuff, aren't you?'' she teased.

Joe pretended not to care. ''I am married now.''

Janey looked at him like a TV shrink. ''So I see.''

''So what should I do?'' Joe asked seriously.

''It wouldn't hurt to ply her with a little dinner. The staff never got to eat at these things, and that goes triple for the wedding planner. Wine would be nice, so would flowers. Clean sheets on the bed, sprayed with a little of her favorite perfume or your after-shave is always a nice touch. You might even go a little crazy and try shaving off that bristly mess on your jaw.''

Joe would do everything but that.

Janey shook her head. "I'm not even going to ask," she said dryly.

Joe shook off the superstition. The fact he'd been growing a beard since he and Emma had come in contact with each other once again had nothing to do with the continuing success of their relationship. What they had going for them now was a heck of a lot more powerful than deliberately engineered luck. Still, if it wasn't broke...why fix it?

He regarded Janey with a patience that was new to him. "Anything else?"

They pushed the cart toward the door. "Candles would be nice. Maybe some soft music."

Joe made a mental note to go out and buy some music Emma would like. All his own stuff tended toward heavy metal, classic rock or alternative. Not really stuff that would get you in the mood. He wanted Emma to be in the mood. He looked at his sister. If ever there was a detail person about this kind of stuff, it was Janey. "I don't want to overlook anything, so..."

Janey tilted her head at him. "If I didn't know better, I'd think you were feeling guilty about something," she teased as they placed the groom's cake on a separate display table.

"Why would I feel guilty?" Joe retorted just as Emma passed by, did a double take and came back.

Eyes twinkling merrily, she looked at Joe. "What was that about guilt?" she asked.

Joe felt a flash of guilt—and that was stupid. He had nothing to feel remorseful about where Emma was concerned. Just because he hadn't told her about Tiffany stopping by or confided his continuing unease where the TV interviewer was concerned, did not put him in the wrong. He was protecting his wife, that was all. And protecting her was what he was supposed to do.

Unfortunately, he wasn't sure Emma would see it that

way. Especially given the way she was looking at him now.

Knowing she already had enough on her plate, and now was not the time to hit her with a confession, Joe flashed his choirboy smile. Covering, he clamped a hand on his sister's shoulder. "Not my guilt, Emma. Hers." Joe looked down at his sister and continued with stern but heartfelt advice, "Janey here is remorseful because she's not supporting her son's interest in hockey the way she should. And that is a very bad thing."

Janey scowled up at Joe, with a look that said, "Talk like that will get you into trouble every time, baby brother." She turned back to Emma. "Ignore Joe. I most certainly am. He's just being a pea-brained athlete, as usual."

"You wish," Joe grumbled right back. Janey was cruising for trouble with Christopher, given her current unsupportive attitude for Chris's love of sports, even if she wouldn't admit it.

Emma smiled, shook her head. Relaxing, she backed off. "As much as I would love to stay and witness the continuation of this sibling bickering, I've got work to do."

Joe grabbed her and kissed her forehead. "Everything looks great."

"Thanks."

"I'll see you at home. Tonight."

Emma warmed at the heat in his smile. Looking as if she couldn't wait to make love to him again, too, she murmured sweetly, "It should be around ten-thirty."

"Okay," Joe said, unable to keep himself from kissing her again. He gave her a reassuring squeeze. "And good luck."

Knowing Gigi Snow, she was going to need it.

Chapter Thirteen

"Is Benjamin here yet?" Michelle asked.

Emma watched, pleased, as the stylist finished pinning up Michelle's hair. "Yes."

"And he's getting dressed, too?"

Emma nodded. "In the suite, on the other side of the staircase."

"What about the groomsmen?"

"They're all here, too," Emma soothed.

The makeup artist hired to do Michelle's makeup looked pained at the bride's continued restlessness. "Honey, please, you've got to relax here or I'll never get your eyes done."

"Sorry." Michelle pressed a hand to her abdomen and took a deep breath. "I just can't shake the feeling that something is going to go wrong today."

Emma knew what the bride meant. She was having the same intuition. But that was probably because Michelle was so nervous. "Would you feel better if I went across the hall and checked to make sure everything is okay in the male quarters?" Emma asked kindly.

Relief softened the pretty features on Michelle's face. "Would you?"

"No problem." Emma consulted her watch, found they were still right on schedule, if not a little ahead. "Just promise me you'll start getting into your dress while I'm gone. The photographer is going to be here in fifteen minutes to take some pictures.''

''I'll see she gets into her gown,'' Gigi Snow declared haughtily as she slipped into the spacious bridal suite. She leveled a disapproving look at Emma. ''Meanwhile, I expect you to do something about those ice sculptures!''

Emma tensed. ''What's wrong with the sculptures?'' She had looked at them half an hour ago and seen nothing amiss.

''The Cupid isn't smiling, that's what!''

Actually, he was, albeit slyly. ''I'll contact the artist, see what he can do,'' Emma said.

And before Gigi could complain about anything else, Emma slipped out of the room.

As she headed across the hall, she saw Mac Hart coming up the sweeping central staircase. He was wearing his sheriff's uniform. His expression was grim and businesslike.

''Where is Benjamin Posen?'' Mac got straight to the point.

Emma swallowed. She had convinced herself Benjamin wasn't guilty after all. Max's expression said otherwise. She looked at Mac steadily. ''Can't it wait? He's getting ready for his wedding.''

Mac took her aside, his expression stern but unrelenting. ''I'm afraid not.''

Silence fell between them. Emma knew if she didn't tell Mac, he would find Benjamin on his own. ''He's in the groom's suite,'' she said.

Although it wasn't necessary—Mac knew the Wedding Inn as well if not better than she did—she led the way to the door and knocked. Benjamin opened it. He was clad in his pleated white shirt and tuxedo pants and was in the process of fastening his suspenders.

He looked from Emma to Mac and back again. The blood began to drain from his face and a bead of sweat broke out on his forehead. ''Don't tell me I'm doubleparked,'' he cracked.

Mac put a hand on Benjamin's shoulder and turned him toward the wall. "Benjamin Posen, I've got a warrant for your arrest for the burglary of the Holly Springs Country Club pro shop and a dozen residences." Mac reached for the handcuffs at his waist. Taking one of Benjamin's wrists, he clamped them on.

"This is a joke, right?" Benjamin said, perspiring profusely now.

"Afraid not," Mac said somberly, securing Benjamin's hands behind his back. While the groomsmen looked on in stupefied silence, Mac went on to read him his Miranda rights. The groom chose not to remain silent, despite the fact that anything and everything he said could potentially be held against him. "You can't do this," Benjamin stated in a low, ticked-off voice. He glared at Mac. "I'm getting married in less than an hour!"

"Should have thought about that before you hired those professional burglars to steal all those golf clubs," Mac said.

The color drained from Benjamin's face once again as across the hall, on the other side of the staircase, the door to the bridal suite opened.

"We know you masterminded the thievery—your buddies in crime have been singing like canaries to the district attorney since dawn this morning. They even led us to the cache of goods taken from my brother Joe's place."

"So Joe's going to get his hockey memorabilia back?" Emma asked.

Mac nodded. "Near as I can tell, it's all there."

Thank goodness, Emma thought. She knew how much that stuff meant to Joe. Especially the Gordie Howe practice jersey his father had given him, before his father died.

Gigi Snow stepped out. She stared at the group gathered in the hall. "What in heaven's name is going on here?" she demanded. Gigi looked at Mac. "Tell me you aren't arresting him!"

"Arresting who?" Michelle demanded. Forgetting for a

moment she wasn't supposed to see the groom before the wedding, she, too, swept out into the hall, in her wedding gown. She was followed by a bevy of bridesmaids, in expensive designer gowns. Michelle stared at her husband-to-be in shock. "Benjamin…?"

"I'm going to call our attorney!" Gigi Snow already had her cell phone out of her purse. "I promise you, we'll sue!"

"Don't bother." Benjamin spoke to Gigi but never took his eyes off his bride. His expression radiated sorrow and apology. "Sheriff Hart has every right to be here." He turned to Mac, his face blotchy with humiliation. "Let's just get out of here, okay, before anyone else sees," he pleaded in a low, strangled voice.

Mac nodded. "Fine by me." Mac led Benjamin off in handcuffs.

A sobbing Michelle tried to follow. "Tell me this is all a terrible mistake!" she demanded of her fiancé.

Benjamin swallowed hard, a mixture of shame and embarrassment on his face "I can't, Michelle. I'm sorry."

Mac pushed on. Benjamin didn't look back.

A stunned and still sobbing Michelle, surrounded by her wedding party, fled back into the bride's suite. The door slammed after them.

Gigi Snow glared at Emma. "How could you let this happen?" she fumed. "You should have kept Mac Hart out of here!"

"How?" Emma blinked in dismay. "He's the sheriff!"

"I don't care who he is." Gigi flailed about, creating even more of a scene. "My daughter is supposed to get married in less than an hour. Guests are going to be arriving any minute! What are we supposed to tell people?" she shrieked.

"That the wedding has been postponed?" Emma suggested calmly.

Gigi stared at Emma vindictively. "This is all your fault! Do you hear me? I'm going to sue you and the

Wedding Inn! And furthermore, if you think I'm going to pay one red cent for this utter catastrophe—''

Mason Snow appeared at the foot of the stairs. Expression grim, he charged up to stand beside his wife. "Be quiet! If the charges are true, Mac Hart has done us a favor! We don't want our daughter married to a common criminal!''

Gigi Snow moaned and buried her face in her hands, looking even more distressed. "Oh, Mason, what are we going to tell our friends?''

More important, Emma thought, what were they going to say to their only daughter?

"WHAT ARE YOU DOING HERE?'' Joe demanded when Emma walked into the master bedroom at four-thirty that afternoon.

Emma had an even better question. "What are you doing?'' And why did he look so guilty, as if he'd just been caught in the act of she didn't know what.

Clad in nothing but a pair of running shorts, looking like he was fresh out of the shower himself, Joe said, "I'm stripping the sheets off our bed.''

Emma liked the sound of that—*our bed*. "I can see that,'' she said dryly. Just as she could see, in the well-sculpted muscles of Joe's shoulders, arms, pecs and abs, the benefits of Joe's physical conditioning. Emma edged closer, noting how defined his hair-roughened legs were, too. "The question is why?'' Joe hated housework and by his own admission only did laundry when it was overflowing to the point of ridiculousness.

"Um, because…''

Inhaling the fresh soap-and-shampoo scent of him, Emma waited for him to finish. To her dismay, Joe looked even more like he had just been caught with his hand in the cookie jar.

"…because I have it on good authority that clean sheets are always nice?''

"If not the way to a woman's heart?" She grinned at the tinge of self-effacing humor in his voice.

"Exactly." Joe dropped what he was doing and came over to enfold her in a hug. "And you didn't answer my question." He ruffled the top of her hair playfully. "Shouldn't you be presiding over the Snow-Posen wedding reception about now?"

Briefly, Emma let her head rest on the solid warmth of his chest. "If there had been one, sure." She frowned, recalling. "Only there wasn't."

"A reception?"

"A wedding. Didn't Mac call you?" She searched his face, finding none of the happiness she would have expected there.

"About…?"

"Your stuff," Emma said.

Joe shook his head.

"Mac found your memorabilia in a storage facility rented out by Benjamin Posen." Emma went on to explain about the confession of his accomplices and Posen's arrest, as the mastermind of the theft ring, the canceled wedding and Mr. and Mrs. Snow's understandably upset reaction about their daughter's botched nuptials and choice of bridegroom.

Listening, Joe groaned in sympathy. "So what did you do about all the guests?" he asked.

"Your mother and I called all the guests we could. Most showed up. We had to notify them at the door and offer them something to eat or drink."

"How many took you up on it?"

Emma wrinkled her nose. "Nearly everyone. But it was so awkward, no one stayed long."

Joe looked her up and down. "You look exhausted."

No kidding. "I could really use a long hot bath."

Already reaching for the button on her suit jacket, Emma started toward the master bath, then stopped when she saw the loose bouquet of roses on the counter, the bags of candles, and bath soap and lotion.

Joe sauntered up to stand beside her. He looked proud as well as rueful. "I was going to surprise you with an evening of total pampering," he told her gently as he stood behind her, kneading the tense muscles of her shoulders. "I had it all planned out."

Loving the feel of his hands on her, so sure and gentle, Emma leaned into his luxuriant touch. Did he know how to give a massage! Reluctantly, she turned to face him, letting him know with a glance on that score she was just as sorry things hadn't gone as he'd planned. "Only I arrived," she reminded.

"Some six hours early." He didn't even try to hide his disappointment about that.

Emma made a teasing face. "Want me to leave and come back later?" She could act surprised.

"Are you kidding?" Joe winked at her sexily, like her leaving was the last thing he wanted. "We'll just get started early."

That said, Joe put his hands back on her shoulders and guided her into the bedroom, obviously looking for some place for her to sit down. It wasn't easy, given the habitual mess in there. He picked up the towering stack of dirty clothes from the chair in the corner and tossed them willy-nilly onto the dirty sheets already heaped on the floor at the foot of their bed, for later transport to the laundry room.

"Let me at least draw your bath," he said.

Emma was pleased enough at the effort he had already put into taking care of her. "I can do it."

He scowled at her in mock indignation. "Sit down." Tightening his grip on her, he propelled her into the chair. "Then while you soak, I'll finish cleaning up in here. And get the bed made and stuff. Give me a chance," he told her confidently. "I can still pull this off. You'll see."

Emma shook her head, feeling both amused and pleased as he disappeared into the master bath again.

Thinking it might be time for a little romantic surprise of her own, Emma toed off her heels, rose and reached for the zipper on her skirt. And that was when she looked down and saw the hint of leopard-print satin and black frothy lace peeking out from beneath Joe's pile of clothes.

Heart pounding, Emma reached for it and then stared down at it, wishing like heck she hadn't.

"OKAY." JOE ADJUSTED THE roses in the vase, lit half a dozen candles, turned off the spigot and barreled back out of the bathroom. "I'm all ready for you now." He stopped at the stricken expression on her face and asked, "What is it?"

Emma held out a sexy leopard-print black-lace thong he had never seen her in and, still looking at him as if he were lower than a snake belly, glided graciously forward. "Suppose you tell me," she stated almost too calmly as she dropped the undergarment into his palm and folded his fingers around it.

Knowing he was supposed to see something nefarious here, even if he wasn't sure what, Joe unfolded the skimpy fabric and glanced down. Front and center of the lingerie was an embroidered black heart with the initials T.F. The only T.F. Joe knew was Tiffany Lamour.

"Where did you get this?" Joe demanded, confused. And why did Emma have it?

"Near the top of your stack of dirty clothes. Right under what you were wearing yesterday, or maybe it was the day before."

Joe had an idea where Emma was going with this. "I don't know how it got there," he told her gruffly, not liking the accusation in her dark green eyes one bit.

Emma arched her elegant brow. "Don't you."

He hated the sarcasm in her tone, almost as much as the raging disbelief on her face. "No. I don't."

The muscles in her cheeks tautening haughtily, Emma spun away from him. "Don't play games with me, Joe."

He caught her by the shoulder before she could go two steps and whirled her right back around. He clenched his jaw. "I'm not playing games with you, Emma." He stared down at her furiously. "I did not put it there."

"Then who did?" Emma volleyed right back, looking like she wanted to deck him. "Tiffany Lamour?"

Without warning, Joe flashed back to Tiffany's request she use their powder room before she left. As he recalled her dashing up the stairs while he went back to the family room to get his cell phone and keys, he felt his gut tighten. Damn it! He had known that witch was up to something. But like a fool he hadn't pursued the alarm bells going off in his head.

Emma tossed her head indignantly. "This is what she was acting so smug about last night, isn't it? Why she gave you such an easy interview?"

Joe swore to himself repeatedly, knowing he'd been a fool to withhold anything about Tiffany from Emma in an effort to protect his wife. Because had he told Emma the whole story, they wouldn't be having this discussion now. "It's not what you think," he said quietly. And if Emma would just calm down for a second, he could explain.

Emma regarded him contemptuously. "You're telling me she wasn't here, in our bedroom."

"She was. Obviously. But—"

"Nothing happened?" Emma echoed sarcastically.

Silence fell between them. Joe had only to look in Emma's eyes to know she didn't believe he had been true to her. Her lack of faith in him stung.

"She just left her panties here as a souvenir, a promise of things to come, is that right, Joe?" Emma threw up her hands in disgust. She shook her head, moisture glistening in her eyes. "How stupid do you think I am? I know what goes on behind the scenes, how women throw themselves at you and every other pro sports player! I know—" her voice broke slightly, before she got hold of herself "—that there isn't anything a groupie won't do for a handsome and sexy and successful guy like you. And yes, I put Tiffany Lamour in that category, too."

So did Joe. Not that it really made a difference. Tiffany had wanted to get back at him, to really screw up his life for turning down her standing invitation to bed her. Now, finally, with Emma on the scene, and an oh-so-discreet misplacement of Tiffany's monogrammed leopard-print black-lace thong, Tiffany had. The whole ruse was so pathetic and predictable, it was almost laughable. Except Emma wasn't laughing, and neither was Joe. Because Tiffany's mean-spirited shenanigans had pointed out a glaring lack in his relationship with his bride. One Joe would have preferred not to see, or ever know about. "You really think I would sleep with that spoiled little witch?" he asked Emma, eyes stinging. You really think I'm that pathetic, that untrustworthy, that short-sighted and foolish?

Emma pressed her fingers to her temples. "I don't know."

Hurt ached through him, more potent than any play-off loss he had ever endured, even the one that had his team falling just short of the Stanley Cup. He glared at Emma, frustrated that he hadn't let himself see this coming, when he had known all along, that she was more of a good-time gal and a fair-weather friend than a devoted wife who would endure anything to be with him.

Oh, sure, she was happy as could be as long as things were going well. But the first time they faced any kind of hardship or opposition, she was all too ready to head for the exit even as she began to wonder if he was really up to the challenge, after all. And her lack of confidence in him—in the two of them—devastated Joe. "I've never given you any reason to distrust me in that regard," he said coldly. Wasn't it enough he had the task of proving himself over and over again in his profession? Was he going to have to do it in his personal life with Emma, too?

"You're right. To my knowledge, up to now, you've never cheated on me," Emma declared flatly, as if that hardly mattered. Just as if everything Joe had done to try to prove himself to her, prove his devotion and his love, barely counted, too.

"But?" Knowing there would be plenty of time to nurse his pain later, he focused on staying angry.

Emma regarded him with more tranquillity than she had any right to possess under the circumstances. "You have put me second to your career in the past," she reminded him with a weariness that seemed to come straight from her soul. "And my parents made it pretty clear to you that your professional life would suffer if you didn't somehow protect me from ugly gossip and get Tiffany Lamour to back off. That's why you married me all over again, why you made us move in together, instead of insisting on a divorce. Because you wanted to protect your position as up-and-coming star player of the Carolina Storm hockey team."

Like any of that meant anything when compared to his marriage! Or what he thought his marriage had been, Joe amended bitterly to himself.

He glared at her, making no effort to hide his building resentment. "Next thing I know you'll be accusing me of sleeping with you for that reason, too." Like he was that lame and selfish and, yes, stupid!

Hurt flashed in her eyes. "Well, it did make me happy," Emma insisted, her soft lips twisting cynically. "However briefly."

And didn't that just say it all, Joe thought.

Damn it. He'd had people doubting him practically all his life. His mother—indeed, his whole family—had never thought he could make it in pro hockey. They'd only been humoring him when they had agreed to let him go off to the junior leagues and try. His coaches had all been skeptical, too. He'd had to work his ass off, day after day, year after year, to prove otherwise. And even then, there had been and were still plenty of doubters. Sports columnists who felt he either wasn't performing up to par or was playing well past his natural ability, and hence would soon crash and burn, or show his true colors and end up at the bottom of the heap where he should have been all along.

Joe had thought what he and Emma had was different. That she saw him, not as other people figured he was, but as he was. Flesh and blood. Real. All too human, and as capable of making a mistake as the next person. But also as capable of love and tenderness and devotion. He had opened himself up to her, told her stuff he had never told anyone else, given her his whole friggin' heart, and for what? To find out she was as full of doubts about him and his character! The unexpectedness of her betrayal hit him like a stick to the knees, made him want to double over and howl in pain.

"Which makes it all the worse!" Emma continued, pacing, upset. Her frustration spilled over to poison the room. She turned wounded eyes to him, abruptly becoming as hysterical and overemotional as he had expected her to be all along. "Damn it, Joe, how could you do this to me, to us?" she cried in frustration. "Don't you understand by giving in to Tiffany Lamour's sexual demands that you've destroyed every ounce of trust between us!"

She shook her head, talking as if he were no longer in the room. "No wonder you were in such a hurry to change the sheets just now!" Obviously berating herself for being such a fool, she clenched her fists at her sides. "No wonder you looked so damn guilty when I walked in unexpectedly this afternoon. Is this what you were doing while I was at the wedding today? Is that why she went so easy on you in the interview last night? Did you make a deal with her before the taping—to sleep with her today?" she demanded ludicrously.

Joe was tired of defending himself. Tired of proclaiming his innocence. As far as he was concerned, Emma either believed him or she didn't. And she damn well didn't.

"I'm sorry you feel this way." He pushed the words between his teeth.

Emma abruptly went very still. Hands balled tightly in front of her, she traded contentious glances with him, then asked, slowly and cautiously, "Meaning?"

What else? Joe thought with a weariness that came straight from his soul. "I'll have my lawyer call your lawyer."

Stomach churning, he turned on his heel and headed for the door. He had to get out of here before he said or did anything they would both regret. Because right now, he felt like putting a fist through the wall. And then some.

THE CALL FROM HELEN HART, requesting that Joe stop by the garden center to pick up several bags of fertilizer, topsoil and several flats of vegetable plants came via cell phone message early Sunday afternoon. Her plea wasn't unusual—Helen used all her sons for heavy lifting, and since Joe had been out of town for numerous years, he knew it was his turn. So Joe borrowed Mac's pickup truck and did as she bid.

Trying not to think about what a mess his personal life was now in, Joe turned into the private driveway at the north edge of the Wedding Inn property, and drove through the trees that separated the house from the rest of the manicured grounds.

As he expected, his mom was waiting for him.

She came out of the two-story, seven-bedroom transitional home and met him in the driveway where a wheelbarrow stood at the ready. As always on summer days when she wasn't working, she was dressed in old clothes—jeans, gardening clogs, a wide-brimmed straw hat and an oversize man's work shirt.

"Thank you for doing this." She smiled at him gratefully.

"No problem." Joe unlatched the gate and began unloading. He caught the thinly veiled concern in his mother's eyes as he handed her the flat of radish plants she had asked for. He swore inwardly. There were no secrets in Holly Springs. "Cal told you, didn't he?"

"What?" Helen was all innocence as she carried the flat over to the garden bed she had prepared for planting.

Joe tried not to think about how stiff and sore he was from trying to sleep on a too-short sofa. "That I bunked at his place last night."

Helen inched on her garden gloves. "Your brother didn't say a word."

"But you know," Joe persisted as he set a bag of topsoil down on the grass next to the rabbit fence.

Helen shrugged and picked up her hoe. " I saw your car there last evening and again this morning. And since it was highly unlikely you were paying Cal a social call that lasted all night, when you and your new bride have a home just five minutes away, I had to wonder what was happening with you and Emma."

Which was why, Joe thought, she had called him over there in the first place. Joe went back to the pickup and tossed a forty-pound bag of fertilizer and another of planting mix onto the wheelbarrow.

"Especially since she apparently slept on the sofa in her office at the Inn last night," his mother continued as he neared her again, not about to let the subject drop.

Joe's brow furrowed. He had left the house specifically so Emma would have a place to sleep, until they could figure out how to proceed from here.

Joe dumped the bags onto the ground with the others. "What did she have to say about that?" Joe asked gruffly, aware his own foul mood was worsening with every second that passed.

"I didn't ask her. I'm asking you." Helen adjusted the brim of her gardening hat. "So what's going on with you two?"

Might as well get it over with. "Exactly what everyone

expected to happen,'' Joe muttered, as if it didn't matter in the least, in any case. "We split up."

"Why?"

Why do you think? Joe used the sleeve of his T-shirt to wipe the sweat from his brow. "She doesn't trust me."

Helen knelt beside the garden bed, trowel in hand. "In what regard?"

Joe watched his mother tap the bottom of a green plastic cup so the starter plant would slide out. "In the being faithful to her regard," he said.

Helen paused, whatever she was thinking well hidden. "Did you cheat on her?" she asked cautiously after a moment.

Good to know everyone had a lack of faith in him these days. "No I did not."

Helen sat back on her heels, the plant and attached dirt still in her hand. "Then why would she think you had?"

Joe clenched his jaw. "A woman I am not interested in left an item of her clothing where Emma was sure to discover it."

Helen narrowed her eyes. "What kind of item?"

He swore inwardly once again. "A thong, if you must know." Could this get any more embarrassing?

Apparently not, judging by the way Helen winced.

"Unfortunately, it's not the first time something like this has happened to me," Joe continued sagely, ready to lay it all on the line, if only because he really needed someone to talk to, and he hadn't felt like confiding details like this to Cal. "And because of what I do for a living, it probably won't be the last. If Emma can't handle that—well…" Joe shrugged, making a great show of indifference. "That's her problem."

"And yours." Helen scowled disapprovingly.

"Not necessarily."

Helen put down the plant and stood. When he tried to walk away, she grabbed his arm. "Joe, you can't end a marriage because of a simple misunderstanding."

Who says? Joe thought bitterly. "Listen to me, Mom. I can't be married to a woman who doesn't believe in me." Who would think even for one red-hot second that I am capable of something like that.

Helen dropped her hand. "So you're saying because Emma let you down, it's over."

"Right," Joe said emphatically.

"Wrong."

Joe stared at his mother. She had scolded him for a lot of things growing up. He had never heard that particular tone in her voice before. The tone that said if he didn't do the right thing before the end of the day she was taking him to the woodshed. "You married Emma for better or for worse, Joe Hart!"

This was definitely the worse, Joe thought.

"And the two of you need to understand there are going to be times when you fail each other," his mother continued emotionally, tears of empathy suddenly brimming in her eyes. "It's moving past those times, finding the strength and will to forgive each other that adds real staying power to your love."

Joe sighed. *If she really loved me...or had faith in us...* With effort, he tried to explain how it was to his mom, who in her own way was an absolute romantic because of the abiding love she still had for his dad, even though his dad had been gone for twenty years. "If I thought we had a chance of making our marriage last..." But he didn't, Joe thought firmly. It was that simple.

"Well," Helen scoffed, looking extremely irritated with him once again, "it's a good thing you didn't apply that kind of attitude to your hockey career, Joseph Hart. Or you would not have ended up where you are today, that's for certain."

There she went, with the given-name stuff again. "What's your point?" Joe demanded harshly.

Helen trod closer. "My point is that you made up your mind hockey was going to be your profession when you were only ten years old. You had plenty of chances to change your mind and quit, but you didn't, Joe. You stuck with it, despite all the obstacles—and there were plenty of them—in your way. Why?''

Joe shrugged, aware this was the first time he had really felt his mother's respect. ''Because it felt right.''

''You just knew,'' Helen paraphrased for him.

''Yes.''

''Like you knew when you were only nineteen that Emma was the only woman for you,'' Helen said.

Joe swallowed. Leave it to his mom to put it like that. In a way that couldn't help but conjure up all the love he was trying so hard to forget, and make him feel broken-hearted and at a loss all over again.

Helen touched his arm, gentle now. ''I don't believe those feelings you had for her then have ever changed.''

They hadn't, Joe thought. That was the hell of it. They hadn't. Even now…

''Your hard work and commitment toward your career really paid off,'' Helen continued persuasively, searching his eyes.

It would have taken a moron not to see where this lecture was going. Joe was no moron. ''You're saying I need to devote myself to my marriage, and Emma, in the same way,'' Joe said in a rusty-sounding tone, recalling his mother's earlier advice to him, too.

Loving someone doesn't magically happen…it's a decision you make every day.

Helen nodded, then reached over and gave Joe an encouraging hug. ''If you love her, Joe, if Emma truly is the woman for you, then you need to forget your pride, forget the angry words and stick with her, too.''

Chapter Fourteen

Emma was making up the final bill for the Snow-Posen wedding-that-wasn't Monday morning, when a rap sounded on her door. She looked up, hoping against all common sense to see Joe.

Instead, Benjamin Posen was standing there. He was dressed in his usual suit and tie, but the look on his face was unerringly grim, and there were circles under his eyes indicating he hadn't slept.

"Got a minute?" Benjamin asked.

Still unable to believe the charming man was a mastermind to a robbery ring, Emma put down her pen and nodded slowly. She could tell by the defeated set to his shoulders and the apology in his eyes, he wasn't here to do any more damage.

"I'm trying to make amends with all the people I've hurt," Benjamin said in a low, discouraged tone.

It wasn't going to be easy. He had a lot of people to see. But then, Emma thought, maybe that was what Benjamin needed to do to get back his dignity. Having handcuffs slapped on, being taken away in a squad car and thrown in jail had to have been a heck of a wake-up call.

Emma couldn't overlook the crimes Benjamin had committed, but she could forgive him. "Have you spoken to Michelle?" she asked gently.

Benjamin shifted his weight and ducked his head in

shame. "She won't see me. Neither will her folks. In fact, they took out a restraining order against me."

Emma had figured Gigi Snow would be vindictive. No one humiliated her family that way and got away with it.

Emma leaned back in her chair. "I'm sorry."

Ben shrugged, his expression hardening. "It's to be expected, I guess. Nobody wants a son-in-law with a criminal record."

"Do you have one now?"

Benjamin nodded and raked a hand through the neatly trimmed layers of his hair. "My attorney entered a guilty plea for me this morning. No sentence has been handed down yet, but because I was able to return all the stolen goods, the district attorney is going to ask for two to five years' community service and a hefty fine in lieu of a jail sentence. The D.A. figures I would be of more use helping underprivileged youth and going around to schools, talking to kids about how easy it is to take a wrong turn, than working in some prison laundry. They think kids will listen to me when I tell them I lost my job, my house, my cushy life and my fiancé."

With his sales-and-marketing background, Emma knew he was likely to be a very effective spokesperson against crime. She figured the rest of his life was going to be a lot harder for him to deal with. "That's a lot of loss to handle at one time." Emma knew how hard it was just to lose a husband, when you still had a career you loved to fall back on.

Benjamin ran a hand over his face. The sorrow turned to acceptance. He sighed and went on to reveal in an uncharacteristically self-effacing tone, "The odd thing is I'm a lot happier now that I'm no longer trying to be something or someone I'm not. I think I've realized for a while now that my marriage to Michelle was not going to work. I just didn't want to admit it to myself. I couldn't get along with her family. They loathed me."

"What about Michelle?"

"She fell in love with a marketing whiz, an up-and-comer. Now that I'm no longer that person—well, let's just say there's no chance for reconciliation there, either." His jaw hardened with determination. "But that's okay. I've got a lot of work to do on myself before I get involved with anyone. And as far as my legal difficulties go, it could have been a lot worse. Believe me—" he released a tortured sigh "—I know that."

Emma knew what it was like to make a mistake. Behave one way and wish you hadn't. "What happened?" Emma asked sympathetically, indicating he should take a chair. "How did you get mixed up in something like this?"

Benjamin shook his head in silent but heartfelt regret as he sat and stretched his legs out in front of him. "I've been asking myself that all weekend. You met my parents. You saw how modest my own upbringing was."

Emma nodded. "I gathered, yes."

"I just wanted more for myself. That's why I went into marketing and business in college—because I felt there was more money to be made in those fields—why I chose to work in an exclusive country club and sell golf memberships to the wealthy. I figured my chances of falling in love with a wealthy young woman were that much greater." He sighed. "I didn't bargain on how hard it was going to be to keep up with a family like the Snows."

No kidding. "They put a lot of pressure on you to help finance the wedding to Michelle."

Benjamin grimaced. "I think, in a sense, they were trying to make me cry uncle, but I was stubborn. I was not going to let Gigi or Mason Snow tell me I wasn't good enough for their daughter, no matter what I had to do. And I quickly realized I couldn't begin to afford on my own what Gigi was asking me to fork over. So I began casting around for a way to make a lot of money quickly. I put some money in the stock market. Unfortunately, the stocks I purchased were high risk as well as high yield and that didn't pan out.

"In the meantime, two men came in to the country club looking for landscaper jobs. I was given the task of interviewing them, but I was told from the get-go that we weren't going to hire them, because they had criminal records for breaking and entering and grand theft. When I asked them why they had done it, in the course of their interviews, they said, 'Because it was so easy.' Well, those words stayed with me, and I got to thinking about how expensive the golf clubs were that a lot of the members used, and how easy it would be to steal them. I told myself we weren't really hurting anyone, since most of them had insurance on their clubs. So I began tipping off the two thieves, telling them when people were going to be out of town, and when that still wasn't enough, I helped them break into the pro shop at the club."

"Joe's memorabilia…?"

"I was there when Helen asked him to take it home. I had no idea how much it was worth, but I was desperate. Gigi was ordering all those orchids from Hawaii, and then the first batch was stolen at the airport. It was such a mess. I panicked. Or maybe I wanted to get caught, so I'd have no choice but to end the madness. God knows I was having a hard time living with myself, with what I had turned into. I wanted a way out from all the dishonesty and the constant fear I was going to get caught." He paused. "Tell Joe I'm sorry, too. If you see him before I do."

"I will," Emma promised, struck by the courage Benjamin was displaying. She didn't know if she would be able to hold her head up half as high under similar circumstances.

"What are you thinking?" Ben asked.

Emma sat back in her chair. "I admire your ability to make such drastic changes."

"Yeah, well," Ben sighed, obviously thinking of his night in the Holly Springs jail, "if there's one thing I've learned this weekend, it's this. If you're headed in the wrong direction—U-turns are allowed."

BENJAMIN POSEN'S PROPHETIC words stayed with Emma, long after he had left to continue his round of apologies. His life had been turned upside down with his arrest. He could have cowered, felt sorry for himself, made excuses for his behavior, become a permanent victim, but he hadn't. Instead, he had taken a good hard look at himself and owned up to his mistake. He had realized he didn't really love Michelle, that he had wanted and needed a way out, and had seen—however subconsciously and inadvertently—that he had gotten one.

And if Benjamin Posen could do that…why couldn't she? Emma wondered as she slid the completed bill for Gigi and Mason Snow into the envelope and sealed it.

Not that their situations were at all the same, Emma thought as she put the stamp on the envelope. No. Her marriage had crumbled because she hadn't possessed the courage to ignore the evidence to the contrary and believe in Joe. Because she had been afraid to tell Joe how she really felt, how deeply she was in love with him.

Instead, she had hurled the accusations that she had known were sure to make him walk out on her. And take with him the possibility of ever being hurt—or loved—by him again.

Emma sighed as she turned off her printer and began the process of shutting down her computer. Two days had passed. She was as lonely and heartbroken as could be. And until this moment, too stubborn and proud to do anything to reverse the situation.

There was no guarantee, of course, that even if she went to Joe now and tried to take it all back that her attempt at reconciliation would work.

But if she didn't try, Emma told herself firmly, she would never know. And Emma didn't think she could stand that.

Finished for the day, Emma reached for her handbag and set it on her desk. And that was when the footsteps sounded outside her office. Emma looked up to see Mac,

Dylan, Cal and Fletcher Hart stride into her office. Her heart began to pound. Something had to be up for all four of Joe's brothers to show up. Especially since Dylan—a sportscaster for a TV station in Chicago—was rarely in Holly Springs these days. The only sibling missing, in fact, besides Joe, was Janey Hart, the only girl in the bunch. "Did we have an appointment?" she asked Joe's four brothers dryly. "Because I sure don't remember one."

Cal grinned with the assurance of the orthopedic surgeon and sports-medicine specialist that he was. "We figured you would say that," he drawled.

Fletch came around behind her. His hand on the back of her swivel chair, he eased her away from her desk. "What are you doing?" Emma asked. Fletch was the town veterinarian, and known for his easygoing, good-guy demeanor, but right now his eyes had a distinctly mischievous glint.

"Helping you out of your chair, of course," Fletch teased.

Emma struggled against the gentle, persuasive hold Dylan had on her elbow as he helped guide her to her feet. "Why?" She looked into Dylan's extremely telegenic face.

"So you can go with us, of course."

Emma stopped right there and refused to budge. "Where?"

Looking as if he had expected her display of recalcitrance all along, Mac came up on the other side of her and took her other elbow gently in his hand. "Oh, we think that would be best left as a surprise," he murmured in her ear.

Emma scowled, beginning to be a little peeved. It was one thing to be led around by Joe—he was her husband, after all. But by all the men in the Hart clan was something else indeed!

"Suppose I don't want to go?" she asked sweetly, wondering if Joe was involved in this, too. Or was he going to be surprised—perhaps unhappily so—just as she was by his siblings' unexpected appearance.

The brothers exchanged looks, communicating silently. "Then we'll convince you otherwise," Cal said eventually.

"And if I can't be convinced? Then what?" Emma demanded, beginning to understand what Janey meant when she sometimes complained about being overwhelmed by all the "testosterone" in her big, lively family.

In response, Cal, Dylan, Mac and Fletch just grinned.

Emma sighed, beginning to get the picture. "I'm going whether I like it or not, aren't I?" she asked.

They nodded in unison. "We knew you'd catch on quick," Mac said.

"LISTEN, GUYS, I KNOW YOU probably mean well," Emma said as Fletch's SUV pulled up in front of the Storm practice facility. She was beginning to get butterflies in her tummy. A lot of butterflies. "But I don't think this is such a good idea."

"You're telling us you don't want to see Joe?"

Of course she did. Even as hurt and angry as she had been, she had missed him terribly the last two days. But that didn't mean she wanted an audience when she and her estranged husband did meet up with each other again.

"I'm saying Joe may not want a cheering section for this," Emma specified as she hopped down from the back seat.

"Actually, he does," Mac told her soberly.

And sure enough, when the other four Hart brothers escorted Emma inside, Joe was waiting for them in the locker room.

The first thing Emma noticed was that Joe had shaved off the play-off-style beard he had been sporting since they had come back into each other's lives. What did that mean? That they were finished? That their love affair-cum-marriage of convenience was over? And Joe wanted witnesses to that effect? And why was he dressed in workout shorts and T-shirt?

Before she had a chance to ask, her father and mother walked in, along with Coach Thad Lantz and sports attorney Ross Dempsey.

"What's this all about?" Emma asked, looking straight at Joe.

Expression implacable, he looked at everyone in the room as he answered, "You'll all see soon enough. Please. Get comfortable." He switched on the television. Dylan fiddled with what looked to Emma like some high-tech recording equipment. Suddenly, the screen was filled with a picture of the weight room on the other side of the building. Joe hustled off as Dylan pushed the record button. Silence fell. A minute later, Joe appeared in the weight room. They could hear every sound in the room as he began using one of the weight machines. He'd done about ten reps when Tiffany Lamour appeared on the screen. Dressed as beautifully as always, in a form-fitting red sheath and high heels, she looked like a tomcat on the prowl. "Peculiar place for us to meet," she drawled.

"Where would you have preferred?" Joe shot back acerbically as he moved on to the next machine. "My bedroom?"

If Tiffany was surprised by Joe's hostility, Emma noted, she did not show it. "I notice you didn't say *our* bedroom," Tiffany pointed out with a smug smile.

Joe turned and looked at Tiffany. He made little effort to hide his anger. "That's because Emma left me."

"Really." Tiffany looked even less surprised.

Grimacing, Joe worked the muscles in his calves and thighs. "She wasn't very understanding about the leopard-print thong with your monogrammed initials." He paused to wipe his face with the end of a hand towel. "Pretty clever of you, putting it on the chair, along with the rest of my dirty laundry, where you knew she'd find it."

Tiffany laughed victoriously. "I thought so." Eyes fastened on Joe's face, she edged nearer. "I'm surprised, though, that she didn't trust you."

"Well, she didn't," Joe said gruffly as he got up abruptly and moved on to the next workout machine. "And now we've split up, thanks to you. The irony of it being, of course—" Joe huffed as he sat down on the bench seat "—that you and I didn't *do* anything."

Tiffany shrugged as she continued to follow him around, like a cat in heat. "Not for lack of trying on my part. As I recall—" she curved her crimson lips "—I gave you *several* opportunities to seduce me."

"Yeah, well, I didn't," Joe said even more impatiently.

"Your mistake," Tiffany said coldly.

Joe paused, studying her. "So this was payback? Is that it?"

Tiffany shrugged and sat down opposite Joe, crossing her legs at the knee and exposing a lot of thigh. "Call it whatever you like."

Joe began another set of reps. "I call it blackmail and extortion—albeit of the sexual variety." He let the handholds of the machine go abruptly and leaned back, against the shoulder and neck rest.

"Come on, Joe." Tiffany stood and sauntered closer. When Joe merely looked at her, she leaned over him and rubbed her hands across his chest in a way that made Emma want to go tear her hair out.

"You're not going to be the first to humor me in exchange for some good publicity. And you certainly won't be the last," Tiffany cooed as she slipped her hand beneath his shirt. "All you have to do is take me to bed and I'll be good to you from here on out."

Abruptly looking as if he couldn't stand Tiffany touching him any more than Emma could, Joe gripped Tiffany by the arms and set her away from him.

It was his turn to look smug and in control. "Actually, Tiff," Joe drawled, as contemptuously as the blackmailing reporter deserved, "I'd be willing to bet I am the last man you'll ever do this to."

Tiffany narrowed her eyes at him suspiciously. "The hell you say."

He pointed at the ceiling in the room in the direction of the discretely positioned recording equipment. "Smile. You're on camera."

THE SCREECH OF FURY TIFFANY let out was both vicious and short-lived as Joe took her by the elbow and propelled her out of the room. "Let's go meet our audience," the group in the room heard him say as the two moved off camera. "I think you'll find this fun and informative."

A minute later, he and Tiffany walked into the locker room. She glared at the group assembled there. Her fear turned to anger, then contempt. "I'll sue," she threatened.

"I wouldn't advise it," Joe's lawyer, Ross Dempsey, said. "'Cause then we'd have to countersue and this whole nasty mess might become public."

"And I'd for sure have to arrest you for blackmail and extortion," Mac Hart said.

Joe looked around. He had no compunction about piling it on. "A lot of witnesses in this room, Tiffany. Not to mention the lovely videotape we just got of your confession."

She folded her arms in front of her defiantly. "What do you want from me?"

"For starters, an apology to me and Emma and everyone else you've hurt."

Tiffany did a double take. No one in the sports world talked to her like that. "You've *got* to be kidding."

Joe looked at Ross and tilted his head indifferently. "Guess you're going to have to file those papers, then."

"Wait." Tiffany held up a well-manicured hand. She looked at Ross Dempsey and spoke as if underlining every word. "This isn't going to be necessary. I'm sorry. Joe. Emma," Tiffany said politely and insincerely. Her end of the deal held up—in her mind, anyway—Tiffany turned to Dylan, who was standing at the recording equipment. "Now I'd like the tape," Tiffany said, holding out her hand.

Joe and Dylan exchanged looks. "I don't think so," Joe said.

"That tape is our insurance," Saul Donovan agreed, stepping forward to take the floor. "Because I'm putting you on notice right now, Ms. Lamour. If you ever do anything like this again to any of my players or any other athletes, your shenanigans will become known, not just to the NHL, but to the entire viewing public."

Emma knew her father meant it. And more, he had the clout—as one of the team owners—to pull such a threat off.

"You're all nuts," Tiffany muttered beneath her breath. She glared at them, then stormed out of the room.

Silence fell in her wake.

Wow, Emma thought. Joe had certainly taken care of that problem.

"That all you needed from us?" Fletcher Hart asked.

Joe nodded. "Thanks for coming, everybody, and serving as witnesses to what happened here today. But now, if you don't mind, I'd like to talk to *my wife* alone."

SILENCE FELL AS EVERYONE streamed out of the locker room. Joe shut the door behind them, then turned back to Emma. He had never looked more handsome, nor more unapproachable. Given the grimly serious expression on his face, she wasn't sure what was on his mind. But she knew she had to take the lead before he did anything rash where the two of them were concerned that would consign them both to a life of misery. She stepped toward him, hands spread out in front of her. "I'm sorry."

He slouched against the door and folded his arms in front of him. "I figured you would be," he said.

Emma eyed him cautiously, unsure of his mood. Was

he as ready to forgive her for her mistakes as she was to forgive him for any he had made? Emma bit her lip uncertainly, then forced herself to go on. Aware her knees were trembling, she looked him in the eye. "I should have believed you." She swallowed hard around the ache building in her throat. "I should have trusted you to be faithful to me. To us."

"Yes." He straightened and swaggered laconically toward her, not stopping until they stood toe-to-toe. His amber eyes were shrewdly direct as they locked on hers. "You should have. The question is, why didn't you?"

As much as Emma would have liked to blame it on her father—his warning about the temptations faced by players—or the "test" he had insisted Joe pass—she knew in reality that had little to do with her reaction. Aware she had never felt more tense or full of bittersweet anticipation in her life, Emma shrugged. Looked deep into his eyes...and her soul. "I don't know," she answered finally, aware her voice had taken on a husky tremor. "I think it had less to do with you than me, really."

"Because?" He searched her eyes, looking ready to understand.

"Deep down, I guess I didn't think I could hold on to you." It hurt as much to say the words as it did to think them, but she forced herself to go on, anyway. "I didn't before. So..." Her voice trailed off in heartfelt regret. Aware she was very close to bursting into tears, she let her hands fall to her sides.

Joe lifted a hand to her face. With the pad of his thumb, he brushed away the tears trembling on her lower lashes. "Before we were young. And foolish," he reminded her huskily, the passion he had always felt for her gleaming in his eyes.

Emma took his hand in hers. "I'm still foolish sometimes."

He wrapped his arms around her waist, brought her closer yet. "I think we can work on that."

Emma splayed her hands across his chest. She could feel the thundering of his heart—it matched her own. "I think we already have," she told him tremulously, then rushed on, ready at long last to tell him all that she felt. "I love you, Joe. I know I've never said that to you before. And I don't know if you'll ever love me back, but—"

He grinned. Then erupted into a full belly laugh.

Emma flushed. This wasn't exactly the response she had hoped for. And yet…he looked happy. Happier than she had ever seen him.

Joe tangled his hands through her hair, lifted her face to his. "Damn, Emma," he said in a voice that sounded as if it were brimming with joyful tears. "Don't you know how much you mean to me?" he demanded hoarsely, tightening his arms around her possessively.

Emma had hoped. And now she was crying!

Joe stroked a loving hand down her face. "You're my reason for getting up in the morning, my reason for coming home. My reason for smiling!" He searched her eyes, all the passion and tenderness she had ever hoped to see in his eyes. "I've never felt the way I feel about you for anyone else, and I never will again."

Hope rose within her. "Does that mean you want to stay married to me?" she asked softly, searching his face.

"Only on one condition," he warned gruffly, his beautiful eyes brimming with emotion.

Emma was ready to grant him anything. "Name it," she ordered huskily.

Joe put his hands on her shoulders and held her in front of him, his protective, possessive hold telling her every bit as much as his low, forceful words. "No more walking out when the going gets rough—for either of us, Emma. And no more accusing me of not loving you with all my heart and soul, because I do."

Emma couldn't think of anything better than spending the rest of her life with Joe. "I promise," she whispered emotionally, love filling her with blissful emotion. "I'll never doubt you—or us—again.'' Because now she knew. They were meant to be together. Not just temporarily. But forever.

Tightening his grasp on her, Joe brought her closer yet. ''And no more letting circumstances, or careers, or anyone or anything else break us apart. 'Cause we're in this for the long haul, Emma,'' he told her seriously. ''For better, for worse. From this day, this moment, for the rest of our lives. We're husband and wife. Not just legally, but—'' he touched his chest and hers ''—in here. In our hearts.''

Nothing could have sounded better to her. Emma hugged Joe back tightly, her lip trembling as the joyful passion she had been holding back spilled over, inundating them with the warmth and comfort of their love. ''I promise.''

Joe smiled and took her all the way into his arms once again. Her body warmed as they touched and they kissed. Deeply. Passionately. Sweetly. Until every doubt Emma had ever had faded, replaced by the love in her heart. And his. And she knew for certain that everything really was going to be okay.

Joe broke off the kiss reluctantly, linked fingers with her.

Emma had only to look into his eyes to know what was on his mind.

''What do you say we go home, Mrs. Hart?'' he teased, lifting her hand to his lips.

Emma grinned as he kissed the back of her hand.

Then she guided his palm to her mouth and caressed it tenderly. ''I say yes,'' Emma whispered as she kissed his hand again, and then his lips.

And then they did what they both wanted—they went home.

* * * * *

Coming to Harlequin American Romance in
December 2003,
look for the next installment in
Cathy Gillen Thacker's
captivating new miniseries
THE BRIDES OF HOLLY SPRINGS
*Weddings are serious business in the
picturesque town of Holly Springs! Everyone
knows the grandiose Wedding Inn is quite a
sight to behold in this neck of the woods.
The Inn is owned and operated by matriarch
Helen Hart, the no-nonsense steel magnolia
who has also single-handedly raised five
macho sons and one feisty daughter. Now all
that's left is getting all her headstrong
offspring to march down the wedding aisle!
Turn the page for a sneak preview of THE
SECRET WEDDING WISH—the second book
in* THE BRIDES OF HOLLY SPRINGS.

Chapter One

Janey Hart Campbell saw the Hart family posse coming as she turned the closed sign in the window of Delectable Cakes. Knowing full well the last thing she needed was an emotional confrontation with all five of her very big and very opinionated brothers about her excessively sports-minded twelve-year-old son, Christopher, she ducked back out of sight of the old-fashioned plate glass windows and hightailed it to the back of her bakery. Grabbing purse and keys, she dashed out the back door and ran smack into the tall man standing on the other side of the threshold.

Immediately, Janey became aware of several things. The wall of testosterone she had just crashed into was a lot taller than she was. Probably six foot four or so to her five-foot-nine-inch frame. Not to mention all muscle, from the width and breadth of his powerful chest and shoulders, to his trim waist, lean hips and rock-hard thighs. He was casually dressed, in expensive sneakers, old jeans and a short-sleeved white cotton polo shirt that contrasted nicely with his suntanned skin. He smelled awfully nice, too, like a mixture of masculine soap and fresh-cut Carolina pines. His dark brown hair was the color of espresso, thick and curly, shorn neatly around the sides and back of his head. Longer on top, the three-quarter-inch strands brushed the top of his forehead.

Individually, the features on his long, angular face were

strong and unremarkable. But put together with those long-lashed electric-blue eyes, don't-even-think-about-messing-with-me jaw, and the sexy mustache that topped his sensually chiseled lips, the mid-thirty-something man looked good enough to put even someone like Mel Gibson to shame. More curiously yet, the handsome stranger was staring down at her as if he had expected her to come bursting out of her shop and run headlong into him.

"They said you were going to do this," he murmured with a beleaguered sigh.

Finally, Janey had the presence of mind to step back a pace, so there was a good half a foot of space between them. "Do what?" she demanded, aware her pulse was racing as she stood staring up at him.

He planted a big hand on her shoulder. "Run."

"And we were right, weren't we?" Dylan Hart said in the same know-it-all tone he used during his job as a TV sportscaster, as he rounded the corner of the century-old building.

"Pay up," Fletcher Hart insisted, entering the alley that ran behind Main Street and sauntering up to the stranger.

"Don't forget. You owe me a beer." Cal Hart—who was still wearing his physician's badge from the medical center—grinned victoriously.

Janey glared at Cal. "Don't you have a surgery to perform or an athlete somewhere who needs your sports-medicine expertise?"

"Nope." Cal smiled. "I'm all yours. For the moment, anyway."

"Great," Janey groused. Just what she needed after an entire day spent baking wedding cakes for this weekend's nuptials.

Mac Hart shook his head at Janey. For once, he was without his Holly Springs sheriff's uniform and badge. "When are you going to learn you can't avoid your problems by running away?" Mac chided.

Janey folded her arms in front of her. Just because she

had fled North Carolina once, in her teens, did not mean she was going to do it again. At thirty-three, she knew what she wanted out of life, and it was right here in Holly Springs, North Carolina, the town she had grown up in.

But not about to admit that to her nosy, interfering brothers, she sassed right back, "I don't know. Seems to me I've been doing a pretty good job ducking all of your phone calls."

"And look where it's gotten you," Joe Hart pointed out disapprovingly. Clad in running shorts and a T-shirt bearing the Carolina Storm insignia, her only married brother looked as if he had just come from one of his summer-conditioning workouts.

The mystery man Janey had run into arched his brow. "Maybe we should take this inside?" he suggested mildly.

"Good idea," her brothers concurred.

That swiftly, Janey found herself propelled out of the July heat and back into the air-conditioned comfort of her shop. To her consternation, the sexy stranger was still with them. Janey wrinkled her nose at him, wishing he weren't so darned cute.

"Do I know you?" she asked cautiously, perplexed. Now that she studied him some more, he looked awfully familiar. As if she had seen him on TV, or in the newspaper, or a magazine, maybe. Certainly, he carried himself with the confident authority of someone used to being recognized and then thoroughly scrutinized.

Janey's brother, Joe, rolled his eyes in exasperation. "Oh, for Pete's sake! This is Thaddeus Lantz. Head coach of the Carolina Storm professional hockey team. The one I am now playing for!" he reminded her.

"Oh, yeah." Janey bit her lip as her eyes slid to Thad Lantz's, then held. Now it was coming back to her. As well as the reason she had not wanted to recognize the savvy strategist...

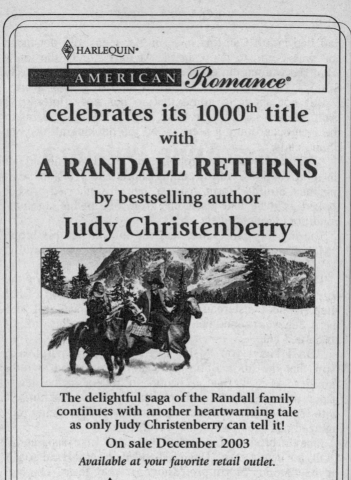

HARLEQUIN®

AMERICAN *Romance*®

celebrates its 1000th title
with

A RANDALL RETURNS

by bestselling author

Judy Christenberry

The delightful saga of the Randall family
continues with another heartwarming tale
as only Judy Christenberry can tell it!

On sale December 2003

Available at your favorite retail outlet.

HARLEQUIN®
Live the emotion™

Visit us at www.eHarlequin.com

HAR1000

HARLEQUIN®

AMERICAN *Romance*®

is thrilled to bring you the next three books
in popular author

Mary Anne Wilson's

delightful miniseries

Just for Kids

**A day-care center where love abounds...
and families are made!**

Be sure to check out...

PREDICTING RAIN?

HAR #1003

January 2004

WINNING SARA'S HEART

HAR #1005

February 2004

WHEN MEGAN SMILES

HAR #1009

March 2004

Available at your favorite retail outlet.

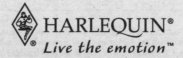

HARLEQUIN®
Live the emotion™

Visit us at www.eHarlequin.com

HARJFK

If you enjoyed what you just read,
then we've got an offer you can't resist!

Take 2 bestselling
love stories FREE!
Plus get a FREE surprise gift!

Clip this page and mail it to Harlequin Reader Service®

IN U.S.A.	IN CANADA
3010 Walden Ave.	P.O. Box 609
P.O. Box 1867	Fort Erie, Ontario
Buffalo, N.Y. 14240-1867	L2A 5X3

YES! Please send me 2 free Harlequin American Romance® novels and my free surprise gift. After receiving them, if I don't wish to receive anymore, I can return the shipping statement marked cancel. If I don't cancel, I will receive 4 brand-new novels every month, before they're available in stores! In the U.S.A., bill me at the bargain price of $3.99 plus 25¢ shipping & handling per book and applicable sales tax, if any*. In Canada, bill me at the bargain price of $4.74 plus 25¢ shipping & handling per book and applicable taxes**. That's the complete price and a savings of at least 10% off the cover prices—what a great deal! I understand that accepting the 2 free books and gift places me under no obligation ever to buy any books. I can always return a shipment and cancel at any time. Even if I never buy another book from Harlequin, the 2 free books and gift are mine to keep forever.

154 HDN DNT7
354 HDN DNT9

Name	(PLEASE PRINT)	
Address	Apt.#	
City	State/Prov.	Zip/Postal Code

* Terms and prices subject to change without notice. Sales tax applicable in N.Y.
** Canadian residents will be charged applicable provincial taxes and GST.
  All orders subject to approval. Offer limited to one per household and not valid to current Harlequin American Romance® subscribers.
  ® are registered trademarks of Harlequin Enterprises Limited.

AMER02   ©2001 Harlequin Enterprises Limited

eHARLEQUIN.com

Your favorite authors are just a click away
at www.eHarlequin.com!

- Take our **Sister Author Quiz** and
  we'll match you up with the author
  most like you!

- Choose from over 500
  author **profiles!**

- Chat with your favorite authors
  on our **message boards.**

- Are you an author in the making?
  Get advice from published authors
  in **The Inside Scoop!**

- Get the latest on **author appearances**
  and tours!

*Want to know more about your
favorite romance authors?*

Choose from over 500 author profiles!

**Learn about your favorite authors
in a fun, interactive setting—
visit www.eHarlequin.com today!**

INTAUTH

HARLEQUIN®

AMERICAN *Romance*®

proudly presents a captivating new
miniseries by bestselling author

Cathy Gillen Thacker

THE BRIDES OF
HOLLY SPRINGS

Weddings are serious business in the picturesque town of
Holly Springs! The sumptuous Wedding Inn—the only place
to go for the splashiest nuptials in this neck of the woods—
is owned and operated by matriarch Helen Hart. This no-
nonsense Steel Magnolia has also single-handedly raised
five studly sons and one feisty daughter, so now all that's
left is whipping up weddings for her beloved offspring....

Don't miss the first four installments:

THE VIRGIN'S SECRET MARRIAGE
December 2003

THE SECRET WEDDING WISH
April 2004

THE SECRET SEDUCTION
June 2004

PLAIN JANE'S SECRET LIFE
August 2004

Available at your favorite retail outlet.

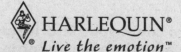

HARLEQUIN®

Live the emotion™

Visit us at www.eHarlequin.com

HARHS